LOVE OF DANGER

LOVE OF DANGER

A WESTERN TRIO

MAX BRAND®

FIVE STAR
A part of Gale, Cengage Learning

GALE
CENGAGE Learning™

Detroit • New York • San Francisco • New Haven, Conn • Waterville, Maine • London

GALE
CENGAGE Learning™

LIBRARY OF CONGRESS CATALOGING-IN-PUBLICATION DATA

Brand, Max, 1892–1944.
    Love of danger : a western trio / by Max Brand. — 1st ed.
      p. cm.
    ISBN-13: 978-1-59414-693-0 (alk. paper)
    ISBN-10: 1-59414-693-4 (alk. paper)
    I. Title.
PS3511.A87L68 2008
813'.52—dc22   2008027476

First Edition. First Printing: October 2008.
Published in 2008 in conjunction with Golden West Literary Agency.

CONTENTS

THE TERRIBLE TENDERFOOT 9

THE GENTLE DESPERADO 89

THE TIGER 173

EDITOR'S NOTE

Throughout his writing career Frederick Faust featured series characters in his contributions to magazines. Among these creations are Bull Hunter, Ronicky Doone, James Geraldi, Chip, Speedy, and Reata. Faust's output in 1927 was decreasing from what he had published in the first half of the decade, but still constituted eight serials and twelve short novels. All but three serials appeared in Street & Smith's *Western Story Magazine,* his biggest market. Among the short novels was "The Terrible Tenderfoot" (7/2/27) which introduced readers to Robert Fernald, the young protagonist who rights wrongs and who appeared in two more stories: "The Gentle Desperado" (7/16/27) and "Tiger, Tiger!" (7/30/27). At the beginning of the first story Fernald finds himself at a crossroads. Having been raised on stories of adventure, he decides to begin a pilgrimage into the world "where God and Satan engaged in visible conflict," and, when he meets up with a Mexican con-man, Pedrillo Oñate, he fast becomes a legend for his ability with a gun. All three stories appeared under Faust's George Owen Baxter byline. Since their original publication in *Western Story Magazine,* this is the first time that these stories have appeared in unabridged form.

★ ★ ★ ★ ★

THE TERRIBLE TENDERFOOT

★ ★ ★ ★ ★

I

In a little house under the shoulder of a hill lived James Dinsmore, but his favorite dwelling, that in which he had his spiritual being, was a low, round-headed tree on top of the shoulder of the hill. There he could weave a lariat, looking from time to time toward the piled mountains on the one side or the heat mists of the desert on the other; there he could ponder his plans for another prospecting expedition among the higher peaks, and there, also, he could lie on his back and look through the branches at the blue sky or the pure white clouds. There had been a time when he spent more energy and hours on the trail of lost mines than he did dreaming on his hill, but, after he turned fifty, he began to relax, and thus it was that he was lying on his back looking up through the branches when Robert Fernald came up to him and called out: "Hello, Uncle Jimmy! Here I am."

Dinsmore started—guiltily, one might have said—and with one hand he combed the disorder and a few dead leaves from his magnificent beard, and the other hand he extended to greet the boy.

Dinsmore replied to Fernald's announcement of his arrival: "And so you are, Bobbie. And I'm glad to see you. Sit down . . . wait a minute . . . lemme see you walk."

"No," sighed Robert, "I still limp. The doctor says that I always will."

"You were a fool kid to ride that mustang," declared Dinsmore. "Sit down here, and tell me about yourself."

Robert sat down obediently upon a rock.

"Lemme see your diploma," said Uncle James.

"I left it below in the house."

"Why, kid, you don't seem very proud of it. Is it everybody around these parts that can sport a college diploma?"

"It doesn't mean much, really," said Robert gloomily. "You don't have to know a lot to skin through a college course. But I suppose that law will be different. You have to work in the law school, they say."

"Let the law go for a minute," said the older man in some haste. "But here you are, twenty-two . . . sixteen years of studying and grinding behind you . . . and tell me what you have been specially doing with yourself? What studies were . . . ?"

"I was too light for football," said Robert with a greater sigh than before. "I tried pretty hard, but I kept on getting broken up. It seems that I smash rather easily. But the coach kept me on the squad all season," he added, lifting his head a little. "And in the last game he almost sent me in. But that would have been just sentimentality," he went on more gloomily. "Too light, couldn't get distance with my kicking . . . and my eyes, you know. . . ."

His voice trailed away. Robert always intended to be stoic, but sometimes he slipped a little.

"Then I went in for boxing," he continued.

"Did you get licked?" Dinsmore asked rather anxiously.

"Not in my own class," said our hero, setting his jaw in a way that made it seem not quite so soft. "But when I went out of it . . . I . . . was knocked out . . . three times."

"But if you beat everybody at your weight, kid, you were champ at that figure."

"What good is a lightweight?" asked Robert fiercely. "What good, I ask you? What good in the world?" His head fell. He prodded at a rock with the toe of his shoe and gouged the leather without stirring the stone.

"You can spoil your shoes, kid," said Dinsmore, "but you can't move a whole porphyry dyke. Well, you didn't do much at boxing, then?"

"Nothing at all," said our hero.

"What else? Rifle team again, I suppose?"

"Oh, yes."

"And pistol team, too?"

"Yes."

"Matter of fact you got a medal or something, I think?"

"You'd laugh to see the shooting we do," said Robert, smiling without mirth. "Perfect guns, perfect ammunition, but men in these days aren't like the men you used to ride the plains with, Uncle Jimmy. They've fallen off a lot."

"Lemme see," said Dinsmore. And then he tossed a 25¢ piece a few yards away.

Robert produced a heavy automatic with an easy gesture—as though the gun had been dropped into his hand. And he hardly looked at the 25¢ piece as he said: "Oh, of course, with a target as big and as close as that. . . ." He fired.

"By jumping Jupiter!" cried Dinsmore. He leaped up and came back with the blasted coin—one half of it was blown away.

"Even then, you see," remarked the boy, "I couldn't make a center hit."

Mr. Dinsmore did not seek elegant speech. He said: "Well, what the devil do you want? The world with a fence around it?"

Robert looked up at him and smiled. "You always want to make me feel that I'm someone," he said. "You always want to make me happy. But I know . . . I don't forget. You and Buffalo Bill and Wild Bill . . . why, you could hit a dime at twenty or thirty paces every time."

"I . . . ," began Mr. Dinsmore, and smoothed his beard with haste.

"I've worked for hours nearly every day," said Robert. "You know . . . practicing the draw . . . and snap shots . . . and yet I can't hit a dime with a quick shot at twenty-five paces. Not more than once in four times . . . or hardly that. You see, I simply haven't any talent. I simply haven't!"

Dinsmore said nothing. He took out a great black square of chewing tobacco and bit off a liberal chunk on which he began to work so rapidly that it seemed as though he were eating it.

Robert raised his head and looked across the heat mists of the distant desert. He was not seeing the desert, however—he was seeing the future. "You always knew that I wouldn't make good in this country," he said, "but I always hoped that someday, if I worked very hard and patiently, I'd be able to box, and wrestle, and ride, and shoot, and be able to go hunting, and really live, the way you did in the old days. I've studied trailing, for instance, by book and by magnifying glass. But I haven't the eyes for it. Even these glasses won't completely help. I can't shoot the way real men can. By instinct, you know. I can't ride a real outlaw mustang. And now that I have this bad leg, I can't run all day like an Indian. In fact, of all the things that I wanted most to do and to be, I can't say I've succeeded in a single one. And I see that I'm a failure."

"How many men can ride or shoot with you, kid?" asked Dinsmore with great heat.

"The world is filled with dubs and fools," said Robert bitterly. "What good is it to be a shade better than most? I could handle the boys my size with the gloves. I could go through the welterweights, and most of the middleweights. But when it came to the really good big men, they beat me. They . . . they flattened me. They hung me on the ropes. I did well for two rounds with our middleweight champ. Then he knocked me right onto the ropes. It didn't hurt. But I was just weak. 'We'd better stop, Bobbie,' he said. 'I don't want to hurt you.' Ah, Uncle Jimmy, did anyone ever have to say to you or to Buffalo Bill or to Wild Bill such a thing as that? Can you imagine it? *'We'd better stop, Wild Bill, because I don't want to hurt you.'* Why, it would have killed Wild Bill . . . the shame of it. But I'm not made of such fine, sensitive stuff. I haven't even the pride of a real man. I . . . I just confess that I'm beaten, and I give up. So I'm going to give up the West, and I'm going to settle down to three miserable years in the law school. . . ."

"Hold on, lad," said Uncle Jimmy. "The fact is . . . I hate to say it . . . but the real fact is that the funds have run out. I can't keep on sending you to school."

"Not to school?" echoed Robert.

Mr. Dinsmore combed his beard vigorously. "Bobbie, the money's all gone," he said, and he looked sadly across the desert and shook his head.

II

When Bobbie saw that the old way was ended and that he was come to the crossroads, he was silent for a moment. Then he murmured: "I didn't suppose . . . I thought, you know, that Father had left me enough. I thought you said so, Uncle Jimmy?"

"Did I?" said Uncle Jimmy, growing rather red. "Fact is . . . I was always a fool about talk. But you see . . . I didn't want to have it on your mind. I just wanted you to finish up your college course and . . . I dipped into my pocket pretty deep to manage the thing."

"That was like you!" cried Robert. "But I want to know what you've spent, and you shall have every penny back that you. . . ."

"Hey, hold on, will you?" said Mr. Dinsmore, growing redder and redder. "It's all right, I say. Don't get excited. But the money's used up. Finally . . . well, someday I'll strike it rich and pay you back everything that. . . ."

"Pay me back what, Uncle Jimmy?"

"Pay you back? What am I sayin'? Bobbie, you don't think that I would take anything that was yours? You ain't accusing me of stealing from you what . . . ?"

"Stealing?" Robert exclaimed, his eyes filling with tears—as they often did when he was moved. "Good God, sir, don't make me out worse than I am. You've been a father to me. Accuse you? There's nothing under heaven that I trust so much as I trust your honesty and goodness, Uncle Jimmy."

He clasped the brown hand of the prospector, and Uncle Jimmy muttered: "Don't be a fool . . . let it go . . . it's all right. Only . . . didn't mean to have it turn out like this . . . but there was the money, and it went . . . not enough left for me, hardly . . . I mean, not enough left for me to do what I wanted for you. Always considering you, kid, from the first."

"Yes, yes," said Robert. "And to think that you've been depriving yourself while I idled through college. . . ." He stopped and mopped his forehead. "But I'll go to work," went on Robert, "and I'll be able to pay you back before long and. . . ."

"Hold on! Don't run away with yourself. Let the horses do that," replied Uncle Jimmy. "Maybe there's enough left . . . I mean, maybe I could rake enough together to give you a flying start on that law course and you could raise something from some of your rich friends back East to see you through without giving up what . . . what are you dreaming about now?"

"Maybe it's fate," suggested Robert in an awed voice. "Maybe it's fate that has stopped my work in school because perhaps, after all, I could learn to fit into the big things out here in some small way. I don't aspire to be such a man as you and Wild Bill. I only want to do some small thing . . . some free thing. The right sort of thing, even if there isn't much to it. I don't know what would be the best way to begin. But I think that I should begin by going to the spot where my father lies buried, Uncle Jimmy. Don't you think that that would be best? A sort of pilgrimage, you understand?"

Uncle Jimmy pointed a brown forefinger at the boy.

"You stick to books," he said. "Don't you go wasting your training and your brains. . . ."

"You don't think that I could do anything real," acquiesced Robert sadly.

"Oh, hang something real," said Uncle Jimmy. "Is it real to toil in the sun, and get sand down your throat and in your eyes, and have sore feet and a sunburned neck, with a danged mustang stumbling under you?"

"You want to make it seem nothing," said Robert with his wistful smile. "But I've heard the truth from you. I know the wonderful, free, big life that's to be found in the mountains and the desert. The sort of a life that you and Wild Bill. . . ."

"Oh, damn Wild Bill," the prospector said.

Robert was shocked. Not by the oath but by the name to which it was coupled. "I suppose," he said sternly, "that no one during Wild Bill's life dared to damn him."

"Oh, well," said Uncle Jimmy, "let's go down and cook a snack for supper. Can you eat pone, kid? Or are you plumb above it?"

They went down to the shack, where Robert made the fire in the crazy cast-iron stove while Uncle Jimmy Dinsmore mixed corn pone and sliced ham. As the ham sizzled on the stove, Robert stood outside the door in the cool of the evening and whistled in a high, weird key, and all the animals of the place came hurrying as to a familiar call.

There was a shambling mule, a lump-headed mustang, a jennet, and a couple of goats that were kept for milk today and meat tomorrow—but tomorrow never seemed to come for them.

They gathered about the doorway, and from Robert eagerly received various tidbits. As for the goats, they would have eaten the hand that fed them. Their cruelty always hurt the feelings of Robert a little, but such was his faith in the ultimate goodness of this beautiful world that he found no difficulty in fitting a few ugly facts into the general harmony of all things.

"Now, kid," Uncle Jimmy said after supper, while Robert washed up, "lemme hear what you gonna do with yourself out yonder on that desert."

"I'm going first on a sort of pilgrimage," said Robert, "to the very spot where my dear father. . . ."

"Hum!" said Uncle Jimmy.

". . . . and to think," said Robert, his voice quivering with emotion, "that I've come to this age without going to see. . . ."

"And after you get there?" said Dinsmore.

"I don't know exactly. I'll find something to do. You know, one must have faith."

"Faith? In the desert?"

"Oh, yes," said Robert with the quiet of conviction, "because without faith there would be no friendship, or love, or kindness, no trust in the world . . . there would be no religion, there would be no God in heaven."

Robert looked up, and a greasy frying pan dripped gray water on his trousers, unregarded.

"Now, look here, and I'm gonna tell you something," said Dinsmore, "and the fact about the desert is that you ain't seen nothin' but the edges and the trimmin's of it. You've gone onto it because it was a lark, and the desert don't pay no attention to kids out havin' their game and their fun. But when you go onto the desert because you have to, then it's likely to be different. It's a treacherous, sneakin', good-for-nothing thing, a desert is. Just when you think you got it patted and petted and smoothed down and sleepy, it just nacherally opens up and swallers you alive. And you never can tell what's stealing up behind to hit you when you ain't looking. No, kid, the desert is like a whole cage full of starved painters. That's how much I would trust it, and nobody with real good sense would ever want to have nothing to do with it at all."

To doubt his uncle's words never occurred to Robert. But he had already discovered that there were certain contradictory moods and humors in the older man that must be outwardly respected, although they need not be taken to heart too seriously. After a time he said: "But tell me, Uncle Jimmy, why you still get onto the desert whenever you can?"

Mr. Dinsmore gathered his brows. "The trouble with you youngsters . . . you all got to argue things. Got to find out for yourselves. Well. . . ."

He left something dire unsaid and fell into a brooding gloom, from which he roused himself only when Robert suggested: "Uncle Jimmy, what about a yarn?"

"I ain't feeling like yarning," declared Dinsmore. "I ain't feeling like making up . . . remembering, I mean. . . ."

"I'd like to know, though," said young Robert, "about that time you started on the trail of Spotted Antelope. . . ."

"The Comanche? Yep, I remember that and. . . ."

"No, no! The Sioux."

"Well, didn't I say he was a Sioux?" asked Dinsmore, frowning again.

Robert was silent. He could feel the spell beginning to take effect; the atmosphere altered; Uncle Jimmy was donning a robe of dignity and impressiveness, and many an evening in the past had this ceremony been repeated.

"I was sitting with Kearsarge Pete in his lodge, and his squaw had laid some boiled buffalo tongues in front of us. I remember that Kearsarge laid into her for not roasting them tongues. He was feeling kind of mean at her because the day before a cracking thunderstorm blew up and she had sacrificed her best dress and a couple of strings of beads to the Sky People to keep a thunderbolt from hitting the teepee. But her and Pete had a kid, and she was kind of soft about it. Pete reached over and picked up a fine pipe and begun stuffing it. 'Pete,' I says, 'that's a medicine pipe, or I hope I'm a liar.' 'Chief,' he says, 'say it in English. I don't want the girl yonder to hear.' So we drifted into English. 'There's a yarn that goes with that pipe,' he says, 'and it takes a back trail to the Sioux . . . and, by the same token, I'm gonna take that same back trail with my feet and not with my tongue only, one of these days. . . .' "

Softly, moving with utmost precaution lest he make a sound, Robert slipped to his bunk and clasped his hands behind his head. He closed his eyes to the drab little shack and the star or two glinting through the wide edges of the hole up which the chimney passed. The melancholy night wind of the mountains was beginning to sing and brought down from time to time the voice of a wild hunter, the sob of a puma, or the hunger call of a coyote coming out of Bender Pass, and savoring the tales of rich plenty that the wind carried up from the lowlands.

As it was now, so had it been before on how many and many a night.

If he waked, the steady, strong voice of the narrator would continue almost endlessly. And if he slept, what he had heard would pass into reality in his dreams.

Robert could not help smiling a little in the dark, for he thought of the deluded millions who toiled and fought and hoped in the great cities, although the greatest of their fancies would have shrunk to nothing in this Western land. For how can men build great thoughts when they have not been able to conceive an appropriate stage for their imaginings?

Robert's breathing grew more and more regular. Indian ponies, a winter storm, a perilous crossing over an iced river, an avalanche bursting down a mountain slope, the yellow eye of a campfire looking kindly up from the heart of a black valley— such things passed into his mind with the words of the narrator. And then by one step of natural magic Bobbie left the cabin and the sound of Dinsmore's voice and crossed the threshold of a world of beauty where God and Satan engaged in visible conflict, for half the inhabitants of this dream world were stainless heroes and half were possessed of a fiend. Here battles to the death were rewarded by undying honor and love; women with souls more pure than their chaste and lovely faces smiled upon him; he walked beside heroes, not as their equal, but as a glad attendant, a servant, a worshiper of their nobility.

From that Homeric slumber he was roused at last, by cramping cold in all his limbs, and he raised his head to see the rose of dawn streaming through the open door. The beauty of the morning and the snoring of Uncle Jimmy filled the cabin with an equal power. He glanced at the open mouth and grizzly, unshaven face of the prospector, and then hurried into the open air.

The grand procession of the mountains assured Bobbie that all his dreams were true, and he hurried down the slope to take his morning plunge. The pool was sheeted with thin ice along its margin, but, if one wants a cold bath, the colder the better, and is he not a fool who quarrels with the provisions of our mother, Nature?

So thought Robert, and with his heel he broke the ice.

III

To Robert it would have been sacrilege to start his pilgrimage after sunrise. Only base, laggard souls will let the sun precede them on their journeys. The sacred enthusiasm sustained Robert even through a breakfast of cold bacon and stale pone washed down with ice water from the creek, until Uncle Jimmy roused and reared himself upon one elbow.

"You stirrin'?" he asked.

"The early bird, Uncle," said Robert brightly and cheerfully.

"These here early birds," said Uncle Jimmy, "are bothered a lot by indigestion. Gonna go fishing?"

He learned then that Robert's instant determination was to start for the grave of his father and thence into the world.

"But maybe you'll find the world before you find the grave," suggested the prospector. "Comanche Corner is a dead town, kid, and it died almost as long ago as your dad. But I'll tell you where it lies."

It hurt the boy a little that his uncle did not attempt to persuade him to linger in the shack for a few days at least, for there is nothing that fortifies an enthusiasm so much as argument, but Uncle Jimmy surrendered at once. He took a bit of charred wood and sketched a map on the floor beside his bunk. A chimney butte to the north, and the bed of the vanished river crossing the plain. There he would find Comanche Corner. God knew how many days' ride away; Uncle Jimmy did not.

But what he did know was that he had $500 in his wallet and that it must go into the pilgrim's pocket. Robert made stout resistance, but finally submitted because he saw that Dinsmore seemed eager to make the gift, and even heaved a breath of relief when Robert accepted. Besides, Robert knew full well that in the work that he was about to undertake gold was little more than dirt.

So he took the money, clasped the hand of his dear benefactor and guardian, and strode off down the mountainside with a pack on his shoulders, a rough staff in his hand, and a Colt automatic that launched seven shots at one pressure of the trigger in a clip holster under his left armpit. So had Wild Bill, of deathless memory, worn his weapons when in the prime of his glorious career. And even if a man cannot himself be great, he should follow the best examples.

Robert walked for seven hours that morning. His limp grew worse and worse and his feet sorer and sorer. At first he did not want to pause to remove his shoes because it would cost so much time to dress the painful feet, and after that he did not want to take off his shoes because he was a little afraid of what he might find.

He began to suffer dreadfully, but tasted joy in enduring this torment, for he felt that he had entered the fire that was to change the metal of his nature and give it the finer and sterner quality that it required. He believed in pain; he believed that it had a purifying property. If that were true, by the time he reached the first village in the foothills, all taint should have been washed from Robert's soul.

He hobbled into the dining room of the hotel and the waitress hooked her thumb over her shoulder. "Beat it, kid," she said. "No hand-outs for bums, bindle stiffs, or tramps royal here. Not in this joint, baby!"

Robert looked upon her in hurt astonishment, but then he saw that she was a woman and that she was young. Therefore she must be good.

He flushed a little, not because of her rudeness but because of his first harsh thought. "I beg your pardon," said Robert. "I don't blame you for mistaking me for a beggar. I should have brushed my clothes before I came in." He backed out, and went to find the pump at the back of the building, while the waitress turned toward a man who sat at the long table eating busily. Above his hat mark his hair was brown; below the hat mark it was white with dust, and all the back of his shirt was also white with dust.

"Bud, did you see that nut?"

"Naw, but I heard him," said Bud. "Gimme some coffee, will you?"

Hebe had vanished, however. Presently she was hanging out a back window watching our hero soaking his feet in a bucket of cold water. She saw; she nodded with a knowing air, and without a single question she went to her own room and came down with a strip of cotton cloth, washed and worn to the texture of the softest down.

"Wrap 'em up in this," she said, "and here's some lard to rub on the skinned places."

Fernald looked up to her again and flushed even more crimson than the sunburned tip of his nose. He lifted his hat and said in his timid voice: "You're terribly kind to me. You're terribly kind," he repeated. He was thinking of the first hard thought that he had had of her and could have sunk into the ground in his mortification, because, for an instant, he had doubted gentleness, kindness, charity in woman. It was a rather broad and freckled face that looked down at Robert, but it seemed beautiful to him.

"*Aw*, it's nothing," she said, and vanished to get the coffee for Bud.

But when Robert had struggled into his shoes again—they seemed a size too small by this time—and sat in his turn at the dining table, the girl served him with heaping portions. Twice she lingered near him until he looked up with his wistful smile.

"What made you do it, kid?" she asked.

"I don't understand," said Robert.

"*Aw*," remarked the waitress, "you been pounding your feet to pulp for nothing, or just fun, maybe?"

"It's foolish to have one's feet give out so soon, isn't it?" he admitted seriously. "But I don't quite understand what. . . ."

"Nothin'. Nothin'," she said in haste. "I'm a sap. But you never can tell . . . the birds that come through this town."

She hurried to the kitchen and came back quickly with a white breast of cold chicken. "Stow that under your ribs, kid.

24

It'll stick to 'em, I guess."

When he had finished his meal and paid for it, he begged her to accept $1 for her kindness. Not that it was a reward for her goodness.

She crinkled the bill between thumb and finger. It was real, and she turned from Robert to put the money in a place of security.

He asked if she could tell him where he could buy a horse.

"I can tell you, honey. Everybody in town has got a horse to sell. All crooks. My stars, when you think what a lot of yeggs there are when it comes to selling a horse. But I tell you what you do. You go to Hank Chandler at the far end of the town. He's got a little paint horse that'd be a regular sweetheart for you. He'll ask you three hundred. If you pay him more than a hundred and a quarter, you *are* dumb. Oh, that's all right." She followed him to the front door. "Is there a *she* in why you left home? You don't understand? How old are you? Well, never mind. Are you coming back this way again? So long, honey. Now, you take care of yourself. And . . . hey . . . you better get a hat with a wider brim, or you'll have that nose burned right off your face!"

Robert, hat in hand, looked earnestly upon the speaker. The face, he felt, was beautiful, but he wished to look past the face into the lovely soul. He looked, and he felt that he saw the truth.

"I shall never forget you," said Robert softly. "I never shall forget you."

The waitress watched him out of sight. "*Aw*," she said, "I'm gonna have a heartache for you, baby face."

Robert walked in a rosy mist, to the farther end of the village. Hank, the horse dealer, sat on the top rail of his corral and talked about the pinto.

Robert heard that this was the one horse that Hank had

learned to love. This was the one horse that his family loved.

"Lord pity me if the missus should ever hear of me sellin' this pony," said Hank, turning up his eyes.

Robert caught his breath. "I hope that no act of mine . . . ," he began. "I wouldn't wish to be a cause of friction."

The dealer scratched his chin and looked askance.

"But I see that you got an eye for a horse, my son. And them that knows 'em should have 'em. I'd give that horse away to you for five hundred bucks."

"Isn't that odd?" said Robert. "It's exactly the sum that I have in my wallet." He took out the sheaf.

The dealer steadied himself on the top rail and, rather hoarsely, added: "And I wouldn't mind throwin' in a bridle, kid, at that."

The money had almost changed hands, when Robert quite suddenly remembered. "But," he said, "I'm under instructions not to pay more than a hundred and twenty-five dollars for that horse. I'm sorry that I forgot."

The dealer dropped heavily from the fence to his feet. "A hundred and twenty-five damnations," he said. "Are you kiddin' me?"

Robert drew back a little. "I'm very sorry," he said. "I don't want to waste your time. I admired the horse so much . . . I forgot about the price limit . . . but thank you for letting me see. . . ."

He had reached the road when a loud bellow called him back.

"I'll make it two hundred," said the dealer, "and make it even. Dog-gone me if I'll be able to face the wife, though."

Robert hesitated. The voice of the waitress was still in his ear, but, after all, it was only an extra $75, and he really was ashamed to think of such a paltry sum in the presence of a man who was wounding the tender heart of his wife. Moreover, Robert knew horses, had worshiped and ridden them since childhood, and the pinto was made like a watch—neatly and filled with springs, and all his parts fitted together as by the skill of a jeweler. He would never see fifteen hands, and his blood was pure ragamuffin from the plains and the mountain desert, whereas Robert, in his dreams, never mounted anything less than a coal-black charger of at least seventeen hands, but, after all, Robert was himself some ninety pounds short of his wishes and could content himself with a lightweight pony.

He paid the $200 without more ado. He bought an old saddle, too, and a bridle, and saddlebags, and a slicker. The individual prices seemed small, but the aggregate was oddly large.

"But who told you," asked the horse dealer, eying the little sheaf of bills that our hero was restoring to his wallet at the end of these transactions, "who told you that paint horse ought to go at a hundred and twenty-five?"

"The lady in the hotel," said Robert. "The lady . . . who waits on the table."

"That cross-eyed, flat-faced calico!" cried Hank. "I'll teach her to. . . ."

"Don't!" Robert snapped.

"Don't what?"

"You mustn't, you know. You mustn't speak of a lady in such language."

"I mustn't?"

He roared so loudly that a tremor passed through Robert, and then, looking earnestly upon Hank, he saw that he was in the presence of one of the evil ones of the world.

"Good Lord!" cried Hank. "Are you crowin' at me, kid? A youngster like you! Can't I call that . . . ?"

"Not another word," said Robert firmly. He raised his hand, his left hand, and shook a warning forefinger.

It seemed that Hank was paralyzed with fear. Alas, he was

only paralyzed with rage and astonishment. Then, with the flat of his hand, Hank smote the bare cheek of his young customer.

Hank's was a heavy hand, and it shook Robert to the toes, but not so much as he was shaken by another consideration. For in all the frontier tales that had flowed from the lips of Uncle Jimmy, Robert hardly recalled a dozen clenched fists—certainly no blow had ever been struck with the palm. No, in the mountain desert, guns blazed instantly when men quarreled, and, as the flames leaped, lives flickered and went out. And he, Robert Fernald, had been deemed worthy of no greater insult than a blow, flatling, upon the cheek.

Rage turned his hand to steel—that hand that had been ready for the draw—and shooting it up and over from the hip, Robert lodged the knuckles fairly on the point of Hank's chin. It was Robert's favorite punch, in which he had been schooled by the boxing instructor until that gentleman, contented, swore that the blow could win money in any ring. It was as nifty a right hook, he declared as ever extracted teeth.

As for Hank, he acknowledged the magic touch by falling on his face like a log, and Robert left him lying there, mounted the pinto, and cantered down the street. But even when he was far from the village and the open country received him, Robert's cheek burned hot with shame, as a knight would have blushed who had been smitten with the flat of the sword.

IV

Riding was a grateful relief to Robert Fernald after the agony of his last miles afoot, but life on the back of the pinto was by no means perfect. The horse had the beauty of an Arabian, the eye of a lion, and the soul of a mule. He knew all of a mule's tricks: how to arch his back so that his canter bumped the brain of a rider into a dizzy haze; how to stiffen his legs so that his trot racked every bone of him in the saddle, but, having gained his point and been allowed to walk, he went swiftly and sweetly, well nigh as fast as the dog-trot of an ordinary cow pony. But when he felt that a day's march had been completed and that a good camping place had been reached, he was apt to go dead lame. So much so that he could barely hobble on three legs, and exhaustion made him stumble again and again until his dainty nose almost touched the dust of the road. At the first of these compulsory halts, Robert spent an anxious hour massaging the useless legs of Pinto, but no sooner was the little horse turned out to graze than he began to frolic here and there and chase crows with the joy of a reckless boy. So that the first grave doubts entered the mind of Robert, and by the time the third stage of the march was completed he was forced to admit with much sorrow of soul that Pinto was a very knowing and bad-hearted pony.

There is only one way of conquering mulishness, and that is by giving a strong taste of the whip from time to time, and by that means Robert learned how to smooth the gaits of Pinto, although every time he flogged the horse, he sighed with compunction.

The foothills sank behind the pair, turned from brown to blue, and melted at last into the loftier masses of the mountains. They were in the desert. Mesquite or greasewood or cactus was the only vegetation, and so scant and so pale was it that it seemed no more than an occasional smoke drift lying low along the ground. When the sun was two feet above the horizon, it had the force of midday heat, and at noon it withered and scorched the very soul. There were dangers for horse and man in this travel, but Robert had charted the water holes in his memory and he was able to knock over a meager, leathery jack rabbit now and again. As for Pinto, if he had the mental traits of a mule, he had also the physical toughness of a mule. A good bellyful of water once a day lasted him, or, for that matter, he could campaign with one drink in forty-eight hours, for he was of the true desert strain. Break the tougher spikes from the outside of a branch of cactus, and Pinto would devour the rest with neat, small, but patient bites. He was equally patient in gathering grass that had no more substance than streaks of spider web, and upon the end tufts of any growing plant he was willing to dine without complaint. No schooling could teach a horse such desert manners, but a hundred generations of tough ancestry had equipped the mind and the body of the little stallion. Where an ordinary animal would have wasted away, Pinto was growing fat and laughing at the ardors of the journey.

Robert's feet were healing now, and were perfectly comfortable in the stirrups, and the trip was turning out so much less arduous than he had expected that he began to feel like a conqueror, and like a conqueror he rode into a little desert village that came upon his horizon.

He could see no reason for the town. There was no visible supply of water. The houses were a handful of adobe huts surrounded by no gardens with any touch of greenery. There seemed no more juice of life in the place than in so much dead rock, and at every rising of the desert wind, the town disappeared in a cloud of dust. But people were living in this town, people strong enough and wise enough to have made their way to a greener land. But alas for human misery, as well. Barely had Robert entered the town than he saw a one-armed Mexican beggar seated cross-legged in the full blast of the sun and holding out his hand like a shallow cup, asking alms.

Robert dismounted. Even to a beggar he would not speak from a height: "Poor man," he said gently, "are you utterly desolate?"

The Mexican rolled up dull, black eyes. He was a pudgy figure, with stomach resting heavily upon his crossed legs. "Ah, *señor*," he said, lifting his hat to the questioner, "God gives and

God takes away."

"True," said Robert, with a sigh. "But one has patience. One endures."

"That is true, also. One endures, if one has courage. I think you are very brave."

"I? I have only the heart which God gave me. No man has more. But how did you lose your arm, my friend? And don't keep your hat off in this sun."

"It was a little matter of dynamite. We talked, some friends and I. Was dynamite *muy diablo?* A little dry stick, like clay, how could it be *muy diablo?* I offered to hold a stick in my hand while it was set off."

"Good heavens!" cried Robert. "But did your friends allow you to risk your life?"

"No great risk, *señor.* I held the stick around the corner of a house. However, there was this little accident to the arm. It seemed that dynamite was, after all, *muy diablo!* Well, we learn by experience. One cannot be born with all knowledge, *señor.*"

"And that is true, also. Here is a little money. I am not rich or I would make it much more. It will buy you a few meals." And he gave $50 to the beggar.

The brown-faced man came to his feet with a bound. "The Holy Virgin watch and bless you, *señor!* May she be with you like your shadow. May you have ten children, all sons. May your wife never grow old. I, Pedrillo Oñate, foresee that these things shall be. Kind *señor,* my prayers shall be raised for you every day of my life."

Robert hurried away. For $50 was not much, and yet it made gratitude run like water from the heart of this poor man, whose loud voice still cried praises and blessings after him.

"May each of your ten sons marry a rich wife, and may the ten wives die young! God give you peace in your old age! May you . . . !"

Robert cantered Pinto around the next corner and breathed more easily when the voice died away behind him. He was flushed, happy, his soul uplifted. Why should charity be commanded, when to give is such a joy?

There was a little hotel in this town—two squat huts, joined by a structure of galvanized iron. Bread would have baked in the frightful oven of that dining room, but the advantage of the heat was that one's appetite departed even before the food was brought.

Robert staggered gasping from the room at last, and went to the stable to watch Pinto finish his rations. Then he groomed the little horse with loving care, saddled him, and started down the street—when, behold, seated at the wayside, cross-legged, his smoky hand extended for charity, was Pedrillo Oñate. Robert did not dismount this time.

"Friend," he said a little sternly, "do you not know that there is a point when he who asks for alms becomes a professional beggar? Beware, Pedrillo Oñate, lest some one should apply the term to you."

"It is my little father!" cried Oñate, unabashed and smiling up expectantly to Robert. "Ah, kind *señor*, I thought that your beautiful, swift horse had carried you away from this city of hard hearts. I thought that I never should see you again except in my dreams. But you are brought back to help the wretched, relieve the distressed, and aid the poor."

"Ah?" Robert said, a little staggered by this bland flow of words.

"It never can be said of my little father," said Pedrillo, "that he saw a hungry man. . . ."

"Oñate," said Robert severely, "have you eaten fifty dollars' worth of food and are you still hungry?"

"Alas, *señor*, I tasted no more than a single glass of beer. I began to think of what I should eat, but it was not fated that I should touch food. There is such a thing as fate, *señor.*"

"It is true," admitted Robert.

"And fate ruled that I should be robbed of your charity."

"Robbed?"

"All the saints witness for me."

"You have reported to the authorities, then?" asked Robert.

"Would the authorities listen to a poor Mexican? 'Dog of a greaser,' they would say to me, 'out of our sight.' "

Robert suddenly began to grow very pale. "Is it possible that there are such men in this town?" he asked.

"What am I? I am useless. I have only one arm. Why should they consider me? No, they kick me from their paths."

"Who robbed you?" Robert asked in a trembling voice.

"It is a story, *señor,*" said the beggar. "When I looked down at the fifty dollars that you had given to me, I said to myself . . . 'It is the will of heaven that Pedrillo Oñate should be made rich this day.' Yes, food for five months lay in my hand. My heart swelled. For five months I could do nothing but pray for my little father. But then I had another thought. It was enough for me, but for my ancient father and my poor mother . . . alas, even a son with one hand still must think of his honored parents, *señor.*"

"It is true," conceded Robert. "And I honor you for that thought."

"Do you, in truth?" said Pedrillo, with a little glitter of insight in his eyes. "Ah, but the poverty of my poor father and my mother. Bent and sick and unable to work. For what sin they are punished no man can tell. Their lives have been as straight as a ruled line. Every day one of them hears Mass, and both of them go to church on Sundays. But still they are bent with trouble, and yet they submit to the will of our Father. Who are we to question Him?"

"I see that they are good people," Robert said. "My heart

aches for them. But what had they to do with the disappearance of the fifty dollars?"

"I am coming to that. When I thought of them, I said . . . 'You, Pedrillo, may grow fat on this money, but what of your parents?' But everything that the little father has touched is blessed. This money can grow. God will turn it into a great sum. And at that moment I passed the saloon, smelled the cool, fragrant beer, and heard the clinking of the glasses. I went in, and, in a back room I saw the gamblers playing blackjack. 'It is the will of God,' I said, 'that I should play in that game.' Hastily I swallowed my beer. I hardly stayed to pay for it. I entered the other room and sat at the table. And just as I had expected, so it proved to be. The blessing of heaven was on the money of my little father. From fifty it turned to a hundred, and from a hundred it turned to two hundred. And all that money I pushed into the center of the table. I was dealing. I won. I was about to take in the big stake . . . and then suddenly a drawn gun looked into my face. They snatched the money from me. They kicked me from the place. See, *señor*, where a spur tore my coat. So I must sit here again and beg, and my poor father . . . my poor mother must. . . ."

Pedrillo began to weep with heavy sobs, but through his fingers he was watching Robert's face.

As for Robert, he thrust his hand inside his coat, but he did not bring forth the wallet. He merely touched the butt of his automatic and made sure that it worked softly and smoothly in its spring clip.

"Now where is the saloon?" he asked.

"It is that fourth house, little father."

"Come there with me."

"Little father, what are you about to do? They will beat me if I go in. They will speak lies. They will call me a thief and a scoundrel. All three of them will kick me. . . ."

Robert turned slowly away. The way of duty lay before him, as clearly seen as any sunlit path. There were three gamblers in that house of dark deeds. And he must oppose them all. But in the olden days, when had Uncle Jimmy turned from facing such odds as these? Moreover, Robert thought of the good old people, the father and the mother of Pedrillo, and his heart swelled.

When he entered the saloon, three men stood before the bar with little glittering glasses of whiskey before them. The back room was empty, so these were the culprits. And one of them was speaking, with a chuckle.

"I knew he was as crooked as a snake, but I passed the boys the wink and we lay low and watched him deal. Dog-gone me, Joe, it's a sight to see that one-handed deal and I dunno how he works the cards, but finally. . . ."

"I beg your pardon," Robert interrupted.

They jerked their heads around at him.

"Mister Pedrillo Oñate," said Robert, "has been robbed of two hundred dollars in this place. I have come to beg you to return his money."

The three looked soberly at him; they looked at one another; they smiled.

"Kid," said one of them, "are you the new sky-pilot? This ain't your church, though. Take the air, boy."

Robert blushed. "Gentlemen," he said, "I do not wish to use force."

"He's drunk," explained one of the three. "Throw the little fool through the door, Charlie, will you?"

"Well"—Charlie grinned—"maybe it is my turn." And he strode toward Robert.

What a thrill of glory passed through Robert at that moment. There could be no question of mere fisticuffs now, for the odds were three to one. He was afraid. He was hideously and shudderingly afraid, but at the same time he had the joyful assurance that he would not be too afraid to fight.

"Friends," Robert cried, "fill your hands!"

Was it not the old time-honored formula? In those words the immortal Wild Bill had addressed his foes before he fired and slew. And, as Robert spoke, he snatched out his automatic with the speed of long and arduous practice. But, for all his speed, he had time to note that the three were not reaching for their guns. He changed his aim from head to hat, blew the sombrero of Charles into the air, and sent it sailing the length of the bar.

The bartender dived for shelter; falling bottles *crashed* like an echo to the *booming* of the gun, and then the room was still. The three tall men at the bar had gripped the handles of their guns, but they had not drawn.

"Gentlemen," said Robert, "will you kindly take your hands from those guns? Unbuckle your belts, if you please, and let them fall. And remember that I am watching you. My next bullet will be for a head and not for a hat."

Watch he did, and in tense excitement, waiting for the first twitch of gun from holster. But, to his bewilderment, there was no such movement from any of the three. Pale, silent, with lips compressed, they slowly unbuckled their belts and let them fall, guns and all, to the floor.

It was the only safe way of disarming enemies; Wild Bill had never used any other method.

And now three helpless men stood before Robert.

"Who has the stolen money?" asked Robert.

"What stolen money?" asked Charlie with an oath.

"Don't be a fool, Charlie," said another. "Pass out your wallet. He's got the drop on us. Do the watches go, too, kid?"

"Do you consider me a robber?" said Robert, growing very red. "You, if you please . . . count out two hundred dollars on the bar."

It was done. $200 in a stack of rather battered greenbacks lay upon the bar. Robert scooped them up and put them in his pocket.

"Kid," said Charlie, "I don't make out your play, but, if you want your name in the paper, this'll get it there. And I'll be immortally danged if you don't get something else besides a headline!"

"Sir," Robert said with the surety of absolute virtue, "I have taken not a penny more than you stole from the helpless Mexican. And if I seem to have taken an unfair advantage of you, you can take up your guns one at a time and we shall settle the matter here and now."

They were tall men; they were rough men. Their hard hands seemed surely to know every trick of battle and no fear seemed to live in their bright, keen eyes, so Robert waited a moment in breathless suspense. And yet not a move was made. It was odd, but when he saw that nothing more was to be done at the moment, Robert backed to the door and through it into the street.

The moment the door closed, a storm of cursing, shouting, and wrangling began inside the building. He expected to see three fighting men, guns in hands, rush into the street crying for vengeance. He wanted very much to turn his back and run to Pinto, so he forced himself to remain on guard, gun in hand. No one appeared. The storm seemed confined to the interior of the barroom, so Robert restored the pistol to the clip beneath his left armpit, and went hastily to his horse.

V

Around the corner Robert caught sight of fat Pedrillo Oñate fleeing at full speed, but a shout stopped the Mexican, who turned and threw up his hands as though he expected a bullet the next moment.

Other people were hurrying from their houses, and some of

them had caught up a shotgun or rifle as they came. There was no doubt that this little town could prove itself a hornets' nest if it were roused. But the citizens paid no attention to Robert; they looked toward the saloon, from which the shot had been heard and in which the voices now were raging. And Robert felt it was safe enough for him to canter Pinto up to the Mexican.

"Ah, *señor, señor!*" cried Pedrillo, close to tears. "Did I not tell you that they would drive you out with bullets and with curses? God forgive me for the danger in which you have. . . ." He paused.

Robert was extending to him a hand crammed with paper money.

"They gave me the two hundred dollars which they stole from you," said Robert. "And, after all, it seemed that they were not very violent men."

"San Miguel protect us!" breathed Pedrillo, his black eyes making perfect circles. "One of them is Charlie Bent. Violent men, *señor*. They will destroy us both. They gave you the money?"

Dust had gathered on Robert's glasses. He took them off and wiped them clean, at the same time regarding the Mexican earnestly. "The fact is," he said, "that they seemed very unwilling to use their guns. After I had shot off the hat of this Charlie Bent, they became extremely reasonable. I think, Pedrillo, you will find that they are men of good hearts after all."

"Shot off the hat of Charlie Bent?" Pedrillo said, turning pale—that is to say, a shade of sickly greenish yellow. "Ah, *señor.*" He took the money that was offered to him, and his fat fingers stumbled as they counted it. He stuffed it into his pocket.

"You have a horse fleeter than the wind, little father," he said. "But what will become of poor Pedrillo? They will tie me to the tails of wild mustangs. They will drag me to death through the cactus. They will shoot me by little bits. Ah, *señor,* think of me, guard me, protect me. What use is the bone you give a dog if the dog is to be kicked to death for taking it?"

Pedrillo Oñate had only one hand, but, nevertheless, he understood how to make with it gestures as eloquent as any two hands could have managed. Now he pressed up to the shoulder of Pinto and caught Robert's sleeve.

How could one resist such an appeal?

"Come with me, then," said Robert. "I'll protect you if I may. But I don't think there will be any need of protection. You see, they haven't come after me as yet."

"I know them as a man knows fire," Pedrillo stated in a voice that quivered with emotion. "The scars of the anger of *Señor* Bent still are on me. Take me with you, kind *señor,* my father, my master. . . ."

Tears streamed down the brown cheeks of Pedrillo, and Robert was overwhelmed. Pedrillo, with a speed and endurance amazing in a man of his fat, ran from the town, and Robert rode behind him as a sort of rear guard, taking care that they were not followed by danger. There seemed not the slightest chance of this, however, until they topped a rise of ground, heaped up about some stone that broke through the flat face of the desert. Then, glancing back, they saw a cloud of dust sweeping toward them from the village.

"There are seven men!" cried the fat fugitive. "Mother of mercy, fly with me, *señor!*"

"Perhaps there are seven men," Robert agreed, his heart beating fast while his eyes strained through the cloud of dust, "but it appears to me that we should not fly, Pedrillo."

"Should not? That we should not? Yes, but I will show you how we may run away from them and. . . ."

"That," declared Robert, "is a word that I don't like. I've heard a good deal about Wild Bill, but I never heard that he ran away."

"Wild Bill? The gentleman is not known to me," said the trembling Pedrillo. "I respect and honor him . . . I shall offer a prayer for his soul . . . for if ever he waited for seven such men as those from that town, Wild Bill is dead."

"Treachery killed him," Robert explained gravely, "but he never was badly injured by great odds. And the reason is that heaven fights on the side of justice and goodness, Pedrillo."

"Let heaven be on whose side it will!" cried Pedrillo. "Those men speak with nothing but bullets and they listen to nothing but guns. But if you will ride down that draw, I can show you a way to cover your trail. . . ."

"It begins to appear to me," replied Robert, "that this is a matter that you don't understand. The proper thing to consider is not what may be done but what should be done. However, if you are afraid because of your wretched life, Pedrillo, take to your heels and run for the draw. I forgive you for the desertion."

Pedrillo, in fact, ran a little distance, but he turned back again almost at once to the spot where Robert sat his horse, dauntlessly facing the rolling dust cloud that sped across the desert with seven shadows in its midst.

And Pedrillo shouted: "How can I leave you? *Señor*, little father, are you mad? There are seven!"

"There are seven shots in my gun," said Robert Fernald. "I never should fly except as a matter of strategy. Wild Bill would never. . . ."

The suspicion that there was a little streak of unsoundness in the mind of his patron had no sooner entered the brain of Pedrillo Oñate than he felt that this was the solution of the entire mystery. It explained why the little man had given him $50, and then had entered a saloon and held up three fighting men at the point of a gun in order to take back the money that Pedrillo's crooked play had won and lost for him most deservedly.

For two reasons Pedrillo hesitated to fly. In the first place, he had conceived a real affection for our Robert; in the second, and controlling place, he was by no means sure that he could get away from the townsmen if he trusted merely to his speed of foot, unaided by the help of this mad American. He decided to play a last card. He fell upon his knees in the dust and caught hold of Robert's stirrup.

"Little father!" cried Pedrillo. "It is well for you to stand and fight against odds. If I were a lone man . . . a man free from responsibility, I should do the same thing gladly. But I have the burden of a mother and a father who could not keep body and soul together if it were not for me. Fly with me . . . protect and save me . . . for three people die in my one wretched body."

When Robert heard this, he looked down to the shaken form of Pedrillo that stirred in all its fat folds, and then across the plain to the approaching danger. With all his heart he wished to be perfect in his duty, but Pedrillo's argument seemed a weighty one. He turned his horse with a sigh, and presently was riding toward the draw, with Pedrillo holding to one stirrup leather to give wings to his feet.

It was easy to see why Pedrillo had taken the way to this course of a vanished river. The rocky bed would leave little or no trace of the hoof marks, and the sinuous draw was joined at intervals by shallow little steep-walled ravines—the junction points of other waters in the old days. Into one of these blind cañons Pedrillo led the way and behind a rocky shoulder Robert dismounted and waited.

Almost at once, they heard the *rattling* of hoofs down the draw. The hoofs came near. Pedrillo, on his knees, lifted a pitiful face and folded hands to the God who lived somewhere in the sun-white arch of the sky, and the noise of the pursuers went past them so close that they could hear a horse stumble in the loose rocks and the loud cursing of a startled rider recovering his seat. The danger flowed past them, and the noise died away toward the north. At once Pedrillo was all gaiety and mockery.

"Let them sweat on that trail," he said. "They think that they will have Pedrillo like a fat chipmunk out of wind and unable to run another step. But the chipmunk has taken to the ground. Look, *señor,* some men are born fierce, and some are born strong of hand, but it is better than either to be born wise. I am fat and I have only one arm, but it is easier to follow the way of a snake in its hole than the way of Pedrillo Oñate across the desert." Now they left the draw and hurried across the desert to the west. Robert, unwilling that the fat man should wear himself out on foot, offered him his place in the saddle, and Pedrillo, panting, accepted. No sooner was he seated than Pinto pitched him on his head.

Robert lifted the beggar and was happy to find that he was not hurt. He would have had the fat man take the saddle again while he held the bridle and led Pinto, but Pedrillo resolutely refused.

"Better a sprained back than a broken neck," he informed Robert. "A black cloud still floats before my eyes, *señor* . . . but it is a wise horse that knows his own master. Moreover, a fool, *señor,* knows more in his own house than a wise man in the saddle of a stranger."

So he plodded across the desert, promising that before the dark they would reach a good water hole where there would be, moreover, excellent grass for the horse. In the meantime, they scanned the northern horizon but saw no sign of pursuers returning. In good time, as the hot sun rolled down to the rim of the desert and the northern mountains turned a brilliant blue, they reached the promised water hole. It was a little oasis of trees, a small area of grass, and a spring that came welling above the sands and running a little distance before it was drunk up by the desert from which it had issued.

"Such are the virtues of bad men," said Pedrillo, turning up his eyes. "They themselves devour their own goodness. Let us camp here. If there is food in your pack, *señor*, I, Pedrillo, will cook it as food never was cooked before. Ha, look! If there were only a rifle to gather in the rabbit that God gives us for our supper."

A huge jack rabbit that had been crouching in the roots of a tree near the spring, unable to stand the pressure of fear any longer, had leaped up and fled for the desert, dissolved into a gray streak by his speed.

"Rifles are surer, but pistols are quicker, Pedrillo," Robert said, and fired.

A spray of dust stung the belly of the rabbit, which turned with a frightened *squeak* as though dodging the teeth of a hound. As it turned, the second bullet struck it, and it rolled on the sand.

Pedrillo, momentarily turned to stone, regarded Robert with great, round eyes. Then, without a word, he struck his heel into the sand beside Robert and paced the distance to the rabbit. Here he paused, crossed himself once or twice, and returned thoughtfully.

Pedrillo's meditations kept his voluble tongue silent during all the while he was arranging his fire and preparing the rabbit for cookery, which he did by splitting portions of rabbit meat on long splinters, with bits of smoked bacon interspersed. When he began to turn the spits above the fire, however, and delicious fragrance of roasting meat stole beneath the trees, Pedrillo lifted his earnest eyes to his little father.

"Now it is all revealed to me," he said. "I thought that *Señor* Bent was a fool to let two hundred dollars go out of his hands, but I see that he was a wise man. I shall respect him more so long as he lives . . . may the devil take him quickly. Had the rabbit been a man, little father, at thirty paces. . . ."

He stopped, his teeth chattering in his head. The subject was closed. Still, a change had been wrought in the Mexican's attitude to his companion, and now and again Robert found the dark, keen eyes of Oñate turned upon him as if searching for the solution of a mystery.

The promise of Pedrillo was made good, for never was a daintier meal offered on the desert than this which he prepared; never was tougher rabbit made tender; never was such coffee brewed, even in the tent of an Arab. Its perfume delighted no less than its taste, and its power kept joy in the heart long after the few dishes were cleansed and the two reclined in the cool of the evening. They heard the bubbling of the fountain, a faint music that washed away the long pain of the desert sun; they heard the stirring of the wind through the trees; above the far stars shone down and showered infinite peace upon them.

Pedrillo smoked cigarettes of strong Mexican tobacco. Robert lay still and lost himself in a dream. That day he had come to the very brink of a battle to the death and that battle had been undertaken, he felt, in a just cause. Another day, still greater and more perfect, good fortune would come to him. The night turned a little chill. Robert roused himself, prepared for sleep, knelt on his blankets, and bowed his head. There was a long silence; he was settling himself for the night when Pedrillo said: "Little master, is it true that the *Americanos* also pray?"

Certain recollections of his college days swarmed upon the mind of Robert.

"Ah, Pedrillo," he said, "there are many of us who do not know so much as the meaning of the word . . . but my mother taught me."

Pedrillo was amazed. He whistled a long, gentle note of music and admiration.

"Yes," he said, "it is true that women are good for a few small things . . . and advice to children is among them."

Robert was so stung by this remark that he lifted himself suddenly upon an elbow and threw the damp saddle blanket from him—his better blanket he had of course assigned to the beggar.

"Pedrillo Oñate," he said in a solemn voice, "may God forgive you for slighting mothers and womankind. My own mother died while I was a little child, but from her I learned my first and best lessons."

"That is well," said Pedrillo, who loved an argument, "but what does a woman know that a man does not know better? What does a woman do that a man cannot do better?"

"Woman," Robert said sternly, "gives birth to every new soul. Can man imitate her?"

Pedrillo was silenced for a moment, snapping his fingers with impatience.

"And from women," said Robert, "we learn that the greatest strength is the strength of hand."

"That is true," Pedrillo agreed instantly. "But we could learn the same thing from certain men . . . from a fat one with one arm that I have in mind just now we all could learn that wits are better than two hands."

"Foxes have sharp wits," replied Robert, "but they are caught at last by the wolf or the trap. No, no, Pedrillo, the greatest strength is the strength of love. And that is the lesson that we learn from woman. Shall I tell you something? To this day the love of my mother follows me through the world, and her spirit at this very moment is near me. Yes, yes, Pedrillo, her voice is as clear to me as the breathing of the wind in these trees. Do you think it is a miracle? Well, I'll tell you what I believe . . . that every mother follows every son. The whisper of her spirit is our conscience. Sometimes even the fall of a leaf is loud enough to drown that voice, but, if you practice the art of listening, Pedrillo, you will be able to hear it even above the crashing of guns."

Pedrillo did not answer.

"One can keep the body clean with water," Robert went on, expanding on a favorite subject of his thoughts, "but it is the love of woman that purifies the soul. It isn't an accident that women are called our better halves. They are, in fact. And nothing really good is done that hasn't a woman as its cause." He paused for a reply, and the soft, deep snoring of Pedrillo answered him. Robert was left with the silence and the stars.

VI

Robert fell asleep so late—having been raised into an ecstasy by his high thoughts, by the majesty of the desert night, and by the strength of Pedrillo's coffee—that he did not waken until the rim of the sun rose above the eastern horizon and glared at him with a fierce eye.

He got up with a sense of guilt that made his heart beat.

"Pedrillo," he said, "I have slept too late. You should have wakened me before. . . ."

Pedrillo did not answer; there was no Pedrillo to answer.

At first, Robert thought that the Mexican had gone hunting for another rabbit with which to break their fast, but, when he found that his wallet was also gone, he began to suspect that some other cause was responsible for the disappearance of his companion. And a moment later, when he discovered that his automatic pistol was missing, he knew that the Mexican had drawn the teeth of danger before he fled with his spoils.

For a moment Robert was blinded and benumbed with bewilderment and rage. After that, he set about finding the trail. There was not a trace within two hundred yards of the camp, but then he came on a spot—as he cut for sign—that showed a trail beginning. And, looking back, he now could see where Pedrillo had turned with the patience and the skill of an Indian and obliterated one mark of his feet before he made another stride.

Then Robert saddled Pinto, guessing that the Mexican had not been able to catch the pony. Once mounted on the fiery little stallion, Robert sped down the trail of Oñate like a hawk swooping down the arch of the sky.

Presently Robert came to a point where Pedrillo had taken to a rocky draw such as that in which he sought shelter when the seven were behind them. The natural supposition would be that Pedrillo, once in this covert, would turn away from the direction of the town where his enemies dwelt. For that very reason Robert took the opposite way, for he surmised that the Mexican would double on his course like a hunted fox. Some minutes later he was rewarded by sight of Oñate, trotting steadily down the middle of the hollow.

A thrust of Robert's heels made Pinto leap from the low wall, and he landed with a *crash* at the very heels of Pedrillo, who barely had time to wheel, pistol in hand, when Robert had him by the hair and Robert's knife was at his throat.

In this moment of extreme danger Pedrillo did not attempt a snap shot. Instead, he dropped the automatic and screamed: "*Señor* . . . little father . . . do not stain your hands with murder! It is only poor Pedrillo . . . who means no harm. You kill me already with your terrible look. Ah, *señor,* spare me. Let me speak. Let me tell you. . . ."

He was on his fat knees, his face gray and congealed with terror. Robert dismounted and picked up the pistol. No sooner was it in his hand than half his fury disappeared.

"Now the money," he said.

Pedrillo, with a moan, held out the pilfered wallet and the handful of greenbacks, which Robert had given to him the day before.

"I want my own, and not yours," Robert said in disgust. "Do you think that I am a thief as you are, Pedrillo Oñate?"

"My life!" cried Oñate, waddling forward on his knees, and trying to catch Robert's sleeve. "My life, my poor life . . . my father and my mother, *señor!* You will not murder me?"

"Murder? I shall take you to the nearest town and the sheriff shall have you."

"The will of God be done," said Pedrillo, with a sigh of vast relief. "The will of God be done."

"What a scoundrel you are!" exclaimed Robert. "To rob me and sneak away . . . and the last words I spoke to you were concerning. . . ."

"Woman, *señor.* Do you think that I did not hear?"

"You could not. You fell asleep."

"I? Alas, *señor,* you wrong me!"

"Pedrillo, I heard you snore."

"What?" Pedrillo cried, his eyes wandering from side to side with shifting glances. "What? Snore? I snore, little father, while you honored your poor servant by speaking. . . ."

"Your black hypocrisy does not deceive me," declared Robert.

"But to snore. No, no! *Señor,* you heard my deep breathing . . . which is always a little rough . . . particularly when I am stirred, as I was stirred, little father, when I heard you speak of woman. . . ."

"It is false!" Robert contradicted, losing patience.

"No, no, *señor,* kill me, beat me, torture me . . . I shall continue to swear that I heard every word."

"Then why did you not answer?"

"How could I answer? My heart was too full. You had spoken so beautifully. The thought of my mother stood like a picture before my eyes. I wept. A groan was in my throat . . . here, *señor* . . . I felt the ache of a groan." Pedrillo tapped his fat

Adam's apple to prove his point.

Robert was a little shaken, but he continued to regard the Mexican through narrowed eyes.

"You said that you were trickier than a snake in its hole," said Robert, "and I believe you. But now try to twist or wriggle or writhe away from the manifest truth that you were under some obligation to me . . . that I had at least done enough to warrant kindness from you, and yet you stole my money and left me in the desert without a gun, and in danger of enemies who had been raised against me by what I had done for your sake. This is the fact. Now let me hear how you will disentangle yourself from these plain truths that damn you as a knave, a hypocrite, and an ingrate, Pedrillo Oñate."

"Call me a knave, and a hypocrite, and an ingrate," said Pedrillo, "because what virtue is there in me compared with the beautiful soul of my little father. . . ."

"Stand on your feet and talk like a man," commanded Robert.

"No," said Pedrillo, shaking his head with such violence that the loose flesh of his throat waved back and forth and his cheeks shuddered like twin jellies, "no, little father, I shall not rise until you forgive me . . . and believe me! I am about to tell you sacred truth. May God pour belief into your noble heart."

"Well, tell me what you have to say," Robert said, drawing back a little. At the same time he made a strong effort to banish all his prejudice against this fat, brown fellow. But the effort failed; Robert was a very angry young man. His fingers were tingling with a furious desire to grip the handle of his pistol and. . . .

"Ah, how shall I begin?" wailed Pedrillo.

"With the truth," advised Robert, "because a short, plain truth is better than a whole host of lies."

"With the truth and only with the truth do I deal," said Pedrillo, moving a little nearer on his aching knees. "But alas, alas, little father, this truth is so strange and wonderful and beautiful and strong that even you with your strong and beautiful and wonderful and strange. . . ."

"Stop it!" Robert shouted, stamping with impatience.

"*Señor, señor,*" said Pedrillo, shaking his head, "wise men never understand the strength of their own wisdom. You have filled my ears with such words that I could not sleep . . . I thought and thought. You spoke so beautifully about women that the picture of a beautiful woman came into my mind. I saw her clearly in the night. I said to myself that I would waken you and tell you about her. And then I thought that you must have your rest and that in the morning I would tell you so that you could help her. . . ."

"What woman?" asked Robert.

"The *Señorita* Larkin. I thought of her and her sorrows. Then I told myself that it would be wrong to tell you . . . you had your own business. It was not my part to take you from your way. Then I said to myself that I myself would go and do what I could, and, though it might not be much. . . ."

"What trouble is she in?" Robert asked, more in curiosity than in anger.

"Ah, that I could tell you." The Mexican sighed. "But no! If you considered in your great heart among what dangers the lady lives, you would turn straight north to the Larkin Ranch and you would never stop until you had come to the place, and there you would fight and die for her. No, I never shall tell you how her land is harried and how her cattle are driven away by wicked men. You would go mad if you heard it. But I myself shall go. Only, I remembered that I had little money and no gun. So I took yours, *señor,* knowing that you would want to use your weapons and your wallet for none but such a good cause as this one. I took them, and I hurried away to get to the place. . . ."

"You should have asked me," said Robert. "I tell you seriously, Pedrillo, that another man would have accused you of robbery."

"Robbery?" cried Oñate.

"Well," Robert said, "that is what they might call it. But tell me more of the *Señorita* Larkin."

"But the whole world knows about her," said Pedrillo.

"Not I."

"But you have heard of the Larkin Ranch, of course?"

"Never a word before this moment."

"That is a great pity," said Pedrillo. "Once *Señor* Larkin was like a king in the mountains, his lands were so wide and his cattle were so many. But his *ranchería* lay in the midst of hills and mountains. The ravines that cut them were so many doors through which the thieves could drive away stolen cattle. In the days of the great *Don* Gilberto, he had ways and fighting men to keep back the trouble a little . . . but after his death, the robbers had only a woman to fight, and every year her bands of cattle grow less. 'Give up and go away,' say her friends. 'No,' says the *señorita*. 'Someday a strong and brave man will come to help me, and I shall wait here until he comes.' So still she waits and still. . . ."

Robert listened with his head thrown high and his nostrils dilating a little, in very much the pose of a fine horse that hears the cry of the fox hounds over the hills.

"Do you tell me that no one has gone to her help?" he asked.

"Ah, yes. They have gone to try, and they have failed."

"Failed, Pedrillo?"

"In seven years, seven men have died there."

"This brave woman . . . her sons have died fighting for her?" asked Robert, his voice rising a little in the scale of emotion.

51

"Sons? *Señor,* she is only a girl. She has not twenty years, I think."

"Dear heaven," Robert murmured. "Is it possible that a woman could be such a child and still so brave?"

"She is her father's daughter."

"God forgive all men." Robert sighed. "And such a wonderful and beautiful woman is allowed . . . did you say that she was beautiful, Pedrillo?"

"Beautiful? Alas, *señor,* if I were to talk of her, you would say that even your poor servant, Oñate, is a fool and a boy."

"Ah?" Robert sighed again, his breast heaving.

"Her eyes . . . ," began Oñate.

"No, no," said Robert. "I would not go to serve her simply for the sake of her beauty, but only because she is a woman and in trouble. Tell me, Pedrillo . . . no, first stand up."

"You forgive me, *señor?*"

"Forgive you? For what, my poor friend?"

"Because I dared to take. . . ."

"My money? My gun? But only to give them to a woman who needs them? Pedrillo, I not only forgive you, but I should despise you if you had done any other thing. You have taught me my duty."

"I? I could not."

"Hush. Tell me in what direction we should go?"

"North, north, *señor.* North, of course, in the very direction that I was traveling. But consider that there is a terrible danger. . . ."

"We must not be cowards," Robert advised, "dying in fear whenever duty beckons to us."

"But there is Lefty Tom Gill, leading those man-slayers, those. . . ."

"Lefty Tom Gill!" cried Robert. "Is it the man who raided Black Gulch and shot the sheriff of . . . ?"

"*Sí, señor.* But he is older now, and therefore he is more terrible . . . and his men are chosen from among the worst of all the. . . ."

"Let them be chosen where they will," said Robert, "I have heard of this man before. He was a scoundrel in the days when my father still was living. He has been a scoundrel ever since. And consider, Pedrillo, that if I can destroy him, I shall be doing a work that my father would have been glad to do had he lived a little longer. If I am called to this service by the need of the poor lady, why, it is made sacred, a sacred cause, when I hear that Tom Gill is the villain. I thank God, Pedrillo, who sent you to me to show me what to do."

Pedrillo, having rubbed some of the pain out of his knees, which had been grinding on the hard rocks until they were a torment to him, now mopped his streaming face. He seemed to have grown older. His flesh hung in folds. Only by degrees did he regain a moiety of his former assurance and his normal red-dashed color. Still he regarded his reconciled master from the side with an odd mixture of contempt, terror, and astonishment. He measured the distance between them and the hills as though considering that many things could happen before they reached that goal, and then he cried heartily: "*Señor,* we waste time. Let us go forward."

"True, true, Pedrillo," replied Robert. "Let us go forward. But tell me . . . is it not strange that from the beginning of time women in great distress . . . even in the most ancient books, Pedrillo . . . is it not strange that always they are beautiful?"

VII

Such was the beginning of Robert's venture against the cattle rustlers who preyed upon the Larkin Ranch, and all other ranches in the broken range that fenced the desert to the north.

The way was long, but the cunning of Oñate took them to

every water hole with an unerring instinct as true as that of a wild horse, and the purpose of Robert was not dimmed in its strength and its luster. Only, from time to time, he wished to press ahead at a speed such as poor Oñate could not maintain. For Robert was impatient to be at work yonder with his gun.

So they came to the mountain wall, and, as they labored slowly up the incline, he began to appreciate the superior mountain craft of Pedrillo. For the cañons on either side came to blind walls over which the water poured in a crashing white torrent, and there was no thoroughfare for any creature unequipped with wings. The spur made hard going, but by means of it they wound slowly but securely through the belts of greasewood and cactus, and then through a region of stunted shrubbery, and so up to a level of lofty pines that closed high above their heads and made a delicious shade and coolness along the hills.

While they were still in this region, they came to a summit from which Robert had his first view of the Larkin Ranch. It was in a great bowl with an uneven, rolling bottom, edged by the ragged and deeply bitten ranges of hills and mountains. He could hardly guess at the thousands of acres of grazing land that it comprised, but he knew that the sparkling streams of water and the growth of fresh green grass must make an ideal pasturage. He could see, too, that this was a paradise for cattle thieves, for out of the dark mouth of any cañon that split the mountain rim they could swoop down on a scattered group of cows, and drive them away in comparative security.

There was not one such cañon, or two, but a dozen shadowy recesses opened among the heights.

"There are two things that could be done," said Robert at length. "Either the cañons must be blocked . . . which is impossible . . . or else such strength must be here in the valley that cattle rustlers will fear to come down more than they fear riding into fire."

"*Sí, señor*," said the Mexican. "If that could be done. . . ."

And he smiled covertly and looked straight before him, not daring to turn to Robert lest the latter should see the mockery in his eyes.

They came in sight of the ranch house late that afternoon. A noble cluster of trees stood around it, and it extended two large, comfortable wings like welcoming arms. It had grown by fits and starts, according to the whims of the rich rancher who had planned it. No two portions of it were the same in design, but very patently it had pleased one man, and therefore it would please many others. The great stables, sheds, and barns lay well away from the ranch house, and the fields through which the two travelers rode were liberally dotted with cattle.

"Surely," Robert said, growing more and more thoughtful, "the owner of all this land and cattle is rich and untroubled."

"So one would say, *señor*," said the Mexican, "but often as great men grow they carry a growing mortgage with them. So it is here, and the whole world knows that the *señorita* loses money every year and the banks will not help her any longer."

"Business is a mysterious thing," said Robert seriously. "I have tried to understand it before, but I have given up. We must go faster, Pedrillo. I long to see the lady."

Pedrillo, it must be admitted, was a matchless pedestrian. He could not walk fast, but he never stopped, and, although he perspired incessantly, his shadow never grew less. He was as round, as plump, as smiling at the end of this journey as he had been at the beginning of it.

In the evening they came to the ranch house through the cool cloud of trees that surrounded it, and found Miss Beatrice Larkin walking up and down the long verandah that wound about the amusingly irregular front of her house. A tall, spare youth walked up beside her. Near the front door an elderly lady looked up from her knitting, from time to time, to watch the growth of the evening shadows dancing among the trees.

"It is the sister of the mother of the *señorita*," said Pedrillo, whose eyes were growing round with awe as they approached the mansion.

Robert dismounted and stood at the foot of the steps. Miss Larkin paused with her companion just above him. She was a brown-faced girl, almost as dark as a Mexican from constant exposure to the sun that had also faded her bobbed hair from brown to almost a straw color. She was small and slender, but a great spirit found expression in her keen eyes and restless gestures. At a little distance it had seemed to Robert that she walked and talked like a man, but, when he came closer and saw that Pedrillo had not overpraised her, he lost all power of speech.

"Hello," said Miss Larkin. "Where did you blow in from, stranger?"

Robert merely stared.

"Well, sonny," said Miss Larkin, "what's wrong?"

A lump in Robert's throat was seriously in the way of his speech, but he managed to stammer that he had come from the direction of the desert.

Miss Larkin smiled. Or rather, she grinned, for there was something boyish in her expression.

"I didn't think you came from the mountains . . . and Tom Gill," she said.

That gave Robert a perfect starting point, and he said: "I've come about Tom Gill, Miss Larkin. For I hear that you need help. . . ."

"Help? I need an army," said the girl. "Hold on. Are you Sheriff Matthews's boy?"

"No. My name is Robert Fernald. I have no help to offer

except that of my two hands, you see." He spoke with gravity and modesty.

Miss Larkin looked keenly and quickly into the fresh face that all the strength of the desert sun had not been able to mar, except for the tip of a crimson and peeling nose.

"You came to fight Tom Gill. Is that it?" she asked crisply.

"Yes," said Robert.

Miss Larkin stared. She raised her eyes, and saw Pedrillo in the background, significantly touching his forehead, then she said quickly: "It's mighty fine of you. Tumble your pack off that horse and . . . Martha! Martha!"

A voice echoed from the interior of the house and footsteps approached down the hall.

"Show Mister Fernald to a room. We'll have a talk after dinner."

In two minutes Robert was safely out of sight and sitting, rather stunned, in a large, cool, clean room. He felt, somehow, that his entrance had not been very impressive, but at least he was on the ground and afterward he would find his chance for action. In the meantime, there was Beatrice Larkin. He wished that her voice were a little softer, her step a little less briskly swinging, and her eye less commanding. Nevertheless, in spite of these faults—or perhaps even partly on account of them— she filled his mental horizon.

He barely had time to make himself clean and neat—and look to the condition of his automatic—when he was called to dinner. It took a good deal of effort on his part to answer that call, but when he got downstairs, the atmosphere had changed. He was received with gentleness, almost with pity, he thought. And now and again he was vaguely aware of glances meeting behind his back. But all was kindness and hospitality, and Robert was soon quite at home. The only disagreeable feature was the presence of the ranch foreman, who was introduced as Dan

Parker. He took Robert's hand in a grip of iron and looked keenly, quizzically into his eyes. That grip and that stare kept Robert a little flushed for several minutes and made his heart beat uncomfortably fast. But during the rest of the meal, Dan Parker's head was bowed between his mighty shoulders and he attended exclusively to his food. Miss Larkin was absent-minded and silent, also. Her youthful companion, Fitzroy King, who seemed to be a guest, ventured a remark now and again, but got short answers from Miss Larkin. Only the aunt, Miss Harriet Atkinson, maintained the conversation in a quiet, pleasant voice.

After dinner Miss Atkinson talked for a time with Robert—about himself. He explained to her a few of his ideas. And he told her that he really did not hope to rival Wild Bill, or any others among the truly great, only he hoped that he would be able to do something in a small way. And if he could but meet Tom Gill. . . .

Miss Atkinson listened with wonderful sympathy and understanding; she was sure that her niece was grateful for his help. And perhaps, indeed, he might be the means of lifting the terrible cloud that hung over the ranch.

Robert said good night and went to bed. But after he had passed the door—which was framed with a crack so ample that voices passed easily through it—he heard Miss Atkinson say: "A terribly pathetic case, my dear."

And he heard Miss Larkin answer: "Sad or crazy. I don't know which."

Robert wondered what they were talking about, but he was too sleepy to think things out. He could hardly wait to undress before he was in bed and asleep.

The desert fatigue had left him when the sun rose, and he went downstairs where he met Beatrice Larkin singing as she hurried toward the front door, clad for the day's riding on the range.

"If I may have just a little minute of your time, Miss Larkin," he said, "I'd like to know what you could suggest for me to. . . ."

She hardly turned; she merely waved a hand and said vaguely: "Just rest up for a few days, Mister Fernald." She was gone, the screen door banging loudly behind her.

So Robert went out, feeling rather dazed and down-hearted, and found Pedrillo. Pedrillo was in the best of spirits. He had found a blackjack game in the bunkhouse and his capital had increased in consequence. After talking with Pedrillo, it seemed best to Robert that they should ride the range themselves, drifting far toward the northern mountains. One could not tell when they might come on traces of terrible Tom Gill and his men.

Pedrillo got a bronco; young Robert's armament was increased by a borrowed rifle. They rode out on the plains. By suppertime they returned with nothing gained except a closer knowledge of the land. And so it was the next day and the next. But when Robert came in on the third night, Dan Parker met him.

"There was three hard-boiled gents blew in and said they was looking for you," he declared. "I said that they wasn't. They said that they was, and they described you pretty close . . . you and the greaser. But I give them the run off the place. Only I got to tell you, sonny, that, if any of them three meet up with you, they'll eat you raw, because they're pretty mad. And I'll tell you one more thing. All the time that you're on this here place, I'm watching you, kid, because I don't take nothing for granted."

As he said this, he tapped Robert's chest with a finger like a rod of iron.

It was very uncomfortable, and the worst of it was that it seemed to leave Robert nothing to say. So he went into the house for supper, and that night it occurred to him that his hostess was more than a little weary of his presence. Or was it only that her mind was too much occupied with her own troubles?

For she said at table—where the talk had been rather listless: "If Sheriff Matthews doesn't bring a hundred men and comb those mountains, I'll let the world know that he's a quitter and a coward."

It was a brief explosion, but it made Robert tinglingly glad that he was not Sheriff Matthews.

So, next morning, he rose with an iron determination to accomplish some definite thing. First of all, he hunted out Pedrillo. They had been so much together lately that it began to seem impossible for Robert even to think without the company of the Mexican.

"Pedrillo Oñate," he said, "we're starting for Tom Gill again today. But we're going to change things around. Suppose that you were Tom Gill. Suppose you were raiding this ranch. What would you do? Think it out that way, Pedrillo."

"Ah, *señor*," said Pedrillo, "but suppose that I should think right . . . and suppose . . . God forbid . . . that we should meet Tom Gill?"

"Ah!" cried Robert. "And what under heaven has brought us here, Pedrillo? What was the noble motive that made you . . . ?"

"Alas, *señor*"—Pedrillo sighed—"noble motives will not stop lead bullets."

"I understand you," Robert said scornfully. "But even if your first fine purpose is growing weak, Pedrillo, we must keep on, for I have taken an oath."

"An oath, *señor?*"

"That I never shall leave this trail until I find Tom Gill. God is my witness."

He raised his face and his right hand to the sky—and was well-nigh blinded by the sun.

Pedrillo did not laugh; he was still lost in gloom as they rode across the hills toward the mountains. It was mid-morning before they reached the base of the mountains, and they rested in the saddles, watching two riders drive three or four hundred cows ahead of them.

"We must go to the mountains and live there and hunt there," said Robert. "We never shall find Tom Gill on the plains. They make their raids by night, and by day Miss Larkin's men ride everywhere. See, there are two of them even here at the edge of the range."

"But it is a strange thing, *señor*," said Pedrillo, "that Miss Larkin's 'punchers should be driving the cows toward the mountains. And look, *señor!* They are taking the cows at a trot."

So it was indeed. Why should they be driving those cows in that direction?

"We'll ride up and ask," Robert announced.

"My horse is lame, *señor!*" cried Pedrillo.

Robert turned quickly in the saddle and saw the sickly yellow-greenish color of his companion's face.

"Pedrillo, you coward!" he cried. "You act as though Gill were riding there."

"The virgin of mercy shield us!" moaned Pedrillo. "But if that is not the gray horse that no man but Tom Gill rides. . . ."

"It could not be," Robert said, trembling, but trembling not with fear alone. And the next instant a whip cut on Pinto's flank and sent him bounding forward.

Indeed, it did not take long to tell that these were strange cowpunchers, for, when they saw they were approached from the rear, they dashed at the cows, hurried them into a gallop toward the mountain pass that gaped just before them, and then drew from holsters beneath their legs long rifles that flashed brightly in the sun.

So Robert knew, with an excitement that almost stunned him, that whether or not yonder rider on the gray horse were

Tom Gill, here were two thieves working in the broad light of day.

VIII

He looked back. Pedrillo was following, but only at a hand canter and sitting stiffly in his saddle, rather like an observer than one bent on mischief. And that left two men on Robert's hands. If one of them were Tom Gill, then he was lost, to be sure. But he could not turn back. It seemed to Robert that the ghost of pretty Beatrice Larkin drifted somewhere behind him, an armed ghost, rushing fiercely after these robbers. It was a wild illusion, of course. But it made it impossible for Robert to turn his horse, in spite of his fear.

His was a real terror. Now he realized clearly that he had been on a fool's errand, seeing that Tom Gill was one of those very immortals about whom Uncle Jimmy had spoken so often, one of those fearless, strong, cheerful spirits who laughed at death—and never missed a mark. He prayed that Tom Gill might not be one of the two riders, and at the same time he stopped whipping Pinto forward. There was no need of whipping, however. The little stallion loved a race as well as any creature in the world, and now he had taken it into his heart that this was a race against yonder two riders, and he was giving his best, stretching lower and longer as he increased his stride, and fairly winging his way over the rough ground. Perhaps that longer-striding pair could have distanced him on level going, but not over this sort of running. Besides, they seemed to have no intention of merely bolting. They kept the cows at a gallop, headed for the pass, and now one of them turned in the saddle and pointed his rifle.

For the first time in his life, Robert heard a bullet rip through the air above him—a bullet intended for his own body. And what a difference that made in the sound. He ducked lower; he flattened himself against Pinto's neck. If only the little mustang would go slower. No, Pinto raced on gloriously, madly, his ears flattened with his effort. And every instant they drove closer to the formidable pair. Robert's thought changed. Let him be struck, if struck he must be, in leg or arm, a wound that would topple him from the back of his horse.

Two more bullets sang past him. They missed, and Robert groaned to himself: "They're just warning me away. And when they make up their minds, I'm done for."

Only a mighty sense of shame kept him from reining in Pinto as the little horse streaked across the rolling ground. Robert's thoughts glanced back to the past. It all seemed part of a trick of fate now—the meeting with the waitress and her recommendation—the purchasing of Pinto—the journey across the desert—fate had put him on the back of the mustang so that the horse could, in the end, dash him to his death.

Then something nipped his cheek; that side of his face became numb; there was no pain, but hot blood began to pour down.

He had been hit! He touched his face with his hand, and it came away dripping and crimsoned. Surely now it was time for him to turn back. He had been struck with a bullet. Now even Miss Larkin would take him more seriously. He pulled at the reins.

But Pinto had the bit securely in his teeth and he minded that pull on the reins not a whit, except to shake his head and then stretch it forward.

I'm lost, thought Robert.

He saw the two before him bring their horses to a slow canter, and swing around, with rifles poised.

In desperation he whipped out his own rifle and took a snap shot at the man on the gray charger.

He did not stir from his saddle, but yonder—behold—the

second man had doubled over and dropped his rifle to the ground with a yell that rang far and faint in the ears of Robert. He had shot his first man. Ah, not fatally, thank God. For the fellow had swung to the right, was lying low along the neck of his horse, and was fleeing for his life.

That was not all, for when the man on the gray horse saw what had happened, he pitched forward low on the neck of his mount, and drove to the left into some scattered trees.

It was not Tom Gill, then, for Tom Gill would never turn his back on any man or group of men. It was not Tom Gill, therefore, why might not Robert overtake this rider and fight him to a finish with a chance of victory? The first success had filled him with the same glorious madness that possessed Pinto, and the next moment he was rushing through the trees of that open copse. Again and again Robert had glimpses of the fugitive, and once so near that he could see the strained and desperate expression of a broad-faced man, grizzled with middle age.

Robert thrust the rifle back into the sheath and snatched out the automatic, for when he next had sight of this man, it would be a close thing. The gun was hardly in his hand when he had a nearer view of the flying horseman. He fired, and in answer the pursued swung his gray around and fired pointblank.

The bullet twitched at Robert's coat as it tore through beneath his armpit. As he felt the jerk, he instinctively fired in reply, hardly so much as pointing his own weapon.

The rider of the gray lurched from the saddle and lay on the ground face up, his arms thrown wide. A moment later, while Pinto touched noses with the tall gray, Robert knelt by the motionless body and saw a red streak across the forehead of the fallen man.

Death, surely.

In the quiet that followed the firing, Robert felt that the tall, dark trees were watching and listening, and he was half frightened by the heavy breathing of the horses, and the *creaking* of the girths as their bodies heaved.

It was as if a ghost had voice when the fallen man groaned. Yes, groaned, stirred, and sat up with his hand pressed to his head.

"Thank God," said Robert. "I thought you were a dead man."

"It's a kid," said the other with a snarl. "A pink-an'-white kid. Ten million damnations! Nobody'll believe it. Chuck done for . . . and *me.*"

"You're bleeding still," Robert advised politely. "Will you let me tie up the wound?"

"*Aw,* go to hell," answered the unromantic cattle rustler. "I ain't hurt. I ain't hardly scratched. But," he added, looking at Robert with a horrible leer of mingled pleasure and hate, "if I'd bore a bit to the left, I'd've got you clean, my fine young bird, eh?"

And he pointed to Robert's wound.

It was an excellent remedy for the boy's sentimentality. It enabled him to order his prisoner crisply to his feet; it enabled him to tie the man's hands behind him and make him climb upon the gray.

"Everybody'll know there was something wrong," said the prisoner. "They'll know that a baby-faced brat like you never could have beat Tom Gill in a fair fight."

"*Tom Gill!*" cried Robert. He almost lost his balance and fell from the saddle. "Did you say that your name is Tom Gill?"

"You blockhead," answered Mr. Gill. "Who else in these parts rides Lucky Joe, will you tell me?"

Robert could not answer. Awe, wonder, and a peculiar shame possessed him. For, after all, what Mr. Gill said was perfectly true, and, if luck had brought his rifle bullet a little more toward the center, there would have been a dead Robert Fernald—dead with a bullet through his brain.

Shame-faced, dizzy, and unable to realize what had happened, Robert rode out of the woods with his prisoner, and met Pedrillo riding slowly up.

When he saw this tableau, the Mexican went almost mad with joy. He threw up his one hand. He swayed in the saddle. He crooned in hysterical joy. "*Señor,* my master, my dear brother!" cried Pedrillo. "We have won! They are ours! I rode like mad. I spurred this fool of a bronco. I could not get closer. But they saw that I was coming. It frightened them. Together we defeated them. Ah, *Señor* Fernald, we are famous men."

He continued in this vein for some time, meanwhile tying up the wound in Robert's cheek, which he pronounced no more than a little scratch.

"I only got one thing to ask of you, kid," the rustler said, at length.

"Whatever I can do, I shall," said Robert willingly.

"Then shut the trap of this simp, will you?" asked Tom Gill. "Because hearin' him yap sort of tires me a little. I have et greasers," he added to the Mexican. "I have had 'em for breakfast and for lunch. I have practiced upon greasers before shooting at real men. I have most likely used your pa and uncles and all your brothers for targets, you yaller-faced, cross-eyed, one-handed streak of nothin'."

"Dog of a thief and sneak and coward!" Pedrillo cried. "You know that your hands are tied and that I cannot strike you, or I would shoot you to. . . ."

"Be quiet," said Robert. "As a matter of fact, Pedrillo," he added, "it seemed to me that you were not urging your horse very hard when Pinto was running after the rustlers."

"Not urging the horse? *Señor,* you wish to break my heart!" Pedrillo cried. "See! His flanks are torn by my spurring, and he is covered with whip strokes, welts, bruises. I beat him, I cursed him, I prayed for him, but he would not run. Alas, *señor,* you kill me with your suspicion and your unkindness."

"Now ain't that like one of the treacherous, vile, low-down, sneakin' hounds?" Tom Gill stated, without heat, but rather in calm comment. "Ain't it like one of 'em, I ask you? I never knew one that had enough heart to do for a rabbit. You ain't letting him kid you, are you?"

"*Señor* Fernald!" the Mexican pleaded. "I go mad with shame. Do you permit him . . . ?"

"Be quiet, Pedrillo," Robert snapped. "Go back and head the cattle from the pass."

"It ain't any use, kid," Tom Gill said calmly. "Fact is . . . none of the boys'll have the heart to bother them cows after they hear that I've had a piece of bad luck. They've damned me and hated me and spited me and been jealous and low-down and mean and hateful, but, now that they ain't got me to lead 'em and show 'em what to do, why, they'll bust up and scatter. I laugh when I think of it," he added, his lip curling. "Brave as long as they got a Columbus to show 'em how. But now that I'm gone, they ain't gonna be so brisk. About the whole gang of 'em is gonna slide before morning, I take it. They'll see who was the man of the party."

Tom Gill made this speech with a sort of sneering self-satisfaction, and rather to himself than to Robert, whose opinion of his famous prisoner was sinking mightily with every moment that he listened. Suddenly Gill said: "What name did the greaser call you, kid?"

"Fernald."

"Well, I knew a Fernald in the old days."

"You did?" Robert said coldly.

"But he was a hard-boiled one," went on Tom Gill, "and no kin of yours. There was only one amusin' thing he done, that low-down murderin' hound. And that was to cuss. Dog-gone me if he wasn't a corker at that. I seen him lay dyin'. I wish that it had been my luck to sink the bullet in him that stopped him. But even when he was croakin', with his head in Jimmy Dinsmore's lap, dang me if his cussing wasn't a thing to listen to and remember. Only it was too fast to memorize. But I'll be damned if he didn't leave sixty thousand cold iron men, that four-flusher. He'd hit it rich."

Rage had been slowly gathering in Robert's breast, but rage was displaced by astonishment when he heard this last statement. Mathematics never had been a favorite study with him, but he knew enough to understand that $60,000 at six percent makes $3,600 a year. And the bitter truth was that Uncle Jimmy Dinsmore had never spent half that sum upon him in any year. How, then, could the fortune have been dissipated?

"Sixty thousand?" breathed Robert.

"It sounds like much, kid, don't it?" remarked Tom Gill. "But Fernald left it to a windy old crook named Dinsmore. The outlyin'est man that ever spun a yarn. We used to like to hear Jimmy talk so's we could laugh afterwards. By his fireside he must've killed a hundred men or so. Always talkin' about Wild Bill, who must've died while Jimmy was in short pants. Well, Jimmy must've had a real gay time blowin' in that wad of money. He had a flyin' start right there in the camp. And I'm kind of glad of it, because a four-flusher like Fernald didn't deserve. . . ."

"Mister Gill," Robert said coldly, "you're speaking of my father."

Gill gaped, bit his lip, and then was silent.

When he spoke, it was in a humble tone: "If I had knowed, kid," he said, "I wouldn't have yapped like that. But you ain't got the look of your dad, y'understand? I couldn't guess."

Robert, white with anger and grief, said nothing, and Tom Gill added after a moment: "Me and your dad never hit it off. You put down some of my talk just to hard feelin', will you?"

"And the sixty thousand dollars?" Robert added with a burst

of hope that Uncle Jimmy might have been slandered.

"*Aw,* I seen that paid over in dust and nuggets. I seen it weighed out with my own eyes. So did a hundred gents, besides me."

Robert's cheek began to swell, pressing hard against the bandage. The pain, the loss of blood, the burning heat of the sun beneath which they were riding raised a fever. He began to breathe hard, to wish that the miles to the ranch would quickly disappear. They dragged on, however, with a mortal slowness. In a semi-delirium Robert rehearsed what he had heard. His ideal picture of his father, if not destroyed, was at least tarnished sadly. The admiration with which he regarded Uncle Jimmy Dinsmore now seemed to have been paid to a scoundrel—the worst of scoundrels, who would steal from a helpless child. He shook his head, but he could not shake out these wretched doubts. Robert's magnificent faith in humanity tottered and staggered toward a fall. He could recall now some of the words of Uncle Jimmy—words that that wily man had uttered at their last interview. And Gill's statement seemed gloomily substantiated.

So that morning wore away and deep into the hot afternoon they rode. The Mexican, after lingering with them for a time, had raised a surprising burst of speed and dashed away across the hills in the direction of the ranch house.

"Look at him." Tom Gill grinned. "The rat'll get in there and hog all the credit before you arrive, kid. Now, if that ain't a greaser trick. But I'll sink his ship for him. A greaser have anything to do with the taking of Tom Gill? The whole world would laugh at that, I guess." He added with a scowl: "And if it wasn't for a lucky shot, there'd be one less gent named Fernald in the world, too. You write that down in red, old son."

Gill appeared to view his capture in a magnificent impersonal light, as though it were a matter of history that he could stand

back from and regard as though it had happened to another.
They came at length within sight of the ranch house, and
Robert's heart swelled and the dizzy sickness left him.

He would be a stranger and a slighted guest no longer in this
place, he had reason to think. Look. Even now a dozen or more
people swept out from among the trees and swarmed up the
hills toward him. Among them, on a tall black horse that shone
like polished ebony, came the form of a girl, the wide brim of
her hat flaring back from above her eyes. He could pick out tall
Dan Parker, too, who had been so sternly suspicious. Robert
began to laugh a little weakly, and very happily.

"Gonna be a procession," said Tom Gill. "And why not, I ask
you? Because it ain't every day of the year that a jake outfit like
this has Tom Gill with 'em. Look at 'em come tearin', kid. I tell
you, a week from now everyone of them low-down, sneakin'
coyotes will be talking about how *they* captured Tom Gill. But
I'm gonna let the world know the truth, just to spite their eyes.
It was you . . . and luck . . . that downed me. Aye, come foamin'
and shoutin', all of you. None of you had nothin' to do with
this here!"

IX

Robert knew what a triumph was in the days of ancient Rome.
It made him very happy to have these rough men surge around
him, clap him on the back, hope that his wound was not serious, shake his hand, and tell him that he was "all right." With
conviction they said it, and, being men of few words, their praise
had weight and meaning. They laughed at the pride and conceit
of Pedrillo, but they laughed with the utmost good nature. "The
greaser thinks this is his day," said Dan Parker. "Let him crow a
while."

Robert was very happy, but he was ashamed, too. They were
making too much of what he had done, and he felt a rising

sense of guilt, particularly when they reached the house and young Fitzroy King shook his hand and congratulated him, but even more than that, when he was alone with Beatrice Larkin and her aunt. Miss Atkinson was extremely gay as she looked upon Robert with affectionate eyes and had an air of one who "told you so."

Robert could stand no more. He became more and more depressed, and finally cried out: "I can't let you go on like this. It . . . it isn't right!"

For Beatrice Larkin had said: "I think it's going to mean everything to us. We're going to keep the place together. And that means my father can rest happy in his grave." She said it with tears in her eyes. And now, as he protested, she looked at him with a touch of horror.

"Why isn't it right, my dear boy?" asked Miss Atkinson.

"Because," said Robert, "you make me out a hero, and I'm not. I was . . . afraid all the time."

He brought it out with a mighty effort, his hands clenched. They said nothing. He could see condemnation gathering in their quiet eyes.

"And when I saw Pinto overtaking them, I would have turned back, but he had the bit in his teeth. I couldn't stop him . . . he just thought it was a race."

He made the dreadful confession with a gathering sickness of heart, for, as he spoke, he could see what a sorry figure he had cut in the whole affair. Yet it was a consolation to speak the truth. A weight was lifted from his heart and he exchanged glory for an inward peace. It was very hard though to have his words put out the light that had shone in the face of Beatrice Larkin.

He went on: "Then, when a bullet hit me, why I just wanted to roll out of the saddle and lie on the ground and pretend to be dead."

He could feel their censure, their scorn. Ah, well, he would finish this confession as well as he could.

"Then when I saw that I was being brought right at them by Pinto, I . . . well, I was desperate. I fired at Tom Gill . . . and the bullet hit Chuck and made him gallop away. Then when I saw Tom ride to escape from me, of course that gave me more courage. I didn't dream that it was Gill, or I never should have dared to go after him. I rushed Pinto into the woods and by a lucky shot managed to knock Gill out of the saddle. When I found out his name afterward . . . why, it just about paralyzed me. I wanted to be what you thought I was. But . . . I had to tell the truth!"

When he had spoken, he was left trembling. He could not raise his eyes as he heard the cold, clear voice of Beatrice. "It seems that Pinto was the hero, and not his rider."

"Yes," Robert agreed. "It *was* Pinto."

"*Humph!*" said Beatrice, and Robert shuddered.

"It doesn't seem possible," said Miss Atkinson in a wavering voice, "that there really can be anyone like this." She came to Robert and took his face between her withered hands and made him look up. He was amazed to see tears trickling down from her eyes. "It is possible," said Miss Atkinson. "You . . . you. . . ."

Miss Atkinson hurried from the room, and, as she closed the door, Robert heard her sob. He stood up, shaken to the depths of his soul.

"I'm sorry that . . . that I upset her so. I think that I'd better leave right away, Miss Larkin. Thank you for putting me up."

He got to the door, but there he was caught by the arm and drawn firmly back.

"You inconceivable little idiot," said Beatrice Larkin. "Don't you see it was because poor Aunt Harriet was overcome by your modesty. I even am myself a little. Don't you understand? You haven't done any shameful thing. You've been a hero. Robert

Fernald, write it down, memorize it. You . . . are . . . a . . . hero. You've done the greatest thing that's ever been done in this range of mountains since God raised 'em out of the sea. Go upstairs and lie down and I'm coming along to dress that wound in your cheek for you."

Robert obeyed as one in a dream, and yet it was such a happy dream as it is given to few to enjoy. Everything, it appeared, was all right; he had not done wrong; Miss Larkin had said so. Furthermore, she would manage things—take care of him.

When Miss Larkin came, she found Robert delirious, with an alarmingly high fever. She called in Miss Atkinson, and together they ministered to him.

The two women discovered that, if Miss Larkin remained in the room, the sufferer was quiet and slept, but, if she left, he grew swiftly and astonishingly worse.

"I don't know what it means," said Beatrice Larkin, frowning.

"You dishonest little minx," said Miss Atkinson. "It means that another poor man has fallen in love with you. You know it better than I do."

"I suppose I do," said Miss Larkin. "The poor baby."

"Baby? Hero," said Miss Atkinson.

"Baby," insisted Beatrice, and she patted Robert's hand.

In the middle of the night Robert wakened from a frightful dream and started up, terrified, until by the lamplight he saw that Beatrice was beside him. He clung to her hand and watched her feverishly.

"Is everything all right?" asked Robert.

"Yes," said the girl.

"I haven't made a fool of myself?"

"Don't be a silly child. Go to sleep."

He wakened next morning with a clear brain, the fever quite

gone, his nerves soothed, his strength returned. The poison had been drawn from his cheek, and the swelling reduced. There sat Beatrice Larkin, looking just as fresh and pretty and untired as though she had not had an all-night vigil. Robert looked up at her with worship, and suddenly Miss Larkin looked away.

She went to the window and stared out. "You're a lot better," she said. "If you're quiet all morning, you may be able to come downstairs this afternoon. Are you all right now?"

"It's as though I'd been on a long journey," said Robert. "With you, I mean. I hope . . . I hope I didn't say a great many foolish things?"

The merest tinge of pink appeared in the face of Beatrice Larkin. "Oh, of course you didn't," she said, and left him. But he was not reassured. The memory of spoken words remained in his mind, as though he had been saying: "Without you I shall die."

He got up and dressed with some difficulty, and went down the stairs with oddly unsteady knees. However, he had the consolation that Beatrice Larkin had said that everything was all right, and that he was a hero. He did not dare to examine that idea in detail, yet in the mid-morning he managed to walk out toward the corral, to have a sight of Pinto.

On the way he met the roustabout, the cook, and a cowpuncher; every one of whom hastened to corroborate their mistress' flattering estimate. Robert went on toward the corral, and gradually he began to see that, no matter how the fight with Gill might appear in his own eyes, his exploits of the day before were important things in the eyes of the rest of the world. Tom Gill had been taken to the distant town under a heavy guard and, once that celebrated person was in jail, would not history record that one Robert Fernald, son of Dixie Fernald, had captured him single-handedly?

Pinto put back his ears at sight of his master, but, when saddling was not insisted upon at once, he worked his way to the fence casually, indifferently until his head hung across the bars. "You scoundrel," said Robert. "You ran away with me."

Pinto nipped his master's ear and then tossed his head as though overcome with fear and guilt. But he made no effort to run away.

Robert laughed. His heart was very warm. "We're sort of used to each other, old horse," he said.

X

Dan Parker was not one to sit down and rest after such a beginning had been made in crushing the rustlers. He took ten good and true men into the hills, and in five days they were driving a horde of cows that the bandits had pooled in the upper cañons of the mountains to wait for a good market. There had been glimpses of the outlaws during this raid, but they were flying glimpses of men who scampered away as fast as they could. For it appeared their spirit had left them with the departure of Tom Gill.

So, by the time that Robert was fully recovered, the results of his fight were apparent on every hand. Beatrice Larkin was not secretive, and announced with joy that the banks were now only too eager to supply her needs. And she planned to resume operations on the scale and style that her father had employed so successfully.

"In three years," said Miss Larkin, "why, we'll all be rolling in money."

She made a point of saying this in the presence of Robert Fernald, as though she wished everyone to understand his share in any success that might come to her. She had a plan whereby young Fernald was to be established in the lower mountains with a little group of picked fighting men. Shifting his quarters from time to time, he was to study the mountains and learn the location of the open or box cañons, as the case might be. In case of a cattle raid, fire signals by night or smoke signals by day would tell the sentinels in what direction the drive was heading, and Robert with his outpost guards could rush to block the exit. For such a service as this, Beatrice Larkin would pay most handsomely—not only in cash, but in other ways. For instance, she had extensive timber lands in those tall mountains, and, if they were worked on shares, with Robert representing her interests on the spot, he would be on a direct road to high fortune.

It was not these promises of great opportunities that stirred the blood of our hero, but the chance for action, and, more than all this, the delightful necessity of talking over matters with Miss Larkin. There were two things that he must do before he accepted any post, however. One was to complete his pilgrimage to his father's grave; the second was to visit Uncle Jimmy Dinsmore and bring him sharply to task for his treachery. Miss Larkin was opposed to either absence. For, as she pointed out, Gill was not the only formidable cattle rustler in the world, and all that kept others from establishing themselves was the fear of this new force in the Larkin Valley.

Days slipped rapidly away while Robert strove to make his decision. There was nothing to mar the calm of his life now except that Pedrillo Oñate was expelled from the bunkhouse as a crook by the Larkin cowpunchers. They would have taken more violent measures if it were not that they held his master in awe. Robert called the man before him.

"Oñate," he said sternly, "have you cheated the men in the bunkhouse?"

Pedrillo raised his hand to the sky above them. His voice trembled with emotion. "Ah, *señor*," he said, "when luck runs to a man, is it not true that others grow unhappy? Had an American won so steadily as I, the rest would have hated him, only they would have kept silent. But I am a poor Mexican . . . therefore they drove me out and would have murdered me and robbed my dead body if it were not that I belong to my little father, of whom they are very much afraid."

Robert was sure that Pedrillo was a good man. Yet shadows of doubt sometimes persisted in crossing his mind.

In this unhappy quandary, he walked past the house into a lane of pine trees, where the fallen needles deadened the sound of his footfalls. The unkind god of chance brought Robert now suddenly within sound of voices that came toward him around a curve.

One was the voice of Fitzroy King, the other the clear tones of Beatrice Larkin.

"But the little fool looks at you like a calf," said Fitzroy King. "It's intolerable, Beatrice. Really it is. I've hesitated to speak. I don't want to presume, but, after all, a man wants to shield the girl he's engaged to from any. . . ."

"From what?" Beatrice laughed. "Good heavens, Fitz, he's only a child. I feel like a nurse or a grandmother when I'm with him. I just pity him . . . and I have to talk seriously with the poor dear and make him think he could be useful to me here."

"Pity is the nearest neighbor to love," said Mr. King with the surety of the very young.

"Love little Bobby Fernald? Love that baby?" the girl said scornfully.

Then they came around the corner and straight in view of Robert. He had wanted to slip aside, out of their way. He wanted to save the girl from humiliation. But somehow his feet would not walk rapidly, and he was forced to move like a snail. So here they were before him.

Fitzroy King uttered a stifled cry and leaped back. But Robert was not thinking of him. He was too miserable to do more than note the horror-stricken face of Beatrice.

He slunk away among the trees and made for the house. An agony possessed him—lest he should not be able to leave the place before Miss Larkin returned. He met Pedrillo on the way to the house, and sent the Mexican to prepare Pinto and the newly acquired mule.

He rolled his pack together and, hurrying downstairs, encountered Miss Atkinson.

"My dear Bobby. You seem altogether fit," she said. "What's that roll of blankets?"

"I have to leave suddenly," said Robert.

"Does Beatrice know?"

"Yes," Robert muttered faintly. "She knows."

"Well," said Aunt Harriet, "you'll be back soon. But you don't look so well just now, Bobby. You must sit down a minute. I think that you've upset yourself by carrying that heavy blanket roll. . . ."

Now that the veil had been snatched from his eyes, Robert realized that Miss Atkinson was talking to him as though he were a child—and that all the others always had talked to him as though he were the merest boy.

"Here's Beatrice rushing up the path," said Aunt Harriet. "You'd better wait to see what she. . . ."

"No, no," said Robert. "I must go at once. Only, I want to thank you for your kindness to me. I want you to thank Miss Larkin, too. And. . . ."

"Bobby! What in the world are you talking about?"

Robert fled without waiting for another word to where Pedrillo waited with his mule and Pinto.

Side-by-side they rode away from the Larkin ranch house, and Robert thanked the trees that screened his fleeing form. But there was no pursuit, and he was both sad and glad that he was left alone.

"*Señor*," Pedrillo said suddenly, "you are sick."

"Use your spurs on that mule and stop talking," Robert ordered harshly.

Never had he spoken in such a manner to anyone. Pedrillo, blanched with fear, drove his strong mule to a run, and they rushed headlong down the trail.

Wild, fierce thoughts stormed through Robert's mind. He heard again the words: "Pity . . . baby . . . calf." To him! To the son of Dixie Fernald!

He hoped that the rustlers who he had driven from the mountains by his deeds would now return to the passes and sweep Larkin Valley bare of cattle. He hoped that Beatrice Larkin, crushed and broken, would send to beg him to come back and help her. He would coldly and politely refuse. No, he would return, and extend the strong shield of his might above her, calmly, without scorn, then ride away and let humiliation bow her to the dust. So thought Robert.

But when they reached the edge of the desert that evening and made camp, when the distant stars began to burn through the evening haze, his mind grew pacified. The ache in his heart was less and less. But he knew that it would never disappear entirely. This, then, was certainly a type of noble womanhood.

Night came. Robert could not eat. He lay on his back with his hands behind his head. Pedrillo, unconcerned, consumed a double supper and sang a little between courses as he let out his belt.

The image of Beatrice hung in the darkness above Robert, for the eye of the mind sees both body and soul. He could understand everything more clearly now. She was not to blame. He, like a preposterous fool, had aimed at the stars, but the stars were not for him. She was above him, beyond him. Assuredly she had not meant to wound him.

When he had purged all blame from his thought of her, he felt as though he had healed the wound that hurt him. The scar was his, but the image of Beatrice was more divine than ever. And his love for her grew more perfect because it was hopeless.

So by a touch of natural magic he recovered his faith in womankind, but there remained the terrible breach in the strong wall of his faith in men—there remained the cruel treachery of Uncle Jimmy Dinsmore.

Robert set his teeth and reached for the handle of his automatic. And fell asleep.

XI

A certain recklessness had grown up in Robert's heart and his attitude toward his fellow men.

He said to Pedrillo as they jogged across the desert next day: "What is the name of the town where you were living, Pedrillo?"

"San Joaquin," said Pedrillo.

"Point us back for it then," commanded Robert.

"*¡Señor, señor!* They would tear us both to shreds!"

"Point us on to the back trail for that town," reiterated Robert.

Pedrillo, filled with thoughtful misery, obeyed.

In due time they sighted the wretched handful of hovels that rose like heaps of burned mud out of the sands.

"I wait for you here," whined Oñate.

"You ride in," Robert stated cruelly. "You ride in ahead of me. I shall come behind."

Oñate began to whimper. "You can find trouble enough here," he said. "You can find trouble enough without using me as bait while you fish for it. Do not drive me in."

A silent gesture herded him forward, and Pedrillo went on like one condemned to death.

But Robert seemed merely to take a grim pleasure in his companion's pain. He relented not, and they rode through the main street until there was a loud shout, and Pedrillo, with a shriek of terror, fell backward from the saddle into the dust.

Then Robert saw on the sidewalk the ominous form of Charlie Bent, gun in hand, shouting: "Crawl over here, you greaser! Crawl over here and lemme see what . . . !" Charlie Bent left his sentence unfinished and leaped backward through the swinging doors of the saloon.

He had caught sight of Robert, and, as he leaped, he fired wildly into the air.

Robert missed Mr. Bent by an important fraction of an inch, but split the swinging door from top to bottom. Otherwise, there was no harm done, although Pedrillo was writhing in the street as though both shots had taken effect in his body.

Robert dismounted and entered the saloon, gun in hand.

To the rear there was a sound of many hastening feet trampling through the exit, and voices raised in wild confusion. But in the barroom there was no one save a white-faced bartender, his hands above his head, who cried: "You ain't gonna murder a harmless man?"

Robert took stock of the situation with a mirthless smile. Then he called: "Pedrillo! Pedrillo! Come in here!"

Pedrillo rose from the dust and came in, shuddering with terror. He dreaded nothing in this world so much as he dreaded his young master. And the sight of his obedience was a balm to the soul of Robert. He tapped with the muzzle of his gun on the bar.

"Pedrillo will have a drink," he announced.

With a shaking hand, the bartender poured the potion.

"Drink," said Robert.

"Yes, *señor*," gasped Pedrillo. And he drank.

"What is your name?" asked Robert of the bartender.

"Dick Jones, sir."

"Dick Jones, Charlie Bent drew a gun on my friend Oñate

81

just now. If it were not that I have very important business on hand, I should follow Bent and get an explanation from him. But I am busy and riding fast. I want to tell you that Oñate has come back to live in this town, and live in peace. If word comes to me that anything has happened to him, I'm coming back to learn the details. Will you let San Joaquin know that?"

"Yes, sir," said the bartender. "In your own words, sir."

Robert shook hands with Pedrillo, who was beginning to understand what was happening around him.

"Good bye," said Robert. "Be honest, Pedrillo. But if you have trouble, send for me."

Pedrillo looked at the quaking bartender; he listened to the beat of horses' hoofs departing.

"Ah, *señor*," he said, "I think I can live the rest of my life in this town and never have trouble with any man."

Ten minutes later, Robert rode through the desert on the farther side of San Joaquin; the past was behind him, and in the future he saw only the face of Uncle Jimmy Dinsmore.

In due time, he reached the village where he had bought Pinto, and he had lunch at the hotel. But the same waitress did not serve him. She merely hovered in the background, grinning, nodding, waiting for a scrap of attention, while her employer with his own brown hands served his distinguished guest. He let it be known that the town knew all about Robert Fernald's exploits—the capture of Tom Gill, the shooting of Chuck Renney, and the pacification of San Joaquin. They knew, and they honored the warrior.

Robert thought the proprietor the pleasantest man he ever had met, and the town the most delightful in the world. He was sorry that he had to leave it to ride on the trail of the scoundrel, James Dinsmore.

But that trail had to be ridden, and one day Robert rode

Pinto to the hilltop and looked down on the recumbent form of his uncle.

"Get up!" Robert said in the harsh voice that he had used since that day when he overheard the conversation of Beatrice and Fitzroy King. "Get up and talk!"

Mr. Dinsmore got up, his mouth gaping open in amazement. "Why, Bobbie . . . ," he began.

"You've robbed me," Robert stated brutally, "of sixty thousand dollars. Where's the money?"

Mr. Dinsmore staggered back. One hand grasped at the tree trunk for support; the other went toward his belt.

"And keep your hands free from mischief, sir," Robert said, watching narrowly. "I don't want to be tempted . . . any more than I am at the present moment."

Mr. Dinsmore gasped: "Thief! I'm called a thief? And by a lad I've labored, planned, hoped for . . . good heavens, it's enough to kill a man."

"What's become of the money?" Robert asked firmly.

"You wouldn't believe me," said Mr. Dinsmore. "I'm a thief, so I'm a liar, too, I suppose."

"If you have anything to say," said Robert, "I'll listen."

"Robert," said Mr. Dinsmore, "you ask me for sixty thousand dollars."

"Yes."

"I'll tell you where it is in one word."

Even without a single word Dinsmore was able to say it. He made a sweeping gesture with both hands, indicating eloquently enough that the money had flown.

"It's gone?" Robert said, his eyes narrowing.

"It's gone."

"Well?"

"You never knew Dixie Fernald," said Dinsmore. "But I knew him. You never held his head in your arms while he lay dying . . . but I did. 'Do for the kid everything that I'd do, old partner,' said Dixie Fernald to me."

"Well, what would Dixie have done?"

"I'll tell you. He would've kept on the way that he started out doing. He would've stacked up money on top of money, and he would've made himself so terrible rich that there wouldn't have been ten men in the country to hold a candle to him. I knew that's what Dixie would've done, and, by the time that his kid grew up, why he would've had steam yachts and race horses and such like to waste his time on. So I says to myself . . . 'Doggone me if I don't try to do the same thing for this here kid. Little thanks I'll get if I just keep the money in the bank at four percent.' So I started out to make that sixty thousand grow. Well, kid, I had no luck. I worked and planned and never invested a penny without thinkin' it over first and getting the best sort of information. But the fact was that I just had no luck. And nobody can get along without luck, and you ought to know it. You've gone out and made a name for yourself. You've gone out and dropped Tom Gill and another gent. Well, the world's talkin' about you now. The world is glad to know you. But supposing that you had had a little bad luck instead of good? Suppose that Tom had had a little good luck instead of bad? Suppose that the bullet that knocked him down had been a quarter of an inch wide, and the slug that nicked your cheek had been centered a mite more? Suppose that had happened? Then you wouldn't be here to ask your Uncle Jimmy what he done with the money that he hoped to grow into a million or two for you. No, you wouldn't be here calling me a liar and sneak, and a thief and. . . ."

Dinsmore ended with a groan and covered his face.

Robert looked at the ground. Suppose that he were wrong? Suppose that . . . ?

"Look here. You blew in ten thousand gambling before you

left the town where my father died. You blew it in inside of twenty-four hours," Robert stated.

"I?" Uncle Jimmy cried indignantly. "Who dared to say so?"

"Tom Gill."

"Tom Gill?" Dinsmore said, a little staggered. "Well, he was right. I blew in ten thousand. But how did he dare to say that it was your dad's money?" He gathered more force and warmth. "It was my own coin!" cried Dinsmore.

Robert gasped. "Is that true?" he asked.

"True? I'd swear. . . ."

Robert raised his hand. "Don't swear," he said. "I want to believe you. I don't want you to perjure yourself just for the sake of convincing me. I could do nothing, even if you had spent money that belonged to me. But as it is, I want to believe, Uncle Jimmy, that you didn't do it. I want to believe that you were true to Dixie Fernald."

"Ah, lad, and I was. And even bad as I done, I got you through school, I guess?"

"You did," Robert agreed heartily. He swung to the ground and limped forward. "Shake hands, Uncle Jimmy, and forget that I've been talking like this if you can."

Dinsmore took the proffered hand, but he took it weakly. He was pale and shaking. "I can never forget, kid," he said. "Bein' doubted by you . . . that's a lot worse than I ever thought would happen to me. A lot worse."

"I was wrong," Robert said sadly. "I never should have believed such an accusation against you, Uncle Jimmy. But I've had some hard knocks . . . I've learned to doubt nearly everything. I'm not made of the stuff that you and some of the old-timers were made of. I'm not so trusting. There's bad in me, Uncle Jimmy," he said. "And there's more weakness and badness than people guess, even."

"Weakness?" echoed Uncle Jimmy.

"Aye, and I mean just that. Shall we go down and cook a snack?"

They had supper in the house as in the past. All during the meal Uncle Jimmy was as brisk and as cheerful as ever he had been. After the meal, he launched into a glorious story about Wild Bill and Buffalo Bill and himself.

"Didn't Wild Bill die when you were just a child?" asked Robert, suddenly remembering another bit of Gill's evidence.

"Him? Wild Bill? Oh, you mean Hickok?" Uncle Jimmy said, his voice wavering a little and then recovering. "Of course he did. The Wild Bill I'm talkin' about was Wild Bill . . . Smith. Of course. Dog-gone me, kid, you wouldn't think that I'd mix up the two of 'em, would you?"

Robert breathed a great sigh of relief. He could listen to the story after that. But although it was as perilous as ever, there was something lacking. Robert had tasted reality, and fiction would do no longer. And when he heard the soft snoring of Uncle Jimmy, Robert slipped from his bunk and sat beneath the stars.

He could breathe more freely, more happily there, and suddenly he knew that he could not go back to spend the night in the shack. He left a note in the cabin, then he saddled Pinto, tied his blanket roll behind the saddle, and started across the hills. He had not the least notion where he was going. He wanted to turn his back on all the things that he had been. He had failed, he felt, most signally. The world praised him for defeating Tom Gill, but he knew the fear that had been in his heart. So he rode on this outward trail, asking only that he might encounter some adventure on such a scale that he could prove his courage to himself.

He rode, wistfully watching the stars and the dark, solemn trees. And he felt that it was a dark and solemn world, indeed, through which he rode; yet, here too, were stars, in such lovely women as Beatrice Larkin, and such kind and honest men as Uncle Jimmy! Alas, he had doubted them both. And he bowed his head in misery and in shame.

★ ★ ★ ★ ★

THE GENTLE DESPERADO

★ ★ ★ ★ ★

I

Catalina, sitting half seen among the trees, beckoned Robert Fernald with a scattered gleam of lamps among the shadows. And down he determined to go, and had loosened the reins to let Pinto pick his way through the stones and the shrubbery when he heard the *clatter* of hoofs behind him, and from among the great stones cantered a lean-ribbed mule bearing a ragged, round-faced, one-armed Mexican, who waved his single hand and shouted with joy.

"*Señor* Fernald! *Señor* Fernald! God is good!" he cried. "Little father, I have found you at last."

There had passed many a lonely day and solitary journey since Robert had parted with this man, and his eyes lighted as he took the hand of the Mexican.

"You never should have left San Joaquin," Robert said. "Tell me, has Charlie Bent frightened you out again? Tell me, Pedrillo."

Pedrillo, had he two hands, would have rubbed them together. He rubbed his stomach instead—a fat stomach, which bulged against the pommel of his saddle—and chuckled softly, while his little bright eyes were almost lost behind deep wrinkles of contentment.

"Ah, no, little father," said Pedrillo. "I lived in San Joaquin as safe as a branch on a tree or a rock on a mountain. I could not get into trouble in that place. Everyone in that town is my friend, and Charlie Bent bought me a drink every day to show that he had no hard feeling against me or against you, *señor*. But money is not like seed . . . it does not grow . . . and presently all that I had was gone. Then one day as I sat in the sun thinking, that tall, strong man from Larkin Valley stopped his horse near me. When the dust had blown away from my eyes, I saw who it was and stood up."

"It was Dan Parker," Robert said with a faint smile of pleasure such as came rarely on his face in these sad days.

"It was he, *señor*. 'Where is your boss?' he said. 'I am a free man,' I said. 'Free from work,' he said. 'But where's Fernald?' 'He has vanished,' I said. ' "Vanished" is the right word,' he said. 'He's gone out like a match. I've been riding for three weeks trying to find his trail, but he's gone. Pedrillo, if you can get this letter to him and bring him back to Larkin Valley, you'll never be without a place to hang your hat for the rest of your life.' I listened. It was not the fine promise that stirred me. What did I wish in the world so much as to be again with you? The blind wish for sight, do they not? So have I wished for you, little father. I took the letter. I rode like mad on this poor mule. I hunted like a hawk on the wing, and I have not rested, slept, or eaten since I started a month ago. But here I am. All the hardships are as nothing now."

Robert looked at the fat paunch of the Mexican, but something more important than Pedrillo Oñate was in his mind. He took the envelope that Oñate extended to him, ripped it open with feverish haste, and read the strong, masculine handwriting.

Dear Robert Fernald: You know that when we think aloud, we say all sorts of things, and a lot that we don't mean really. I was terribly humiliated that day when I found that you had overheard. But I was more sad than ashamed, and I still am. I want you to come back so that I can show you I'm not such a shallow, ungrateful person as you think now. There are selfish reasons, too, for wanting you here once more. The same cañons that made a good camping ground for Tom Gill promise to attract other rustlers who may not be so famous, but who can steal just as many cows. You see that I am shamelessly frank. I need you, so that I can apologize, and I need you for the sake of your name and fame.

I want to say other things. But I know that protesting with pen and ink doesn't do much good at this distance. Only I feel like a child at school asking the teacher to give him another chance. Please give me that second chance, Robert Fernald.

Aunt Harriet wants me to send you her warmest good wishes, and whether you come back to us or go on your own way without forgiving me, may the best good luck ride with you.

Beatrice Larkin

When Fernald had finished reading this letter for the third time, he was able to fold it, replace it in the envelope, and slip it into a coat pocket, although he still kept his hand upon it, as though to make sure that it should not slip away from him.

"Miss Larkin is married by this time?" Robert said, looking at the ground.

"Married?" said Oñate. "No, *señor*. And *Señor* Fitzroy King has left the valley and gone back to his home in the East."

Robert looked up. All the west was on fire with the sunset gold and crimson, and one towering cloud stretched a lofty head of flame into the zenith. It seemed to Robert that never had there been a more appropriate burst of color, and the gigantic picture expressed the joy that was in his heart at that moment.

"We take the back trail at once, then," he said. "Or, tell me, Pedrillo . . . you know every pass and hill and trail in these ranges . . . is there no way of cutting through the mountains and reaching Larkin Valley in a straight line from this place?"

Pedrillo groaned at the mere thought. "There is a way," he

said, "but even the eagles hardly dare to take it, and they. . . ."

"We'll ride that way," decreed Robert.

"Ah, little father," cried the Mexican, "consider that I have not eaten a true meal in this month of hard labor . . . and there is Catalina only a step away, waiting for us with tortillas, and beans cooked with peppers and tomatoes, and tender roast kid, and . . . !"

"Silence," Robert ordered, sweeping the summits with a restless glance. "Where does our trail start?"

"Besides," said Oñate, suddenly changing the nature of his appeal, "if we take the short cut, your horse will need grain in his belly to climb the rocks . . . and as for my poor mule, my poor Pancho . . . you see that even now his knees sag. His stomach cleaves to his back. One night in Catalina, and then we shall ride together. . . ."

The coming dark, the high mountains, and the starved look of the Mexican's mule decided Robert. He turned his boyish face toward the village in the valley.

"Very well," said Robert. "We'll ride down, Pedrillo. And in the morning we'll be on the uptrail before the dawn begins."

So they wound down the steep mountainside and into the damp, dark forest. When they reached the Catalina River the last of the sunset light was gone, and one could not tell whether night were young or old, except that the sky was a rich, dark blue, instead of black. Over a staggering, *creaking* bridge, they reached the farther bank and the village that straggled there.

It was supper time in Catalina, so the street was empty. Even the dogs were indoors, waiting for scraps, and the only sounds that Robert and his companion heard were the noises of *clattering* kitchen pans as they passed, or the stamping and snorting of horses beginning to work on their filled mangers, or the far-off scream of swine settling together in family huddles for the sake of warmth.

Indeed it was a crisp night, not altogether so cold as in the upper peaks, but the river damp hung in the air and a chill began to settle downward from the monster trees. They were not the fortune of Catalina, those trees. Far off in the mountains were mines of copper and lead, so the trees were not felled except to build houses. And what houses they were. The mountain winter could beat them with its fierce winds or heap its snows around the walls, but never trouble the sheltered happiness that lived behind those thick walls of logs.

The sensitive heart of Robert expanded with joy as he looked right and left, and every shaft of soft lamplight that fell from door or window touched him like the music of a singing voice. His own happiness was welling up within him; he had cast despair behind.

"Tell me, Pedrillo," he said, "that you never have seen a town as happy as this Catalina. Tell me, Pedrillo, that there can be no cruelty, no suffering, no jealousy, no shame in such a place as this . . . for the honesty and the goodness of these people shine out of their very houses."

Pedrillo lifted his head to sniff a trail of frying bacon whose scent had reached him at that moment.

"Ah, well, little father," he said, "men cannot be any better than God has made them. You carry an automatic under your coat. Perhaps you may have to use it before morning even in Catalina. Who can tell?"

So said Oñate, thinking only of his supper to come and not of what he said. But there are unknowing prophets in this strange world.

II

The hotel was seldom so crowded.

"You can chuck here, of course," said the proprietor, "and you can throw your blankets in the yard if you want to. Or you

95

can go next door and tell Austin Bede that you want a couple of beds. He's always glad to pick up a few pennies. We're full here, though. Carl Lovat's back, and everybody's come in to have a look at him, of course."

In the dining room—for they decided to eat before they looked for quarters—Robert had sight of Mr. Lovat entering—a nervous, sharp-spoken man of forty-five with a clean-shaven face that looked a good deal younger.

"Who is he?" asked Robert, lingering a moment near the door with Pedrillo.

Pedrillo did not know, and he was too filled with expectancy concerning the coming meal to spend any of his energy guessing.

So Robert merely gave him a last warning as they parted—the Mexican to the kitchen for his supper, and Robert to pass on into the dining room. "No one that I know is here," said Robert. "And I don't wish to let my name get about. Remember that. If anyone speaks to me by my right name I'll know that you've let the cat out of the bag. Do you hear, Pedrillo?"

Pedrillo nodded and sighed. One of his favorite diversions was the construction of fables concerning his master—legends designed on such a scale that they filled the ear completely. How much of the wild talk that went through the mountains concerning Robert Fernald originated from these fancies of the Mexican, who could tell? But it made Robert vastly uneasy. He prepared to creep through the world unnoticed, for no matter what foolish things people might repeat about his deeds, he still had not proved himself to himself, and the terrible question haunted him day and night: was he, indeed, a brave man?

That question, which lay like a shadow on his otherwise smooth and boyish face, clung in his thoughts as he entered the dining room at last, and settled himself to thin slices of fried steak, fried potatoes, fried beans, fried sausage, and fried pudding. It was not a tasty meal, and it was seasoned with drafts of the terrible mountain coffee, black as night and terrible as the furies. Down the leathery throats of the frontiersmen who sat around him these viands went in a flood, but Robert looked at them in dismay and hardly could touch his meal. Better, ten thousand times better, the fireside cookery of Pedrillo as they wandered together across the desert. As he minced his food, Robert sighed. For he felt more than ever convinced that he never would make a desert hero—never in a world of constant effort.

There was plenty to occupy him besides the food, however. He had to regard the faces of the men who crowded that table. The diners were jammed in tightly. On either side of Robert a swinging elbow occasionally grazed his ribs with much force. The laughter was like rolling thunder, and the eyes of these unshaven wild creatures flashed and rolled terribly.

The heart of Robert sank more and more. These men did not regard him more than to give him a smile as to a helpless child who had wandered into their midst. No, to a child they would have been kind in a rough way, but as they smiled at him, they scorned him.

He wanted to leap to his feet and shout: "Don't despise me! I'm Robert Fernald! You've heard about me. I'm the man who captured the great Tom Gill. I'm the man who pacified San Joaquin!" But if he did, someone might look at him with a sardonic smile and say: "We know all about you, kid. That was just a lucky shot that dropped Tom Gill. Don't try to talk like a man when you're still no more than a boy."

At the head of this long table sat Carlisle Lovat. When he spoke, all listened. By degrees, Robert began to learn the story of this man. Lovat had been born in the little town of Catalina. He had spent his youth here, then gone away to school, and, although he had returned after his school days, he went back again to the East and there built up a great fortune. It was as a millionaire that he returned to the village. It was as a great man that he came, and therefore the villagers sat in silence when he spoke, laughed when he told a few dry jokes, and nodded their heads almost reverently when he dwelt on the hardships of his youth, and told how he had made a place for himself among the sharp businessmen of the East.

Robert, staring at him, wondered what power lay in money that all these men should revere him so greatly? These bold, strong fellows gaped at Carlisle Lovat as though he had been a minor prophet.

In the middle of the meal, a squat, wide-shouldered man, swaggering into the room, went up to the head of the table. No sooner did he approach than the sheriff, his star blazing on his coat, started up from his chair and called out: "Berners, I'm watching you!"

The other, with a sneering smile, looked up and down the length of the table.

"Seems to me," he said, "that a good many of you gents ain't been doing anything much better than just watching me for sometime lately."

"I've had your lip before," the sheriff said starkly. "But if you're here to make trouble for Mister Lovat, I'll let you know that. . . ."

"He sent for me," said Berners, "or I wouldn't have gone out of my way to talk to him. You sent for me, Lovat. Well, what do you want?"

Robert looked closely, not at Berners, but at Lovat. As for the wide-shouldered man in the rough clothes, he had spotted him instantly for what he was—a gunfighter of a more or less old and unfashionable type. For whereas the more modern dandies of the six-shooter carried their weapons securely, lodged under the coats, this man wore his strapped against his leg, so that, although they might make uncomfortable walking, they were constantly at hand for a quick draw. He wore them very low down on the thigh; the butts struck the palms of his hands, and his fingers could twitch out the Colts instantly. The time-worn and custom-polished leather of those holsters was enough in itself to proclaim the nature of the man who owned them. And Robert knew that he was another of those wandering spirits who "lived by the gun". So he regarded the gunman not at all, having read the entire volume by its binding, so to speak.

He turned, instead, toward the millionaire, much interested by the manner in which Lovat might take the approach of the ruffian. The rich man showed no fear. He merely leaned forward a little in his chair and looked keenly at Berners with a faint smile of interest and appreciation.

"You're the same sort, Laurence," he said. "I see that you've grown up to your promise."

"Is that a slam?" asked Laurence Berners, resting his hand on the back of a chair and never keeping his glance fixed on any member of the group at the table, but letting it wander restlessly here and there. "Are you knockin' me? I tell you, Lovat, that what you got to say ain't any more to me now than it was when we went to grammar school together. I could lick you then, and it looks like I could lick you now, even easier. The rest of 'em in here may kowtow to you and kiss your boots, but I ain't that kind, old-timer. And if you've just called me in to look me over, you've had your look and I've had mine, and I dunno but what you've had a chance to see as pretty a picture as you've showed me."

"Blowed in the glass," murmured someone near Robert.

And that described the vicious nature of Mr. Laurence Berners quite accurately. He had grown old in his ways, and his ways had been thoroughly vicious and bad for so long that they were a part of his soul.

Mr. Lovat, however, did not respond at once to the insulting speech. Instead, he toyed for a time with a large silver cruet that graced his end of the table—an ample carrier made to contain flasks of vinegar and oil, and a mustard pot. It was a most elaborate cruet, such as Robert had never seen before. An enameled tortoise supported a tree, and the massive branches of the silver tree contained the apertures through which the flasks fitted. This treasure had been admired by Mr. Lovat during the meal, and he still touched it as he regarded Laurence Berners with a keen glance. There was neither fear nor anger in his look. Instead, there was a sort of fascination and amusement—even a dash of respect.

"I sent for you because I wanted to see you . . . having seen you, I'd be glad to talk with you," said Carlisle Lovat.

"Talk up," invited the gracious Berners.

"Not here. In my room at Bede's."

"Why should I wait on you there? I ain't a servant of yours, and I don't owe you a penny. As a matter of fact, I'm as good a man as you are, Lovat."

"Or better, perhaps." Lovat smiled.

"Or better, perhaps," repeated Berners aggressively.

"Very well," said Mr. Lovat, "but nevertheless I think that you'll be waiting in my room when I get back to the house. That's all, Berners."

So, dismissing Mr. Berners as if he were a hired clerk, Lovat turned back to his meal. It was very well done. It left Berners balanced first on one foot and then on the other, until finally he vowed, with a curse, that he never would stand about in the room of any man, waiting for an interview. With that he slouched from the dining room. But Robert had no doubt that the gunman would indeed be found in the room of Lovat when the latter was ready for him. It had been a brief scene and apparently a quiet one, for all that the sheriff sank into his chair after it, mopping his brow. And yet, even so briefly, Robert felt that he had had a glimpse of the power of the financier. We may tell the lion by his claw.

Another question rose in his mind. What did the rich man want of Laurence Berners? What honest use could anyone make of such a person as Berners?

III

When Robert left the dining room—before the rest had finished, and while one of Mr. Lovat's tales was in progress—he went straight to the adjoining house of Austin Bede. The lower portion of Mr. Bede's place was given over to his silver shop, and the window, even at this hour, was uncurtained and illumined by an oil lamp, the burner turned low. Behind the glass, Robert saw a glimmering array: some articles, such as candlesticks— who would be using silver candlesticks in Catalina?—and many little figures of animals and men, sometimes singly, sometimes worked into groups of two or more.

It pleased Robert to see these things, just as the heart of a child is gladdened by the sight of toys. And there was a good deal of the child in Robert, to tell the truth. He was about to turn away when he heard voices at the door of the shop, and the subject of conversation was so extremely intimate that he hesitated to advance boldly upon the speakers.

He heard a man saying: "All right, I'll run along. But kiss me good night, Chollie."

And a girl answered: "Say, what a lot you take for granted, young man."

"*Aw,* quit it, Chollie," said the man. "As if I never kissed you before!"

"Look here, Tim," cried the girl, "are you gonna tell the whole town that I'm fond of you?"

"The whole town would be a fool if it thought that I'd hang

around this long without no encouragement," declared Tim.

"I'm sick and tired of this," Chollie said with feeling.

"The minute that you're sick and tired," answered Tim with equal firmness, "I'll beat it and cut for sign on some other trail. But you don't mean it."

"Don't I?" she asked dangerously.

"Sure, you don't. You're gonna marry me, and you know it."

"I know nothing of the kind."

"Aw, but you do."

"Why should I? Dad's dead against it."

"He thinks I'm a loafer," replied the undaunted Tim, "but you know that I'm not."

"You've hung around town and not turned a lick for six weeks," said the girl. "You've been borrowing from friends for two weeks. Ain't that the dodge of a loafer?"

"I quit work," explained Tim, "to take the job of makin' love to you. And dog-gone me if it ain't been enough to keep the hands of any two men filled."

"Keep quiet, Tim. Half the town can hear you boomin'."

"Let 'em hear," he answered. "What I have to say I ain't ashamed of. Are you?"

"That's no way to put it."

"Don't try to be mysterious with me, Chollie. I love you . . . you know it . . . the whole town knows it . . . why shouldn't I tell 'em about it? Let 'em hear!"

"Tim Cavaselle!"

"Look here, Chollie . . . if you get crusty like this, I'm gonna kiss you good bye instead of good night."

"I'll slap your face."

"That's fair enough."

There was the sharp *clap* of a hand against bare skin, and then the noise of a well-planted kiss.

"Tim!" gasped Chollie. "I hate you like a snake."

"*Aw*, you liked it, Chollie. Don't lie to me. Good night, sweetheart."

"I . . . I hope you. . . ."

She could think of no wish bad enough to fit his scandalous case.

And then: "If that skinny runt, Lovat, is making eyes at you, I'll run him out of town the same's I did Dick Fraser."

"Don't be a fool," said the girl. "I wouldn't marry a bank like him. He's nice to me. That's all. Just because he used to court my mother."

"Just because he's set his cold eye on you. Well, I'm gonna give him a warning. I got my doubts of him. I heard him talkin' to your old man about setting him up in business in New York. Does Lovat ever do something for nothing? No, he don't. What does he want back? Why, you. That's plain."

"Tim, you're an absolute fool."

"You take it pretty hard," said the outright Cavaselle. "I guess I've touched a tender spot. But so long, Chollie. Wednesday I get your final answer."

"All right, Tim."

"And I know what it'll be, honey."

"You know nothin'."

Tim Cavaselle laughed loudly, and started to walk down the street, and in so doing he passed Robert, paused, and then clapped a heavy hand on his shoulder.

Robert found himself looking up to a youth of the most heroic proportions.

"You been hearing something, kid?" asked Tim Cavaselle.

Robert was too taken aback to reply for a moment, then he stammered that he had been about to enter the house, but had not wished to interrupt such a conversation.

"The heck you was," said the blunt cowpuncher. "All that you done, then, was to hang around and eavesdrop, eh? But I'll

103

tell you, kid, I don't give a hang if the whole world was to hang around and hear what I've got to say. I don't keep no secrets. I'd just as soon live in a house with glass walls. And the simps and the saps can stand around and see me when they please. But . . . if I catch you doin' this again, I'll take off all your skin and hang it up to dry and make socks out of it."

He turned away from Robert, and went whistling down the street, so little malice did he carry in his outspoken heart. As for Robert, he trembled with excitement and anger at being addressed in such a manner. But often words came to him slowly, and he had been unable to think of a retort for the big man before the other was fifty long strides away. And how could he rush after such a man with resentment, with a challenge?

He was afraid. Not of the fighting skill of the cowpuncher, however, for somehow it seemed impossible that that great lumbering fellow ever could have fought with any weapon other than his hands. It was the largeness of body and of spirit that seemed to Robert still to tower above him like a ghost. And, with fallen head, he went to the door of the shop that the girl was just closing.

She was made on lines ample enough for an Amazon. A big, good-natured, smiling, cheerful girl she was.

"Hello, bud," she said. "What d'you want? Buying something for your best girl, maybe?"

Robert, a little embarrassed, managed to declare that he was not, and that he wanted a room, and for that night only.

"We'll fix you up," said the girl. "Maybe you could do with half a room, eh? Or d'you aim to take full-sized man's quarters?"

Robert drew himself up to the full of his five feet and eight inches.

"Madam," he said, "I need a room, or a bed, or whatever you can give me."

"Hello. Hello," said the girl. "*Aw,* don't get huffy. Step in and sit down, will you? I'll run up and see who's in for the night."

She went off and left Robert in a little back waiting room, at one side of which the owner of the place and the father of Chollie sat at a deal table on which a number of silver articles were displayed. Opposite him was a well-dressed gentleman smoking expensive cigarettes. He held raised in his hand a little silver model of a bronco, lump-headed, hump-backed, ewe-necked, but with legs that, even in the silver, looked all their iron strength and endurance.

"Or this," said the stranger. "This, now, would be a nice trinket to give to my youngster. What sort of a price do you put on this, Mister Bede?"

Austin Bede was a huge man, mightily bearded and with eyes half lost behind a downfall of gray eyebrows. But his shoulders slumped forward and his back was curved out in the fashion of one who has hung over his work too many hours. Yet there was manliness in his face, and in his big, workman's hands there was manifest great power still.

"I'll tell you," said Austin Bede. "There's hardly more'n enough silver in that to make it worth more than . . . fifty dollars, say?"

"Fifty? Hello . . . that's rather steep."

"But as a matter of fact, I don't really want to sell that. I'd rather keep it, Mister Norden."

The other pushed back his chair with an exclamation.

"Very well," he said. "I see that it's no use trying to do business with you, sir. You want to keep all of your best work. And. . . ." He paused, as though recollecting himself with an effort. "I'll have to find other Western trinkets for my family," he said. "Tell me . . . how much of this stuff do you sell in a year?"

"Not enough," admitted the silversmith sadly, "to pay for the metal that I have to use. Not enough."

"Then why won't you sell now?"

"Look," said Bede, taking the silver horse. "I know how other people make these things. Where I served my apprenticeship, any man could turn out some sort of a horse in a week. Yes, a bigger one than this. But the fact is, sir, I spent three months on that horse."

"Three months!"

"Three months," said the other sadly. "Part of the time working . . . part of the time waiting for ideas to come. You have to wait like that. Pretty soon something will jump into your head. It'll be a pleasure to turn that idea into metal. You understand?"

"Very odd talk," replied Norden, "for a silversmith in this part of the country. By the way, how did you happen to settle down here?"

"I found my wife here," replied Mr. Bede. "She liked this part of the world. So I settled here."

"And let your business go to pot?"

"She liked this part of the world," said the silversmith.

"But after she died? If you went to a big city. . . ."

"It would be a bit queer to move away," replied Bede. "You can take the work with you, but you can't take the country that I got the ideas from." He indicated the silver figures—the horse, a mountain goat walking on a dizzy ledge wherein a three-inch cliff of silver was made to give the effect of a dizzy precipice, and a band of antelope behind which, with some artful foreshortening, one was made to guess at the limitless flat of the desert.

Mr. Norden rose. "My good friend," he said sharply, "it appears that you have formed the habit of working for your own pleasure and not for sale. In the meantime, you let your daughter support you by taking in lodgers. Is that the idea?"

The silversmith flushed. His large head sank a little, and he sighed as he touched the delicate form of an eagle perched on a crag of black rock. Robert pitied him. He felt that this man was as far from the rest of the world as he himself.

Mr. Norden, grim with indignation and disgust, as it appeared, stalked angrily from the room and at that moment the girl came back.

"Well, Dad?" she asked eagerly.

Her father shook his head.

"What? Nothing?" asked Chollie, vastly disappointed.

"He wouldn't buy," said the father, "nothing except these." He indicated some of his chosen treasures that stood on the table.

"But you could have sold one of them at least," suggested the girl.

Mr. Bede allowed his head to fall still farther.

"No difference!" the girl exclaimed cheerfully, throwing her arm around the massive shoulders of her father. "We'll make out some way. They can't do any more than turn us out of the house."

The big hand of Austin Bede went up and closed over the arm of his girl. "I'll find money some way," he said. "I'll find it some way . . . before morning."

He said it calmly, but it was a desperate calmness. So that before Robert's eye there was conjured up a terrible picture of attempted robbery, of drawn guns, of battle.

"Ah, I forgot about you," said the girl, turning suddenly to Robert. "I've found a corner for you. It doesn't amount to much, but there's a bed in the place. Will you take a look?"

Robert went unwillingly. There was a great will in his heart to do something for this silversmith and his blunt, bluff, whole-souled daughter. But he had no money, and he knew no way of getting any. Money was what they needed. How much misery in the world is caused by the lack of it, thought Robert.

He was shown to a little chamber that was hardly larger than a closet. It had one small window high up on the wall, and, aside from a cot that filled half of the floor space, it held no furniture. However, it was a place for rest, and Robert accepted it.

"How much?" he asked.

"*Aw,* nothing at all," said the girl. "We ain't low enough to charge a man lodging for a kennel like this one. You take it and welcome, partner."

"But," began Robert, "I. . . ."

She was out of the room before his clumsy tongue could frame the words he wished to speak, and she left him alone in the semi-darkness, for the lantern on the wall gave only a ghostly excuse for light, shining as the flame did through a chimney so thickly smoked as to be almost opaque.

Robert sat on the edge of his bed and buried his face in his hands. He wanted to find some solution of the problem of the silversmith, and he hoped that, if he concentrated, some suggestion might come to him.

IV

There was no great opportunity for Robert to continue his thinking, for presently it appeared that the room adjoining was that same back chamber in which Austin Bede was now sitting with his daughter, and every word they spoke passed easily through the thin partition.

"All that the devil could wish is true," said poor Bede. "I've failed right and left, Charlotte. I've piled up debts, lived almost on charity. I'm a worthless good-for-nothing."

"I'd like to hear another man dare to call you that!" cried Chollie. "But we'll find a way out. I tell you, we'll get some money out of Carlisle Lovat. He's full of it. He's dripping with money, Dad."

"Be quiet!" exclaimed the father. "D'you know Lovat? I do. You never could get something for nothing from him. Get five cents from him, and he'd make you pay for it with your heart's blood. That's his way."

"You let me handle him," said the girl.

"Charlotte!"

"Yes?"

"I command you not to ask him for money."

"Well, we'll see about that."

A very grim tone had the girl as she made her answer. At that moment, without any preparatory knock, the front door of the shop was thrown open.

"Who's that walkin' in so big and bold?" Robert heard the girl murmur.

Then he heard the voice of Carlisle Lovat: "I've brought the sheriff along to hear what I say."

" 'Evening, Sheriff Minter," said Bede. "Take a chair."

"I met your friend, the cowpuncher, on the street," said Lovat. "I mean Cavaselle. He told me that he intended to run me out of town if he found me in this house again. Did you authorize him to say that?"

"Of course not," replied Bede.

"I thought that you didn't, and I told him so. He was angry and threatened me. I told him that I was not a fighting man, but that, if it came to a pinch, fight I would and could . . . and, if he killed me, he would hang for it if money could hire good lawyers. I've repeated all this, Charlotte, not because I'm afraid, but because I mean what I say. And I suggest that you pass along the word to Cavaselle yourself, my dear girl."

All this was spoken almost dryly—certainly not in the manner of one greatly afraid of what might happen to him in the future. Mr. Lovat's nerve was excellent in every way, and fitted him to talk with the roughest and hardiest of the cowpunchers and miners of this rude region.

"There'll be no trouble," Bede said hastily. "Tim's a good

boy, I think."

"Good, is he?" interrupted Sheriff Minter. "I got to tell you folks that he ain't so good as you think. He's killed his man. He's killed his second man. And he's killed his third. Down in Arizona they don't act so kind and cheerful with him as we do up here. He's threatened people before. And he's killed before, too. Oh, fair enough fighting . . . but a killer is a killer. You might let your friend know what I know about him, Charlotte."

"Send your own messengers," Chollie snapped. "If you want to backbite Tim, do it to his face."

"Spitfire, Chollie. That's what you are." The sheriff chuckled. "Now, Mister Lovat, what's next?"

"I'm going up to my room," said Lovat. "And there I expect to find Laurence Berners waiting for me. Sheriff, I'd like to have you wait for me down here, if you don't mind. I haven't much to say to him, but what I have to say may make him pull a gun. I'll just ask you to leave this door open. If you don't see me coming back in ten minutes by your watch, make a break for that room, because the business I have to talk over with Berners shouldn't take more than half that length of time."

It pleased Robert to hear Lovat talk, for he had the manner of a lawyer in court, presenting evidence not to a jury but to an impartial judge. Whatever the business was that took him to Berners, Robert gathered the impression that danger of death never would turn back Mr. Carlisle Lovat.

"You know the sort of a man you'll be talking to," warned the sheriff in a manner that left no room for doubt.

"I know him like a book," declared Lovat. And with his crisp, brisk step he left the room.

"He's got plenty of nerve," the sheriff murmured in admiration. "Berners hates him, too."

"Why?" asked Bede.

"Dunno. Berners hates near everybody."

They talked of other things quietly, calmly. And yet Robert knew that they were thinking of the same thing that made him, from time to time, look at his watch.

But their nerve was better than his. Two men and a girl sat in a room listening for a gunshot, and never once did they betray the slightest anxiety. For his part he counted the minutes trailing slowly away. Eight minutes, nine minutes. . . .

"I think I'll just be stepping upstairs," drawled the sheriff.

"I'll go along," Bede said with equal calm.

"You stay where you are," snapped the official with decision. "I'll do this job by myself or else I'll find out what. . . ."

Here a door slammed in the distance. They heard loud voices. Heavy steps came down the stairs.

"I've told you what I'll do," said Lovat. "You take it or you leave it. Understand?"

"I'll see you hanged. You will be hanged!" howled Berners. "You skinflint, you sneakin' coyote, you fox, you rat!"

"Swear yourself out of breath and back again," replied the other contemptuously. "But in the meantime, don't forget that I have made a proposal to you."

"A low-down, cheap, five-cent. . . ."

"Berners, think it over. You'll be back in the morning to say yes."

Berners, apparently foaming with rage and stamping in his fury, rushed through the room and out of the house.

In the comparative quiet that followed, Robert wondered very greatly what possible business could have been offered by either of these men to the other? He had not liked Mr. Lovat before this. Now he was sharply suspicious. Laurence Berners was a manifest brute. For what can such creatures be used except for brutal business? So argued Robert. And his interest in the complicated interrelation of human beings in Catalina was growing. At least it began to be apparent that all was not so peaceful and cheerful as it seemed on the surface of the little town.

The sheriff wished to know now if Mr. Lovat were perfectly at ease in the town, or if he desired protection of any sort.

Lovat's answer was delivered in a drawling voice. "I'm in danger every minute of my stay here, Sheriff. But I don't want any more protection."

The sheriff departed.

"That was a funny way to talk," said Charlotte, large in accent as in person. "How's your life in danger in this town, Mister Lovat?"

"Wait a minute till I get back. I want to hear the answer!" exclaimed the silversmith. "I'm going for my tobacco."

As his heavy footfall died away, Lovat said to the girl: "I think you can guess where the danger comes from, Charlotte."

"Not me."

"Perhaps, I'm growing old," said Lovat, half serious, half ironical. "But it seems to me that I'm in a good deal of peril. In the first place, there's Berners. He's a dangerous creature if ever there was one. In the second place, there's your father. . . ."

"My father?"

"Look here, Charlotte. You're not a baby. You're a woman and a pretty wise one."

"Danger from my dear old dad?"

"Look at this ring of mine, my dear. Look at the red stone in it. That's a ruby, Charlotte. That stone is enough to keep the wearer in a good deal of danger no matter where he be."

There was a little silence. Charlotte was not committing herself.

"Your father is broke. Worse than broke. That ruby alone would pay his debts and put him on Easy Street for a while. You don't think so? But he knows so. He understands jewels and such things. Now, Charlotte, suppose that he should get it into his head to put a bullet through mine in the middle of the night and just slip this ring off my finger. . . ."

"Carlisle Lovat," said the girl, "I don't mind a joke, even if it's a mighty bad one, but don't talk that lingo about my father. Why, he'd never hurt a chicken."

"Wouldn't he?" Lovat chuckled. "Very well. We'll hope not. But in the third place, I stand in danger from young Tim Cavaselle, who is not such a fool and braggart as I took him to be. He really is capable of murder, it appears."

"You fill the whole town with murderers," Chollie said, yawning audibly.

"Of course I do, my dear," said the rich man. "And in the fourth place, I'm in danger from you."

"Hello! Go on and tell me."

"That's what interests me," said Lovat. "I was only joking when I first talked to your father about marrying you, but now that I begin to take it seriously. . . ."

"Don't be the only serious one about it," Charlotte said coldly. "Who wants you to be serious?"

"The truth is, my dear," said Mr. Lovat, "that you are amazingly handsome, and I can't help thinking about you."

"You're making love, I see," Charlotte said with another of her noisy yawns.

"Odd, isn't it?" asked Mr. Lovat.

Robert had not the slightest desire to rap on the wall and give them warning that they were being overheard. Indeed, he felt that he was not listening to a love scene at all, properly so-called. It was rather a sheer revelation of character.

"Yep," replied the girl. "It's pretty funny. You'll laugh about this later on, I know. But you won't laugh alone, Mister Funnyman."

"By heaven," said Lovat with warmth. "I like you better and better."

"Swearing, too," said the girl. "That proves that you come from the West."

"You young minx," said Lovat with his inevitable dry, rattling chuckle.

"D'you want me to listen to you?" asked Charlotte.

"By all means."

"Then tell me what in the world should make you want to look twice at a girl like me?"

"Youth and good looks, my dear . . . ," began Lovat, only to have the girl cut in loudly.

"That string's worn out, Mister Lovat. Quit it, will you? I know. With your flock of money you could pick out something flying high and handsome. You could have what you want, all dolled up in slick clothes with a Paris face and a trained pair of eyes. Don't tell me I got the looks."

"Haven't you?" asked Lovat, not pressing his point at once.

"I'm not so bad," answered Chollie. "I'm better on a horse than I am on foot, and the first flash of me is better than having me opposite to you across the table every morning and night. Bub, you tack another fifteen years on me and I won't be much to boast about. And you know it. So what's the line and what's the game, Mister Lovat? I'm curious."

"Suppose that I call you Chollie?" he said.

"I don't care what I'm called. Go ahead."

"It pleases me a good deal to call you Chollie. Well, Chollie, the reason I'm more and more interested in you is that there's no bunk about you. You hit from the shoulder and. . . ."

"And that's your own style, I suppose?"

"No, not entirely. Sometimes I'm blunt . . . but not often altogether honest. I'd be a poor man today if that were the case. But, Chollie, I don't give a hang for society and small talk. Not a hang. You and I would have a couple of friends. A good many acquaintances. I'd be good to you. I'd be 'specially good to your father."

"I suppose you'll say you're fond of him?"

"Not a bit. But I'm fond of you, and keeping him afloat would make you stick to me."

"I like your line of talk," said the girl. "It's queer, but it's interesting. Go on."

"After a while, you'd grow interested in running my house, bossing my servants, and amusing me."

"Would I?"

"You would."

"And what about you?"

"I don't think I'd get tired of you. I'm old enough to know what I want. And I always get it . . . and I always keep it."

"Women ain't money, you know," suggested the girl.

"No, they're pretty much the reverse." He chuckled. "But if the worst came to the worst . . . why, marriage is not eternal in these days of Nevada, eh? A divorce never would break your heart. But I'd make you so comfortable that you wouldn't think about it a great deal."

"I'd get money, a safe bunk for Dad, and a chance for him to fiddle away at his silly silver. You'd get a woman to run your house and amuse you . . . if you really think that I'd do that. Is that the deal?"

"That's about it."

"Interesting, all right. But it don't buy me, Mister Lovat."

"Why not? Tim?"

"Yes."

"You love him, eh?"

"He's such a great idiot. Sure I love him."

"Do you think that ends me?"

"I think it comes pretty close to ending you."

"Not a whit. One rarely gets what one wants at the first try.

I'll simply find a way of raising my bid."

"Still talking money, eh?"

"Not altogether money. Just think this over. So will I. Tomorrow we'll talk again."

"Whenever you say."

"Hey, Chollie!" called the voice of her father in the distance.

"He can't find his tobacco," said the girl. "I'll have to get it for him. Coming, Dad!"

"Good night, Chollie."

"Good night."

"Do we shake hands?"

"We do."

"Friends?"

"You bet."

"Well, good night."

"Good night."

Mr. Lovat departed, the girl ran to her father, and Robert lay down on his bed without so much as taking off his clothes.

He did not intend to fall asleep. He simply wanted to close his eyes and review matters in greater detail to see what he could make of them, and this singular combination of Berners, Lovat, Bede, Cavaselle, and Chollie.

But it had been a long day; he had ridden far. Before he knew it, the image of lovely Beatrice Larkin rose in his mind and made him smile with wistful happiness. Another moment and he was soundly asleep. He dreamed an old dream, of riding through the streets of a town where people on either side pointed at him and smiled behind their hands. A most unpleasant dream that had made him writhe and groan in his sleep on many a night before this. He was awakened by the sudden *crash* of a gun, and a loud scream, which stabbed the night, died, and left the world listening.

V

He leaped to his feet and flung open the door of his room. Not a sound in the home. Fear shut off his breathing. A door slammed, and Robert started so violently that it forced a groan through his set teeth. But something must be done if he were worthy of the name of man. He could not tell from what direction the sound had come, whether it had rung through the house itself or come from the outdoors. From the outside, he rather suspected.

He did not wait to get out the front door of the house, but climbed onto the narrow window ledge set high in the wall of his little room, and so worked his way through and dropped ten feet to the ground outside.

There, as he crouched, he saw the broad-shouldered, squat figure of a man climb down the side of the house, apparently handing himself down by a drainage pipe that ran to the roof.

Laurence Berners!

There were not two men in the whole world who had that ape-like silhouette. Robert jumped to his feet and ran in the direction in which the shadow of the man disappeared among the shrubbery. He had barely entered the brush when a huge form towered before him, crashed into him, and knocked him spinning. The gun spun from Robert's hand as he fell, and he heard a deep voice growl a curse as the big man plunged on his way without a halt.

Half stunned as Robert was, he recognized the voice of Tim Cavaselle, the cowpuncher and lover of Chollie.

By the time he had recovered himself and found his gun, he decided that it would be foolish to try to follow Berners at once. He turned back to the house where now a tumult of voices sounded and heavy running to and fro. He entered by the rear and spied a light through a crack in the kitchen door. To that crack he put his eye and looked in through a narrow vista. What he saw was enough to curdle his blood.

For there was Charlotte Bede working with a frantic haste first to reload an emptied chamber of a Colt revolver, and second to clean out the barrel so that all signs that the weapon recently had been used might disappear. Could a girl have fired the shot that caused that scream of mortal pain and terror? Aye, such a girl as Chollie. Now, with her teeth set, her jaw thrust out, and her eyes gleaming with determination, she looked the perfect type of warrior.

Robert, sick at heart and utterly bewildered by this time, slipped away from that point of vantage and hurried along the hall. When he came to the stairs, he found a new subject of wonder. For down those stairs came Sheriff Lew Minter, and before him he drove a tall man whose hands were shackled, a tall and dignified man who was none other than the silversmith, Austin Bede.

"What's happened?" Robert asked of someone who stood by, ferret-eyed with a malevolent interest.

He got no answer.

"Hal!" called the sheriff loudly.

"Aye, aye, Lew!" came the answer from above.

"Don't touch the body . . . don't let anybody touch it till I come back."

"Right, Lew."

The sheriff went on with his prisoner, saying to him: "Just you watch yourself, Bede. I don't aim to handle you mean, unless you make me. Just you watch yourself, will you?"

The silversmith said nothing. There was a quiet dignity about him. He stood straighter—the hump of his labor was gone from his back—and he walked with a light, strong step. He looked fifteen years younger than when Robert had seen him last. He looked younger, and stronger, and capable, indeed, of shooting to kill.

But now a stream of the curious began to hurry up the stairs with a rapid muttering of questions, and Robert joined the stream.

At an open door on the floor above the current pooled itself in a closely packed crowd that stared in on a dimly lighted picture of Hal, the deputy, seated on a disheveled bed with a naked Colt in his hand, watching the door. In the center of the room, face down, a gun loosely gripped in his right hand, lay the body of Lovat, the millionaire. And a little red pool had welled from his heart.

Robert grew faint and dizzy at the sight of it. He drew back and leaned against the wall, feeling very sick, but able to listen to the comments of the bystanders. From their words he gathered the story of what had happened, at least the sheriff's viewpoint.

Lew Minter, disturbed by various things, had decided to be near the house of Bede all of that night, with the result that the instant the shot was fired and before the scream had ceased ringing through the night, the sheriff on rubber-padded soles leaped silently up the rear stairs of the house and came to the door of Mr. Lovat's room. He reached it just in time to meet Austin Bede coming out, and he had arrested the old fellow on the spot on the charge of murder. For one glance inside the room had showed Lovat lying dead.

Motives? The motives were plain. Lovat's wallet and rings, representing a considerable fortune in themselves, had been stolen.

Mystery? Aye, there was mystery, too. For the treasure was not found on the person of the silver worker. The only solution was that he must have thrown his loot through the window of the room into the grass of the yard. So the yard was searched, but not a sign of any booty was found.

Now all these things were done in a very short time, and

Robert hurried to the jail, where the sheriff had barely secured his prisoner and appointed a guard to watch over him. Most placid did Austin Bede appear in the cell, smoking a short-stemmed pipe and staring at the smoke that he puffed forth. To those who crowded against the bars with questions, he returned brief, gentle answers.

Tears filled the eyes of Robert. No matter what the circumstantial evidence might be, men were fools to suspect such a kind man as this.

He managed to confront the sheriff: "I have to offer a little testimony, Sheriff," he said.

"About this shooting?"

"Yes, sir."

"Jeff!"

"Aye, Lew."

"Take down what this gent has got to say. Come in here."

They went into the sheriff's office. The crowd buzzed and hummed outside.

Robert's nerve began to fail him a little. He felt as though he were about to rub elbows with a dreadful peril. He did not like being in there alone with the strong-handed representative of the law, for the mild sheriff had become a terrible man with eyes of fire and a voice that *clanged* like metal.

"Now, you. What's your name?"

"Smith. John Smith, sir."

"Don't gimme none of your aliases, you little baby-faced fool," said the rough sheriff.

Robert caught his breath. "You mustn't talk to me like that, sir," he said.

"I mustn't *what?*" roared the sheriff.

"You mustn't talk as though I were a horse . . . or a dog, sir."

The sheriff glared, balled a huge fist, and then controlled himself with an effort.

"Gimme your right name," he commanded. "And stop yapping like this, or I'll stick you in the jail, too."

"My name is Robert Fernald."

"You are?" the sheriff said. "Tell it to Sweeney, will you? You're the great Fernald, are you?"

Jeff Sweeney laughed sneeringly.

"My name is Robert Fernald," Robert repeated, and he began to blush. He always blushed when he grew very angry.

The sheriff was suddenly interested. "Why, I believe you are," he said. "You're Robert Fernald. I didn't think . . . I beg your pardon, Fernald."

They shook hands, and this minor crisis was ended.

Robert told, clearly and with a painful exactness, just what he had seen—how a man who had the outline of the famous Laurence Berners had come down the drainage pipe, and how, in pursuing him, he had crashed into the fugitive form of Tim Cavaselle and been knocked to the ground in the collision.

The sheriff grinned a little, but then looked serious. "And how did they get out there so fast, if they done the killing . . . either of them?" he asked.

"Could you run up the stairs," countered Robert, "as easily as a man could slide down the drainage pipe from Lovat's room?"

The sheriff was silent, biting his upper lip. "I'll round up Cavaselle and Berners, both of 'em," he announced. And he hurried out to issue his orders.

But although many men hastened to obey these commands, neither Berners nor Cavaselle were apprehended. They had disappeared from Catalina with singular speed. They were nowhere to be found, and the search of the sheriff bagged no trace of them.

There was other evidence that Robert could have given, but he could not find it in his heart to tell how he had seen the girl,

Chollie, so busily employed in the kitchen cleaning and reloading a gun. However, he had done enough to throw considerable doubt on the guilt of the silversmith.

By noon of the next day, when people were over their first heat of angry suspicion, everyone agreed that Bede could not be punished for a crime that might conceivably have been the fault of two other men, both of whom were missing. The important thing was to find the pair of them.

Now Robert saw his duty before him as clear as the face of a shining star.

VI

How great is the power of a name. Here was Robert, a mere nonentity, a shadow of a man, so to speak, creeping mouse-like about the street of Catalina, scoffed at, or noticed not at all. But now it was discovered that he was none other than Robert Fernald. What a difference that made. Men stopped him on the street and spoke to him. He heard his name murmured and felt eyes upon him whenever he passed a group. He could not sit on the verandah of the hotel without having people press up to him and start a conversation on any pretext.

The instant that Pedrillo Oñate found that his tongue was loosed, he made the best advantage of his opportunity, and the praises of his master rang through the town. For the greater the master, the greater the servant, of course. However, there were few hours for such chatter. Business was at hand. Robert had guessed at the proper thing for him to do. The sheriff himself made the suggestion with a proper earnestness.

"Fernald, you're interested in this case. You think that old man Bede didn't do the job. Well, why not help to prove it? We can't prove that Cavaselle or Laurence Berners is guilty if we haven't 'em handy to charge with the crime. They're gathering a jury to try Bede. They'll hang him, too . . . you can be sure of that. Now, suppose that you was to start out on the trail of 'em, and try to bring in one of those fellows. You can have your pick of the best men in the town. I swear you in as a deputy . . . you understand?"

"I understand," Robert said faintly. He began to grow pale, and paler.

The sheriff stared. He knew that here was a celebrated young man, reputed fearless, certainly proved with respect to guns and gunmen. Yet the young man trembled and turned white. What was to be made of such a thing? The sheriff waited. He dared not make up his mind about such a matter on the spur of the moment, and he really was afraid to guess at what was passing in the mind of Robert Fernald.

"How many men would you suggest that I take as a posse?" asked Robert Fernald.

"A dozen. Take a dozen of the best. You might need 'em."

"But," Robert said, "if I took a dozen, the other men that we're chasing . . . they wouldn't have much of a chance, would they?"

"A chance? I don't know what you mean."

"Well, I mean, that they would never have the slightest chance against such a number of men, Sheriff. Then, you see, it wouldn't be good sport to chase them with such a crowd. It wouldn't be fair. Isn't that clear?"

The sheriff looked at his companion with eyes that opened wide. He was seeing something more than the boyish, smooth, pink-and-white face of Robert Fernald. He was seeing a great idea that rather overawed him.

"Would the hunting of those two men be sport to you, my lad?" he asked.

Robert considered gravely. "Not sport . . . but a duty, you know," he said, hunting for words to match the emotion that was within him. "But if you were being hunted, Sheriff, you would want to have your chance against one man, instead of a dozen of course. And there's no . . . there's no honor, you see, in running down a single man with numbers."

The sheriff at last understood, and he smiled a little, his eyes shining.

"It's reputation that you want, Fernald," he said. "I can understand that. Although I should think that what you did with Tom Gill would last you for a while. But if you prefer to tackle this job by yourself . . . why, it's a fact that one man makes less noise and dust than twelve."

Such was their understanding before Robert Fernald was sworn in as a deputy and given a little certificate that entitled him to act in the name of the sheriff, and to call upon the citizens of the state for support in the execution of his duties.

Then Robert went to the stable behind the hotel, and found Pinto dancing in his eagerness to be out. Not that the little horse was a lover of work, but he hated the indoors with a consuming hatred. Then Robert sent for Pedrillo and his mule.

The Mexican came in fine fettle, for he had enjoyed himself greatly in Catalina since the announcement of his master's identity.

"If you were in love with a pretty girl in this town," said Robert, "and you got into a fight here and killed a man, what would you do?"

Without a moment's hesitation the Mexican answered: "I should ride as fast as I could to the house of Juan Patron, up yonder in the mountains, and ask him to let me hide out near his shack."

"Is Juan Patron an old friend?"

"Yes."

"What good would it do you to be so near?"

"Because it would be as hard for them to hunt me near as to hunt me far off. Besides, they would be very likely to override

124

me. Also, I should have a chance to slip back into Catalina from time to time to see the girl I loved . . . if she still loved me. But she would not love me long, *señor*. Ah, a woman is only made for fair weather. She cannot stand black days and. . . ."

Robert had heard enough. He made Pedrillo wait while he went to make inquiries that soon gave him an embarrassing richness of information.

Cavaselle had friends near Catalina. Yes, he had scores of them. It appeared that every man in the mountains either was a friend or an enemy of Cavaselle. There were no neutrals.

"But his best friends?" Robert asked, at his wit's end.

"Old man Dodge, yonder by the Sugarloaf . . . and Chris Hansen on the opposite side of the valley in the narrows between those two summits."

Old man Dodge, it appeared, had instructed the fatherless Cavaselle in the arts of hunting and trapping, and Robert felt that the fugitive might have taken shelter with such a time-tried ally as that—if, indeed, the cowpuncher were not far, far across the mountains before this.

So he and Pedrillo rode out of Catalina, and, passing down the main street, Robert was hailed by a strong voice: "Hello, Bob Fernald!"

It was Chollie Bede, walking with her long, masculine stride and carrying a basket.

Robert reined his horse closer to her and raised his hat.

"Think of you," said the girl, "coming into our house like a mouse. Why didn't you speak out and name yourself, man?"

Robert shifted from the point of that compliment. "Is your father terribly worried?" he asked.

"You'd never guess it," said the girl. "He's sitting in the jail smoking his pipe . . . and they've let him have some stuff to work at, so he's as happy as can be. Or at least he lets on that he is. But nobody ever can get behind Dad's face at what he's really thinking."

"Give him my kindest wishes," Robert said. "And tell him that I know he is innocent. I . . . I even hope that I may help to prove it."

"The deuce you do," said the girl. "How would you manage that, then?"

"By finding the man who did the shooting."

Chollie whistled. "More power to you," she said. "I'm taking Dad his lunch, and I'll give him the good news. It ought to mean more than food to him. You're a kind fellow, Bob Fernald."

"Ah, no," said Robert. "Only, I think that I can tell the good people from the bad, you know."

She shook hands with him, giving him a powerful grip, and Robert passed on up the street. All this was not exactly as he had imagined it. He had expected terror on the part of the prisoner, tears on the part of the girl, but this was no world of tales or books in which our Robert found himself. It was the crisp, noisy, brisk, wide-awake 20th Century, with very little room in it for sentimentality of any kind.

Up toward the Sugarloaf they made their way, he and Pedrillo, with Oñate extremely uneasy. For this was not the direction of Larkin Valley. But his master offered no explanations. They climbed for a little over two hours, and then came to the edge of a pine wood and looked into a rough little swale of ground partly set out in a vegetable garden, with a patch or two of grain growing. In the midst, with tall brush all around obscuring it, was the shack of old Dodge. And there was Dodge himself sawing up a supply of firewood.

Robert reined swiftly back into the woods, and Pedrillo followed softly on his mule. The eyes of the Mexican were big with curiosity and fear when they reached a little clearing in the trees, and Robert halted.

"*Señor,* we have become hunters?" he asked.

"We have become hunters," he admitted. "Manhunters, Pedrillo. Can you help me in a pinch?"

"I can help myself, *señor,*" Pedrillo said, turning green-yellow with unhappy thoughts. "But you cannot ask a man with one arm to help others. I have only this old gun." As he spoke, he pulled from its holster beneath his right leg a short-barreled shotgun of large caliber, and this he whipped up under his one arm, so that he could present the muzzle of his weapon, although he could not aim it except by instinct.

"Give me a close target," said Pedrillo, "and I'll blow it to pieces, *señor.* But I have only one arm. You would never ask me to help with the fighting."

He looked the picture of woe, and Robert smiled at him. In a way, he was glad to have such a coward along with him. It set his own uncertain nerves against an excellent background.

"Now, Pedrillo," he said, "I am going to stay here with the horses. I want you to steal up around that shack and watch it like a hawk, until dark if you have to, or after dark. See if there is any other person in the little house and, if there is, come and tell me about his looks."

"You will not make me fight, little father?"

"Not a stroke."

"When I had two hands," began Pedrillo, "I loved battle. There was never any trouble in San Joaquin that did not have Pedrillo Oñate at the bottom of it. I have had wild adventures, *señor.* Once the sheriff himself came and beat me with a stick . . . and once a crowd wished to lynch me for stealing a horse. I stood with a rope around my neck. So you see that I am familiar with danger. It is nothing to me. Except that God has taken one hand away, and I am useless."

"Imagine," Robert said, "that you have no hands at all, but

just an ear to hear for me and an eye to see for me. Go and watch cleverly and come back to me safely. I don't want to lose you, Pedrillo. What should I do without you?"

Pedrillo was as pleased as a child by this compliment. He went off with his eyes shining. So perfectly did he enter into his part that, one step from the edge of the clearing, he vanished from Robert's sight. A little chill of apprehension even ran down the spine of Fernald, but long centuries of Indian ancestry were working to make the wits of the Mexican skillful in his woodcraft. He faded at a stride into the greenery of the woods, and Robert sat down with his back to a tree and stared at a patch of blue sky high above him. In the distance he could hear the whine of the long saw as old Dodge drew it back and forth through the tough, sappy wood. Nearby the leaves shook and rattled now and then, and noises of flying insects *whirred* loudly into his ears and faded. Robert was beginning to sink out of the strenuous, muscular world of action where naught but great things or brilliant thoughts are possible, into the passive world where the senses awaken and the soul seems to take root like a plant so that we are placed in harmony with life itself, whether the life of a fungus or the life of a mountain. Into that state of mind Robert was passing. Vague but immense emotions rose and faded in his blood. He began to see without effort, and therefore he began to see clearly—the blades of grass and their shadows, the ways of the insects through this minor forest, or the noble heads of the trees, and beyond them the soft drifting of the clouds, born out of haze, melting again in the light of the sun.

In this mood he heard the *crunch* of a footfall, louder to Robert than the crashing of heavy guns. He sat up with a start, and the parting of the shrubbery opposite to him showed him the huge shoulders and bulky figure of Tim Cavaselle.

VII

Robert remembered the old story of the wishing gate, which is at hand when we know it not. Yonder was clever Pedrillo, using his Indian craft to locate a possible second person in the house of Dodge. And here at hand was the wanted man, stumbling fairly upon Robert.

Tim Cavaselle saw the stranger in the clearing as he strode forward, wrenching himself through the brush like one who has such an excess of strength that he need not worry about cunning. He saw, and he reached for his gun, but Tim carried his weapon in the old-fashioned, the very old-fashioned style—on his hip. Robert had jerked out his ugly-faced automatic in the least part of a second, and leveled it at the other, while Tim's hand was still gripping the butt of his gun, half unsheathed.

Cavaselle hesitated. He knew nothing of the identity of this youngster. He was much inclined to despise him. But he could not despise that leveled weapon and the keen eye behind it.

"Don't make your draw, Cavaselle," warned Robert. "You'll be hurt if you do."

Cavaselle growled. He was growing red with anger. "What's into you, runt?" he asked impolitely. "What's into you? What you want with me?"

"Unbuckle your gun belt," requested Robert.

"Kid, you're makin' a fool of yourself."

"Unbuckle your gun belt," Robert repeated. "I tell you, Cavaselle, you murdered a man in Catalina, and then ran away and let an innocent man be jailed. I'd shoot you down with no more compunction than I'd shoot a woodchuck."

Cavaselle hesitated, a black scowl upon his brow. Then he obediently unbuckled the belt—obediently but slowly, as though he were turning many expedients through his mind. But an automatic pistol does not encourage brainwork. The belt and its revolver and heavy hunting knife fell to the ground.

"Walk over to the center of the clearing," said Robert, getting to his knees without removing his attention from his captive.

Cavaselle obeyed more slowly than ever. "It ain't really possible," he declared. "It ain't really possible that I've been snagged by a baby-faced boy like you. Now, what you want?"

The sound of the saw in the distance ceased.

"Talk quietly," Robert advised. "I don't want to alarm Mister Dodge. But I want you to go down to Catalina with me. I want to put you in the jail there and take poor Austin Bede out."

"Bah!" snarled the big man. He strode nearer, menacing.

Now that Robert was on his feet, and his lack of inches was revealed, Tim Cavaselle's scorn increased every moment.

It made the blood of Robert leap. He felt terror at the nearness of the huge cowpuncher, and yet that terror was not unpleasant. It made his breath come quickly, almost gaspingly. It made his mouth pinch together as if from cold. But it kept a singing of delight along his taut nerves. This was the spice with which life needed to be qualified before it was tasty.

"Don't come too close, Cavaselle," he warned.

"Suppose I tell you that I'm not coming down with you?" asked Tim Cavaselle. And he clenched his fists.

"You're not a madman, I hope."

"Well, I'm big enough to take a slug through the body and get in at you," said Cavaselle. "One shot couldn't hardly kill me. And once I laid my hands on you . . . why, I'd tear you in two."

"Would you?"

"Wouldn't I, sonny?"

"I doubt it," Robert said, the striking muscles quivering along both his arms.

"Are you nutty?"

"I think I might even handle you without a gun," Robert stated, his breath taken by his own temerity.

At the mere idea of such an encounter his brain fired with dread, with horror, with terrible joy. His lips began to twitch; his eyes began to glitter.

Have you ever watched a bull terrier before it goes into action? Another dog will howl and growl and rage and rave. But a bull terrier about to fly at a throat is merely gravely attentive. His lips grin back a little. A slight shudder goes through his body. And his whole soul is hungering for the encounter.

So it was with Robert. He was thinking, too. Here was a handicap of a full sixty pounds over and above his own scant hundred and fifty. But against that handicap, he might stack his long training in wrestling and boxing. Skill counts. Although a good big man will beat a good little one, how many times, at college, had he seen the little lightweight wrestling instructor lay a hulking football player helplessly on his back? And how often had he seen the slender boxing teacher floor a charging, tearing, furious heavyweight aspirant to the team. "The thinking you do on the floor is a little surer than the thinking you'll do on your feet," that little pug-ugly used to say as he smiled down at a dazed youth.

So thought Robert now, trembling at his own wild idea and measuring the terrible breadth of Tim's shoulders and the very eloquent depth of his arched chest.

"You might even handle me without a gun?" Tim sneered. "Kid, I would tie one hand behind me and still be ashamed of hittin' you. Why, you little knock-kneed son-of-a-toad, I'd. . . ."

Robert slipped from his coat, and, weighted by the gun it contained, it fell heavily to the ground. He stepped forth into the very shadow of his foe, looking slenderer than ever in his shirt sleeves.

Cavaselle laughed. He scanned Robert from head to foot and laughed again. For he was a little too excited to be accurate in his observations. He saw the pink and white cheeks of Robert, and the head that looked rather too heavy for the neck that supported it, but he failed to see the economy and neatness with which Nature had framed Robert. Your six-footer usually has his flaws of makeup. And even if his proportions are correct, possibly he is not strung together with the same steel wires that bind a smaller man. Steel wires charged with electricity. And so it was with Robert, and all that Nature had given him he had improved wonderfully, for he hid the aspirations of a giant in the poundage of a welterweight.

Yet Cavaselle did not see these things.

"The kid has grit, after all," he said as though to an audience. "But I wouldn't know how to begin with you, son. It'd be like hitting a girl."

"This will take away some of your scruples," suggested Robert, and, stepping in lightly, he struck Tim across the cheek with his open fingers.

"*Aghr-r-r!*" snarled Tim Cavaselle. And he smote at Robert, a good, whole-hearted, sledge-hammer stroke. It missed. By the proverbial and almost the actual yard, it missed.

Robert smiled a little with white, twitching lips.

"I'll kill you," Tim said, seeing that smile. He rushed in and smote again. Furiously with either arm he struck, with arms that had been steeled by labor all his life. But he could not find his mark. It floated before him. He no longer missed by yards. By fractions of inches he failed, and it seemed as though the very wind of his punches was driving before him the frail object of this attack, as a gossamer shred floats from beneath a striking hand.

So Cavaselle smote and grunted and raged and fumed. He drove Robert back across the clearing until the little man's heel struck a root and down he went. Have you ever seen a cat trip and fall? So Robert tripped and fell—and whirled to his feet again faster than a bouncing ball.

But honest Tim had not striven to take advantage of this opening to throw his weight upon his elusive foeman. Instead, he gave back, scowling and cursing, and saw that Robert was fairly planted upon his feet before he charged again.

Robert, however, had been stung to the quick by fear and surprise. He no longer retreated. Under the sweeping arms he ducked, stepped in to meet the heavy rush, and with his right fist he drove to the jaw of Tim Cavaselle. He did not sweep or hack or carve like Tim in his fighting. But he hit from his toes, timing his weight, his lifting power, his energy of nerve and body and hand and leg so that all exploded at the correct instant. And the explosion hit the correct spot—about an inch from the point of the jaw, where there is a full lodgment for the knuckles, and where a properly applied shock is transmitted with all the effective leverage of the long bone of the lower jaw to the base of the skull.

Tim Cavaselle turned halfway around. His rush was stopped. His power was gone. He began to tremble and sway like a great tree that has been cut to the inner core by the axe. His head rolled on his shoulders. His knees bent, sagged, gave way. And he dropped upon them, fumbling at the ground with one hand. His spirit was not beaten or overawed. He cursed the blackness that swam across his brain, and shook his head to clear his wits. But Tim was totally upset, and Robert went to his coat and put it on. His knuckles were sore and were beginning to swell, but, otherwise, he felt no ill effects from the encounter. Yet he felt exactly as though he had been riding a storm wind.

VIII

By the time Robert had settled himself in his coat, Tim Cavaselle was on his feet, shaking his head like a great bull. But so soon as he had recovered himself a little, he showed no resentment.

133

"I understand, kid," he said. "You're a pug, though I'm hanged if you look the part. All right. You've got me. Now what?"

"We go down to Catalina," said Robert.

Tim Cavaselle made a wry face. "Me with my hands tied, maybe," he said, "and you drivin' me in like a cow. No!"

Robert was amazed. "You won't go?"

"No!"

"But look here," said Robert, "you have to, you know. I . . . have the advantage over you, it appears."

"You've got a gun in your hands," Tim Cavaselle said. "Use it, then."

"Do you propose," Robert asked, his eyes very wide, "that I should shoot you down in cold blood?"

"Kid," said the big man, "we all got to die once. Today may as well be my time. But . . . I won't go down with you. If you come at me, I'll tackle you again, and, though I couldn't beat you in a fair fist fight, I'll sure massacre you at rough-and-tumble."

This Robert most devoutly believed. And he regarded Tim Cavaselle with a frown of bewilderment. "I don't know what I'm to do," Robert said at last.

"Think it out for yourself," answered the big fellow. "I'll take my medicine and never yelp, you can bet."

Light dawned on Robert. "It's the girl," he said suddenly. "You don't want to be shamed before her, of course."

"Would you?" asked Cavaselle.

"No," Robert admitted, "I certainly wouldn't. As a matter of fact, I admire and respect your attitude, Mister Cavaselle. But how am I to get you to Catalina? And tell me man to man . . . did you kill Lovat?"

Cavaselle looked at our hero partly in cunning and partly in amusement. "Want me to confess right now and pave the short road to a hanging party?" he suggested.

Robert blushed. "Well," he said, "all that I can do is to take a long chance, it appears. I have to shoot you down here in cold blood . . . and I don't want to do that. Or else I have to take your promise that you'll go down to Catalina and give yourself up. Or. . . ."

"Would you trust me to go down and give myself up?" asked the cowpuncher curiously.

"I think I would," Robert said. "Or . . . we might take an even start and shoot the thing out." He said it wistfully, slowly.

Tim Cavaselle cast a quick glance toward the spot where his gun lay. "Do you mean that?"

"It might be a good idea," said Robert, "if you shoot quite well."

"What?"

"You see," Robert explained seriously, "I am rather an expert with guns. I've spent a great deal of time trying to become one, at least."

Tim Cavaselle burst out: "Well, I'll be hanged, kid, if you ain't the queerest lot that I ever come up with. Suppose you lemme see how much of an expert you are? There's a fool blue jay sitting on the top of that sapling yonder. You might take a drive at him."

"Certainly," Robert said without hesitation.

Instantly the automatic flashed into his hand and exploded. The tip of the sapling was shorn away under the feet of the astonished bird, which dropped a yard downward with a frightened *clattering* before it regained its balance and wheeled on the wing—wheeled just in time to receive a second bullet that tore through its body. A crimson wreck, it dropped heavily to the ground.

"I was a little too hasty with the first shot," Robert said, flushing. "But the distance was so short and the bird so big . . . you see, I was a little over confident."

Tim Cavaselle measured the "short" distance with an accurate eye. "Kid," he said gravely, "you and me are not gonna shoot this thing out with guns because you are an expert. So am I. But you got me beat. Well, you got nearly everybody beat."

"Oh, no," said Robert.

"Oh, yes," said Cavaselle. "I know. What might your name be?"

"My name is Robert Fernald."

"*What?*" Cavaselle broke into loud laughter. "All right," he said, "if you're Fernald, that settles it. Fighting I don't mind. But I sure hate suicide. Fernald, if you'll trust me to go down to Catalina, I'll start right *pronto* and go down. And what's more, I'll tell who it was that sent me."

"But you don't need to," Robert said earnestly. "It might embarrass you, and, besides, it would count more in your favor if it were thought that you had given yourself up willingly."

"You talk more friendly than hostile," Cavaselle remarked.

"With all my heart," said Robert, "I hope that you come through this affair with no trouble. I hope that you're innocent. I . . . I really think you are."

"Do you?"

"Yes."

"If it wasn't me, then it was old man Bede, of course."

"Bede? Oh, no. There was the third man. There was Laurence Berners. I should have started after him in the first place."

"Is Berners mixed up in this?"

"Yes."

Cavaselle whistled, and then exclaimed: "And you're going after him?"

"I suppose that I shall have to," Robert replied seriously, "if you're not the guilty man."

"I'd give ten years of my life," declared Cavaselle, "and I'd give 'em gladly, if I could have a chance to see you and Laurence Berners mix it. There'd be a grand scrap, and nothin' much to choose between you. At least, he wouldn't have it on you much, I guess."

"I hear that he's a really terrible man," Robert said, his eyes growing larger as they had a way of doing.

"Him? Well, they say a good deal about him, but nobody ever has said enough."

"No?"

"I should say not. Oh, I know all about Berners. I've seen him in action. And I was in Tracy right after he killed the three Sherry brothers. I walked into the room and seen the bodies laid out. The three of 'em had come to get him. He didn't even jump for cover. He fought it out with 'em, and he salted 'em all away."

"He killed all three?" breathed Robert.

"Sure, he did. They put four bullets through him. But he's harder to kill than a grizzly. You got to find either the brain or the heart to stop him. His brain is so small that you could easily put it into a walnut . . . and as for a heart, why, the whole world knows that he ain't got one. You and him will have a fine go when you hook up together. I'd sure like to be on hand."

"I suppose that I must take up his trail," Robert said, paler than ever. "But it frightens me a good deal just to think of it."

"Frightens you?"

"Oh, yes. My blood is ice, just to think of it."

"Well, have you got a grudge against Berners?"

"No."

"Has anybody hired you to tackle him?"

"Oh, no."

"Then why do you go at all?"

"I never thought of that," Robert admitted blankly.

"You just give yourself this here little job of running down him and me, is that it?"

"The sheriff asked me to help," Robert responded weakly.

"*Humph*," said Cavaselle. "But look here, old-timer, did it ever occur to you that maybe you was doing this job because you like danger?"

"Like danger?"

"Ain't that possible?"

"I never heard of such a thing."

"The things that we like the most ain't always the sweetest," said Cavaselle. "Whiskey ain't very smooth, but we drink it. Whoever liked the first taste of beer? The same way with danger. Me and most, we stay away from it if we can. But there's some that get sleep in ordinary times. They got to have something rare and big and smashing to wake them up. Why, old-timer, you're that kind. 'Danger,' you say, and you turn pale. But the more you think about it, the more you got to follow the hard trails. Ain't that correct?"

"I don't think so," Robert said, much distressed.

"Well, but I'm right," declared Cavaselle. "And you'll keep on following the hard trails until you get a bullet in you one of these days. You'll get famous, but you'll die young."

It was a very new idea to Robert. He considered it with his eyes wide. Suddenly he could see that it was truth. No man in the world could fear danger more than he, and no man in the world could be more drawn by its fatal attraction. All physical contact with men had been terrible to him—and yet he had gone in seriously for boxing and wrestling. To him, the charge of a heavy football line was like the drive of an infantry regiment. And yet he had striven desperately to gain a place on his college team. Four years of failure, but four years of the most strenuous effort had resulted. And now, here he was in the Wild West, following desperate trails that eventually, as Cavaselle suggested, might lead to his destruction. He saw himself and his future with new eyes. He was the foolish moth fluttering, and danger was the candle flame toward which he flew. He touched a scar on his cheek where the bullet from the rifle of Tom Gill had grazed him on that day of days. Already the flame had singed him badly. Another touch of the fire might destroy his life.

So thought Robert, brooding upon himself and the mystery of his own character, the destiny that was drawing him forward. And he was more frightened than ever before. Except that hitherto events and creatures had filled him with terror, but now he was terrified of himself and of the powers that were working in him.

He looked up to Tim Cavaselle and sighed. "Perhaps you're right," said Robert. "I seem to be in a very bad way. I shall never forget what you've said. In fact, I think I shall have to leave this country of guns and gunmen."

"After you've finished this job, however," suggested Tim.

"Yes, of course."

Cavaselle smiled and said no more. "Shall I start for Catalina?" he asked.

"If you will."

Cavaselle crossed the clearing, picked up his gun belt, deliberately strapped it on, and then left the clearing and proceeded toward the house of old Dodge.

Robert sat down on a stone and felt the weight of a tragic destiny descend upon him.

IX

Three days later, Robert and Pedrillo Oñate were on the far side of Catalina cutting for sign on a grand scale, and still without a trace of Berners to guide them, when a message came out to them from the sheriff of Catalina.

There had been strange occurrences at the trial, in the meantime. For one thing, Bede could give no good account of what had brought him to Lovat's room so late in the night. He claimed that it was a bit of local information concerning trails that Lovat had asked of him that he had suddenly remembered. But when the district attorney grilled him in cross-examination, Austin Bede had floundered lamentably and made an exceedingly bad impression upon the jury.

Now matters were rapidly focusing. It had been proved by the district attorney that Bede was staggering under a heavy burden of debt and that the jewels of Lovat would in themselves have been enough to cancel all he owed, to say nothing of the contents of Lovat's wallet. And then, most crushingly, it was learned that three of the debts, totaling more than $5,000, had been paid off by Bede's daughter a short time after his arrest. How had she come to have so much money?

When Miss Bede was put on the stand and questioned, she simply said that her father always, to a certain extent, hoarded money and that after his arrest he had ordered her to take what he had in savings and, with it, discharge his three largest debts. She had done what she was told to do. Otherwise, she could not make an answer.

She had been a good witness on the stand. But it was pointed out by the district attorney that it would have been utterly strange for Austin Bede to accumulate a hoard of $5,000 when he had been faced with utter ruin, and when several times he had postponed that ruin by making personal appeals to his creditors. Very odd, indeed, for a man who was in this situation to be piling up such a considerable treasure as was referred to glibly by the lawyer for the defense.

"Bede was a man who took in little cash, and who hated therefore to spend it," said the lawyer for the defense.

But the district attorney proved that, on the contrary, Austin Bede was an unworldly dreamer who cared not a whit for money, and who gave it away with ridiculous freedom. Furthermore, at the very time of the trial, did not the silversmith sit in his chair idly thumbing a bit of molding clay? Was this a man to hoard money?

The jury, by their expression, showed to which side they leaned.

$5,000 suddenly had appeared in the possession of the defendant—appeared immediately after he was held on a charge of murder. Undoubtedly that jury felt convinced that the jewels and wallet of the murdered man had made up the sum.

So the coils were drawn closer, momentarily, around Bede. Day by day he sat in the courtroom and saw his chance for life disappearing, but never gave a sign of the slightest concern. And his tall daughter walked as bravely and unconcernedly through the streets of the town as ever before, and was heard to sing in the house of her father.

But men knew that she sang and smiled not because she was happy, not because she was untouched, but because she would not have the pity or the soft sympathy of her fellows.

Such was the case when Cavaselle rode into the town and surrendered himself to the sheriff.

"What made you come down here and surrender, Cavaselle?"

"Fernald sent me."

It made a great sensation in the town—the power of Fernald to do the thing—the honor of Cavaselle in keeping his promise to Fernald.

But what had Cavaselle to do with the case? He was questioned sharply. What had brought him up at such a late hour on the night of the murder? What had he been doing?

He had been unable to sleep, and so he had gone for a walk under the stars.

The jury chuckled. In fact, Cavaselle did not look like a nervous man, or one who would lose sleep, or seek starlight for a consolation.

What really had made Cavaselle get up at that hour? He stuck to his first story. Why, then, had he fled after the murder of Lovat? He had not fled after it, said Cavaselle. He had decided before this that he would ride up to the cabin of his friend, Dodge, and get there by daylight. And that was what he had done. He had not known that he was suspected in connection with the trial until young Fernald told him so.

This tale disappeared in smoke before the district attorney's examination. For it was after the murder, of course, that Robert Fernald had blundered into Cavaselle outside the house. That being the case, what had led Cavaselle to lie in this fashion?

The jury was filled with interest, and the district attorney freely implied, by his questions, that he suspected Cavaselle of being in league with old Bede—Bede to do the murder, and Cavaselle to wait outside the window and receive the loot that the murderer would throw down to him.

Then Cavaselle had disposed of the stolen articles, and placed the money in the hands of Bede's daughter. Or even, suggested the district attorney, he might have placed it in the "hoarding place" and let the father tell his daughter about the money later on. In this manner, all suspicion of guilt would be removed from the shoulders of the girl.

The case was black against Bede. It grew blacker after the clumsy testimony of Cavaselle who, under cross-questioning, became sullen and silent and swore at the district attorney and vowed that he would not testify another word. He was put in jail for contempt of court, and men decided that he would have to stay there until he changed his mind about talking.

Such was the state in which matters were concerning the trial, and the district attorney had unearthed a further bit of valuable evidence as to the reasons that would impel the silversmith to take the life of his guest.

In the first place, it appeared that when Lovat was a young

man in the town, there had been bad blood between him and Bede. Lovat had wooed the girl who married Bede. And now when he returned to Catalina, it was suggested by conversations that had been overheard, that Lovat had taken his lodgings in the house of Bede particularly in order that his display of wealth might humiliate his old rival.

Last of all, the proposals that Lovat had made for the hand of the girl were bared in the court. Rather than let his daughter sell herself for his sake, Bede would kill with his own hand and cut the Gordian knot of his difficulties.

It made a neat case. There were few loopholes. Men even ceased arguing. There was no doubt about the guilt. The only question was: what would the sentence be?

The jury found Austin Bede guilty as a matter of course, and recommended him to the mercy of the court—a recommendation that the court saw fit to overlook. For the judge pointed out that no matter what else could be said in favor of the accused and his long and blameless life, he had destroyed the life of a guest, and that was the greatest of great crimes.

He sentenced Austin Bede to be hanged by the neck until he was dead. And God have mercy on his soul.

This was the information that the sheriff sent in much detail to his valued deputy. He added that if anything were to be made of the possible testimony of Laurence Berners, something would have to be done about it at once. What could young Fernald suggest? Except through the testimony of Laurence Berners, if that villain could be made to testify at all, there was not the slightest chance of saving the life of the prisoner. And the sheriff made no secret of his desire; he wanted poor Austin Bede set free and washed clean of guilt.

X

It was a clear portrayal of the state of things in the town, and it threw Robert into a deep dismay. All that he had done in the sending in of Cavaselle seemed less than nothing. Berners he must get—and how should he go about it? There was no trace of the gunman. No one had heard of him. No one had seen him riding through the country.

Others did not regard this as important. For Berners would very frequently disappear in exactly this fashion, no doubt to appear again far off, do a work of mischief, and vanish once more. Either he vanished to do evil or to escape from the results of evil that he had already done.

But to Robert the thing seemed clear as the clearest sunshine. Berners had vanished because it was his hand that had struck down Lovat, the millionaire, his hand that had stolen the jewels and the wallet, and now, like a black scoundrel, he skulked far off and allowed another man to be condemned for his sin. These were Robert's conclusions, and he wondered that others had not arrived at them.

If only he could get at Laurence Berners. He said to Oñate: "Pedrillo, if you had two hands and could shoot equally well with both, what would you be apt to do? If you could shoot straight and fast with two guns, I mean?"

Pedrillo had finished wiping the frying pan. Now he looked up to the lofty pines that rose above them. "Ah, little father," he said, "if I had two hands once more and could handle a good gun in each of them, first of all I should go back to San Joaquin, to my own town, and there I should make certain men eat dirt before me."

"So?" said Robert.

"I should shame some who have shamed me," Pedrillo said. He took a knife from his belt and dug it deep into a stump of rotten wood that *creaked* as the steel compressed the soft, pulpy wood on either side of the blade.

"You'd knife some of them, Pedrillo?"

"I, little father? No, but I should make them live in fear of knifing . . . as some men have made me live."

"San Joaquin is only a little town, Pedrillo. If you were a great fighter, you would want to go to a bigger place and be a king over it."

Pedrillo considered this suggestion for a moment. "Now and then," he said, "I would ride out to other towns. When I heard that there was a great man here or a great man there, hard fighters, terrible men, then I would ride out and find them. I would strike them down. I would ride over them. I would leave them for the wolves to eat, little father." He jerked the knife from the stump and thrust it back in its sheath. "But I have only one hand," he said sadly, "and every beggar can beat Oñate."

"No," Robert said. "Who dares to treat you brutally, Pedrillo?"

"Because of you, they are afraid," said Pedrillo. "They are afraid that, if they strike me, I may ask my little father to come like a blast of lightning. They are afraid because of you, but if I had two hands, they would be afraid because of me. When I came into a house, men would not say . . . 'Pedrillo, fetch me this. Pedrillo, hurry and bring me that. Pedrillo, I need some tobacco, run to the store and buy some. Pedrillo, catch my horse and throw a saddle on it.' " Oñate became silent, his face distorted with rage and shame and pain. "No," he went on, "they would say . . . 'Señor Oñate, take this chair . . . this one that has the view through the window. And what will you have to drink? Accept this cigar, Señor Oñate. It is an honor to have you in this house. Do not disturb yourself, my dear and honored friend. The sun is hot. My son will be pleased to catch and saddle the horse of Pedrillo Oñate.' So they would speak to me, *señor.* So they would speak to me, and I should listen to them . . . and I should smoke the cigar and turn it slowly between my lips . . . and I should not speak much and I should say the thing that I wished, and it should be done. In that manner I should live, little father."

Robert swallowed his smile. "And always in San Joaquin, Pedrillo?"

"Always in San Joaquin, *señor.* Because in that town, though it is small, I was born. I know all the people. I know their values, as though they were so many coins in my purse. I know the liars and I know the true men. Is that not clear? I should know which men to kick and which men to caress. It is better to be a great man among those who we know than it is to be a great man among strangers. So it seems to me, at the least."

He lighted a cigarette, rolled Mexican fashion into the shape of a cornucopia. He leaned back against the stump and closed his eyes and turned the cigarette slowly between his lips, and puffed it as though it were indeed the cigar of his own story.

Robert smiled again, but he smiled in secret, for he felt that Pedrillo was the testing stone by which he should come, perhaps, to know the mind of the bully and brute, Laurence Berners.

"Very well," said Robert, "but now and then you would need money. How would you get it in that little town?"

"Those who have strong hands may take where they will," said Pedrillo. "Consider. Did you not ride into Larkin Valley and do one great thing, and would not the lady who owns the valley give half her lands if she could have you there to defend the other half? Would she not pay you much money?"

Robert bit his lip and was glad of the darkness that covered his blushes.

"Let us ride there, *señor,*" suggested Pedrillo. "Let us ride there at once. What are we doing here, wandering through the mountains, starving one day and eating the next only because the gun of *señor* my master has found game? Let us go to Larkin Valley where we will be like kings in the land."

But it was not Larkin Valley that Robert had in mind at this moment. He regarded the dying fire; he looked at the solemn trees, gilded and made rosy by the light from the flames.

"Tell me, Pedrillo . . . do you know much of Laurence Berners?"

"Every wise man knows a wolf," said the Mexican. "You can tell it by its track. Yes, I know *Señor* Berners, because I have heard of him and I have seen him. Men cannot help talking about a wolf, particularly if it steals sheep from their cotes."

"What is his home town, or has he one?"

"Yes, *señor*. We all know what his home town is. He lives in the town of Last Buffalo. There was an Apache village there, and so it got that name in the old days. Why do you ask me, *señor*? May heaven forbid that you go hunting that man?"

"I have to go to Last Buffalo," said Robert. "Be ready for an early start. Is it far away?"

"A day's ride, *señor*. But what is to be gained there and what can be done there? Tell me, little father?"

It was plain that Pedrillo dreaded the native town of the gunman as others might dread a wasps' nest.

But Robert dwelt no more on his intentions. "Suppose, Pedrillo," he said, "that you were away from San Joaquin and an enemy came to your home town, and that he rode up and down the streets and defied you and scorned you and abused you and swore that he would kill you on sight. Suppose that case, Pedrillo . . . I mean, if you had two strong hands and if you were the king of your town?"

"Ah," snarled the Mexican. "It makes my blood rage to think of such a thing. As soon as word came to me that the scoundrel was doing this thing, I would come like the wind. . . ."

"But suppose that you were far away?"

"That makes no difference. I would be. . . ."

"Ah, but suppose that you were far off, in hiding. Then what, Pedrillo? Suppose that it was necessary for you to hide because of some foolish thing that you had done . . . say the robbing of a stage?"

Pedrillo smirked. He was pleased by the suggestion that he might have the courage and the adroitness to rob a stage of his own prowess, unaided. "Ah, *señor*, no matter what strong reasons I had for hiding, if I knew that a rascal was in my own home town defying me, scorning me, I would come furiously. I would kill horses in my haste. I would ride night and day, and, when I came to San Joaquin, I would be sure to dash up to the saloon. I would ride my pony through the swinging doors. I would have a revolver in each hand. 'Where is the dog who asks for Pedrillo Oñate?' So I would speak. And the bartender, trembling, would say . . . 'Brave *señor*, gallant Pedrillo Oñate, I have heard the fool boasting about what he would do. It was I that sent the word to you. You will find this braggart waiting for you in such and such a place.' Then I would say . . . 'Tell the fool that I am here, resting, and ready to kill him.' Such is the manner in which I would act. And I would fill that fool and coward and braggart full of lead and have him buried like a dog in a trench."

Robert, listening, shuddered a little. His eyes were big and his heart was small. He slept little that night, but awakened again and again and stared at the clear, bright mountain stars high above and the dimly glistening needles of the pines. But he knew the thing that he had to do, and he would not shrink from it. The bright face of danger drew him as the magnet draws iron.

Tim Cavaselle had been right.

XI

The town of Last Buffalo had originally had every natural advantage to give it protection, and none to give it trade. It stood on a ridge in the midst of a narrow valley, with a streak of white water boiling at its feet on either side. Thus it had been in Indian days, when a tribe of copper-faced warriors made it their permanent headquarters. Then the white men came and took up their residence on the ridge. After a while, they let their houses sprawl down toward the river side as soon as the law was strong enough in the land to make peril from Indians an unnecessary consideration. The twin rivers were bridged, the town grew richer. It grew greater. A fringe of houses sprang up on the farther side of each of the streams, close to the bridgeheads. But there was so much more ground than was needed in this community that every house in the place had at least two or three acres attached to it, and these acres were largely planted to orchard trees, so that Last Buffalo looked rather like a series of little farms than like a town, except that along the ridge there was a semblance of the usual village street—a single lane where the shops, the saloons, the hotel, and a few of the houses were posted.

Pedrillo Oñate was enchanted by the sight of this community. He struck his one hand against the neck of his mule.

"If I were *Señor* Berners," he said, "why should I ever leave such a rich town as this? I would simply stay and get fat and make the people work for me."

They rode across the bridge, watched for a moment how the strong current boiled and frothed around the stone piers that supported the structure, and then went on up the steep slope toward the summit. On either hand the orchards were blossoming; the air was heavy with sweet scent, and Pedrillo, like a happy child, could not keep from laughing and crying out with joy now and again.

But Robert rode with his head raised, his face pale, his eyes large and melancholy as befitted a man who was not, perhaps, more than a few moments from death. So they gained the single business street of the town, which wound uncertainly, following the irregularities of the summit ridge. There Robert stopped a youngster of fifteen who was riding past on a bronco, barebacked.

"Is Laurence Berners in town?" he asked.

The boy brought his horse to a halt with a jerk on the reins. Through the dust cloud raised by the planted hoofs of the mustang as it slid to a stop, the stripling studied Robert.

"Are you a friend of his?" he asked.

"I've only seen him once," said Robert.

"Well," said the boy with a flashing grin, "you'd better not see him again." And laughing loudly at his own impertinence, he galloped off down the street.

"He is right," the Mexican said eagerly. "You should not see *Señor* Berners. What could you gain from him except bullets and wounds, little father?"

They came to a blacksmith's shop, and Robert drew rein. The blacksmith, his forge room filled with milky smoke, was working up his fire. Robert, riding close to the door, leaned from his saddle and called: "I beg your pardon!"

The blacksmith left off his labors at the bellows handle. "What for?" he asked.

"I wish to ask you a question. Can you tell me if Laurence Berners is in this town?"

The blacksmith, in place of answering at once, stowed a fragment of tobacco in one cheek, and then jerked his thumb over his shoulder. "His house is right down the street. I dunno what's in it." After a moment, he added gloomily: "What's more, I don't want to know." With that, he turned his back upon Robert and resumed his work at the bellows.

Robert murmured to Pedrillo as they continued on their way down the street: "I've never met such discourteous people, Pedrillo. What is wrong with them?"

"The questions that you ask them, *señor*. That is the trouble, of course."

"And what is wrong with that question, Pedrillo?"

Pedrillo scratched his fat chin. He chuckled. "If you have a corn on your foot, *señor*, you do not like to have that foot stepped on."

Robert smiled a little wanly. "Ah, well," he said, "I must find out from someone."

The house of the seemingly unpopular Berners stood not far off, a little white-painted cottage, exceedingly neat and trim, with a flower garden in front just beginning to give out spots of bloom here and there, and narrow streaks of color along the winding paths.

When Robert knocked at the front door, a tall woman with a face as hard as iron opened the door, and looked down on him from her commanding height. She did not ask why he was there. She merely stared at him coldly, contemptuously.

"This is the house of Mister Laurence Berners, I believe?" Robert said, his hat politely in his hand.

The tall woman did not answer.

"I came to ask if Mister Berners is at home?" said Robert.

"He ain't," the giantess replied, and stepped back and slammed the door in Robert's face.

He was hurt and bewildered by this treatment, but he was exceedingly glad that Berners was not at home. He sighed with relief, and tapped at the door again. He tapped twice; the only response was the clanging voice of the woman from within: "G'wan and stop botherin' me!"

So Robert took a piece of paper from his pocket and wrote on it:

Dear Mr. Berners: When you come back to your home and receive this note, you'll know that I am waiting to take you to Catalina, where you are suspected of the murder of Mr. Lovat. I intend to stay in this town until you come to meet me, and, when we meet, I shall attempt to persuade you to go back to Catalina with me.

Yours most faithfully,
Robert Fernald

When he had finished this note, he pushed it under the door and retreated rather hastily to his horse, for he had an unpleasant idea that the woman of the house—was she the mother of Berners?—might fling the door open and come rushing out at him.

Once safely in the saddle again, Robert jogged Pinto down the street, and poor Pedrillo in a panic at his side, stammered: "*Señor*, you are not going to have a thing to do with that Laurence Berners, are you?"

Robert made no reply. He only said, when they came to the hotel: "I want my name to be known in this town, Pedrillo. I have to make these people think that I'm a little more than a child, you see? And it will help if they know who I am. Not that I have done much. But you understand, Pedrillo, that people talk a little about the capture of Tom Gill."

"And the taking of that fellow Cavaselle," said Pedrillo. "But, ah, little father, why should the people of this town come to fear you and to know you? Is it not better, if we must stay here, to live quietly, to trouble no one? For if *Señor* Berners should learn that you are here, might he not try to make himself greater by coming down and killing you as he has killed others?"

"Perhaps he may," Robert said. "Perhaps he may. I can't tell."

He gave his horse to Pedrillo. Leaving the Mexican gray with fear and uneasiness, he went up the steps of the hotel and presently was leaning over the register, writing his name.

"Robert Fernald? Robert Fernald?" said the fat proprietor, reading the name. "I've heard of it somehow, seems to me. But I guess I'm wrong," he added, looking narrowly at Robert again. "I guess that I sure must be wrong. Well, come along, pardner." And he showed Robert to a room, a back room, and a dark one, with one little window looking on the rear yard and its unsightly litter of trash and junk.

"What might you be doing in Last Buffalo?"

"I am waiting for Laurence Berners," Robert answered.

"Like fun you are!" The proprietor chuckled. "Ain't you afraid that he might eat you when he comes, kid?"

"Perhaps he may," said Robert.

The proprietor paused at the door and looked back. "Going to do some business with Berners?" he asked.

"Yes," said Robert.

"Not aiming to buy his house, are you? Because dog-gone me if the old woman would move out of it."

"Oh, no," Robert said. "I'm not going to buy his house. But I want to take Mister Berners away with me."

"Take him away? Where?"

"To Catalina . . . to answer a murder charge."

"Hey, what the jumping . . . ? Look here, kid, d'you know who you're talkin' about?"

"I was given the work to do, you see," Robert explained humbly. "So I had to come."

"Kid, are you meaning to tell me that Lew Minter sent you up here all alone to get Berners?"

"Yes."

The proprietor gaped, and then he began to laugh rather blankly, like one who feels that a jest is in the air, although he cannot quite locate the point of it. Still laughing, he retreated down the hall, and Robert sat down in his room and hugged himself, and shuddered, and then smiled in spite of himself. He tried to say that he was not pleased. But pleased he was, and most of all by the thrill that would pass through the bones of this little city when it learned the truth about its new visitor.

XII

Pedrillo had become the master of ceremonies. As such he did the talking for Robert, who refused to talk for himself. There was nothing that Pedrillo wanted less than a meeting between his master and Laurence Berners, but, since he felt that the meeting was inevitable, he decided to make the most of it—which is always an excellent plan.

When it was known that the Robert Fernald was in town, and that he would not chatter freely about himself, all men resorted to Pedrillo. He had drinks free whenever he chose to take them; he became the most important figure in either of the two saloons, and an enchanted circle was held by his tales from morning to night.

After all, Robert had not done so very many things at this time in his life, but every Mexican is a born tale-teller, and Oñate was one of the best. Where fact fell a little short, fancy came to his support. He was not one of the foolish liars who make up their stories out of whole cloth. Rather, he was a restrained artist, who never took more than a grain of truth at a time, and this he used to stain whole gallons of narrative.

Under his adroit handling, the manner in which Robert got Pinto and beat the former owner of that horse became a thrilling epic. And the story of how Robert chased and caught and captured the great Tom Gill was such a matter that Pedrillo could not get through it in a single day of steady talking.

To be sure, Pedrillo overstepped the mark a good deal in all directions, and at last the men of Last Buffalo were inclined to think that he was a windy chap with little truth in him. Then an odd event occurred that fortified all that Pedrillo had said and caused his word to be accepted like gospel.

It happened that, on a day, he described how his master practiced with his guns, and how he, Pedrillo, would throw up stones at which Robert tried snap shots. And his master, according to Pedrillo, never missed.

"How big a stone?" asked a grim-faced cowpuncher who had handled guns all his life. "As big as this?" And he showed a shining chunk of quartz.

"Yes," said Pedrillo, "or even smaller."

"At thirty paces?" said the cowpuncher.

"Yes, *señor*. And that is truth by the. . . ."

"Leave off your swearin'," said the cowpuncher. "You're a liar, greaser . . . and a loud one. And I'm gonna show the town how bad you lie."

So said the cowpuncher and straightaway sought out Robert, dreaming on the verandah of the hotel. He covertly marked out thirty paces from the edge of the verandah into the street. And there he turned and sang out: "You gents!"

"Hello?" came from the idlers.

"I've got a little stone here, and twenty dollars to the gent that can nick it with a bullet when I throw it up. Who wants a try?"

Who would not spend a cheap bullet for the sake of a $20 note? All were willing, except Robert.

The end man of the line who sat in chairs along the verandah made the try first and missed, and the second and the third followed suit. But Robert slipped from his chair and made for the door of the hotel.

"Hold on, Fernald!"

"Well?" Robert said politely, wishing that he were far from that spot.

"Ain't you going to take your chance?"

"No," said Robert, "I. . . ."

"You ain't afraid?" sneered the cowpuncher.

Robert hesitated a single instant, and then stepped to the edge of the verandah. "Very well," he said. "Throw up the stone."

It was done, without waiting for him to make ready. Up spun the shining quartz and hung for an instant at the twinkling crest of its rise. The automatic leaped into the fingers of Robert. He had very little hope of striking the target. It was quite true that he made pistol play at just such marks as this, but it was even truer that he had rarely made a hit. However, it was better to try than to be shamed.

At the very instant that the stone hung at its height, he fired— not an aimed shot, but a snap from the height of his hip. As the gun *boomed,* the rock dissolved into a cloud of brilliant particles and these in turn fell softly to the ground.

Robert went hastily into the hotel, saying that he did not want $20 for a trick such as this. But the town of Last Buffalo gathered instantly to talk over the deed and measure again the distance at which the shot had been fired.

Pedrillo, scared and silent, had watched the trial, well knowing what it meant. When he saw the victory, his joy knew no bounds. But he knew enough to control himself.

"Ah, *señores,*" he said, "I would not see any man throw away his money in such a way. If you were to throw up such stones all day, my master would not miss three times. And those three times would only be because he was careless. You observed, my friends? He did not even aim. He fired from the hip."

"It must have been luck!" gasped the disgruntled cowpuncher, who had offered the money.

A bystander remarked dryly: "The same sort of luck that dropped Tom Gill with a bullet down the side of his head."

Pedrillo was invited back to the saloon. But now he had a more crowded and more attentive audience. Hitherto, the men had been apt to look askance at one another from time to time, and smile a little. But now they listened with a grave interest. They had seen magic. They were willing to believe anything.

Pedrillo was not the man to miss such an opportunity. From that moment, his stories about his master became wilder and more brilliant, but the fictions were delivered with a graver and more matter-of-fact air. It would be hard to say how much of the great reputation of Robert Fernald can he traced back to these same tales, but certain it is that a large part of the wonderful stories that to this day are connected with his name must be traced to the glorious inventions of Pedrillo Oñate in the town of Last Buffalo.

He did not throw off many small inventions. The imagination of Pedrillo moved slowly and along large lines. His creations were put together gradually, surely, and made an imposing whole. They were arranged in such a manner that the auditors were not confused by the number of incidents, and each man, after hearing, could retell the story to some advantage. Practiced listeners and tale-tellers are all true men of the mountain ranges and the cattle country. Every ear that drank in the grand inventions of Pedrillo Oñate formed a memory capable of repeating, enlarging, and furbishing up the details until they shone again. But, when those stories were repeated, if any man sneered or shrugged his shoulders, there was a crushing retort: "I'll tell you what I seen with my own eyes! I seen Fernald stand on the edge of the hotel verandah and a stone was throwed up a full thirty paces away . . . a stone no bigger'n this here. And Fernald with a snap shot from the hip, he blew that stone to bits. I seen that with my own eyes. And so did Ham Strickland, and Hugh Moore, and. . . ."

One touch of reality redeems a world of nonsense. The fame of Robert was made in that instant.

People in the town had a continual question during the first few days. If Robert Fernald really wanted to find Berners and fight him, why did he not go hunting for that worthy?

The answer was both simple and spectacular. Pedrillo, of course, was the source of it. Robert Fernald knew that he could destroy poor Berners. But he didn't want to do it alone, in the desert. He preferred to work where men could see him. His private hope was that Berners would not be foolish and make a fight. Fernald would be pleased merely to arrest this man of violence and take him back to Catalina, there to be examined on the murder charge. But, if a fight there must be, let many witnesses be on hand to note that there was nothing but fair play. Thus spoke Pedrillo Oñate, and the crowd, intensely pleased, heard and rubbed its hands.

The challenge was wafted far and wide across the mountains. Somewhere, it would come to the ears of the proud Berners, the fierce, the unconquerable Berners who they all knew so well. It would come to his ears, and certainly he would kill horses in his frantic haste to get home and defend his reputation.

The sheriff of that county rode in and interviewed Robert. He wanted to see the license by which Robert ventured to take the law into his own hands, and the commission from Minter was then shown.

Said the sheriff: "I've heard of gents laying traps, but I never heard of anybody using himself for bait."

That saying was repeated far and wide. Robert Fernald had laid a trap, and then had used himself for bait. He had established himself in the home town of the gunman, and there with an open taunt was drawing Laurence Berners back to him.

There was a sort of devilish surety and calm about this proceeding that filled the imaginations of men. They waited with held breath until the inevitable word came across the ridges that Berners was on his way, riding night and day, never resting, burning with fury, and swearing that he would blast Robert Fernald from the face of the earth.

XIII

When this great news was heard, then the tidings were flashed to all parts of the neighboring countryside. Were there men who desired to be witness to the gunfight of the ages? Then let them appear in the town of Last Buffalo, for there the great battle was bound to take place. And who was there in the West or in the world that would not willingly have been on hand to witness such a tussle? Last Buffalo began to be crowded. The hotel overflowed. And on all sides, people were asking for a glimpse of Robert Fernald.

He was rarely to be seen. He remained much in his room. In the early mornings and in the late evenings he walked out from the hotel by the back way and went into the woods. There they heard him shooting patiently, industriously. Afterward, people went out to find the targets at which he had aimed, but, according to the Mexican, the bull's-eyes that his master attempted were never larger than the mere twigs of trees.

For Pedrillo had no intention of allowing the fame of his master to diminish up to the very day of the fight. As for the battle itself, Pedrillo knew its result beforehand. Robert Fernald was a brave man and a good shot and a quick one, but Laurence Berners was a ruffian who had lived by the gun all these years. How could Robert be expected to stand before him?

For all the preparations that were made, the coming of Berners was a good deal of a surprise. A horse *clattered* to a halt outside the saloon of Chick Murphy. The swinging doors were thrust open, and there entered a squat, wide-shouldered man, with a lower jaw thrust prominently forward.

It was Laurence Berners, hollow-eyed and haggard from the fury of his long ride.

"Is the rat here?" Berners asked slowly. And he looked up and down the barroom.

There was a general movement through that crowd. Each man stepped back a little toward the wall, as though hoping that some other neighbor might come under the keen scrutiny of the man of war.

No, Robert Fernald was not there. But Pedrillo was there. The fat Mexican was there, and on his lips the name of his master and a fictitious adventure of his master had barely died away.

"There's Fernald's man," said the bartender, who on this eve was Chick himself.

Berners strode down the barroom and confronted the Mexican.

Two things saved the face of Pedrillo. One was the color of his skin, which prevented his pallor from being immediately noticeable. The other was the memory that he had only one hand, and that Westerners would not allow a bully to pick on a cripple.

So Pedrillo raised his head high and waved his one hand with a smile.

"Good evening to you, *Señor* Berners," he said. "I might say that I'm glad to see you here, *señor*. But I cannot. Were I your friend, I'd be wishing you any other place in the world."

"You greasy hound," Berners said, thrusting his face within an inch of the face of Pedrillo, "where's the skunk . . . your master?"

"Do you mean *Señor* Fernald?"

"I mean the fool kid that's been talking big in Last Buffalo. And these saps . . . these flatheads, these wall-eyed suckers, that've stood around and believed him. Why, I'm gonna eat that kid alive. But first of all, I'm gonna make him take water. I'm gonna show him off before the whole dog-gone town. Where's

Fernald, I say?"

Pedrillo was very frightened. But in the attentive faces and the frowning brows of the bystanders, he saw that he would be supported if the worst came to the worst. Men do not strike a one-armed man. At least it is not done on the Western range. Pedrillo knew it, and the solemnity with which these spectators watched the clenched fist of Berners gave Pedrillo more heart. He had all the instinct of an actor. Now he made the most of his great moment, prolonging it as much as possible.

"Look here," said Berners, "are you talkin', or do I have to break you open and read your mind for myself?"

"Ah, *señor*," Pedrillo said, "I understand exactly why you are excited. You wish to meet my master. You wish to show that you are not afraid . . . but, *señor*, my master cannot meet you tonight."

"Ten thousand damnations!" Berners cried. "Is the yaller dog gonna . . . ?"

"There are two reasons," said Pedrillo, who as a matter of fact had received no instructions whatever from his employer. "There are two reasons, *señor*."

"Give 'em," Berners said, "and I'll prove that neither of them is worth a cent."

The Mexican looked shrewdly at this man of war. It was not hard for him to see that Berners was keyed up to the point of finest execution. Let him fight now, and he would be more steel than human. He would fear nothing under heaven; he would have caught a lightning bolt in his naked hands and hurled it back at the sky.

If Robert Fernald were to meet this man and live to tell the story, he must take him at another time. So thought Pedrillo Oñate, and undoubtedly he was right.

"The first reason, *señor*," said Pedrillo, "is that my master does not like to fight with you. He knows that you are brave and strong. But he has met many braver and stronger men. There is no glory to him for killing you. But if you insist on meeting him with weapons. . . ."

"Why," Berners shouted, purple with fury, "I'm gonna . . . I'm gonna shoot him to bits by degrees! Why, one killin' ain't good enough for what I'm gonna do to him!"

"Ah, well," said Pedrillo, affecting to sigh with regret. "You are brave, *señor,* and you are foolish, but my master has told me that he will not force you to fight. You have only to surrender your guns to me, and then promise. . . ."

"Surrender my guns to a greaser?" Berners exclaimed, beside himself.

"Very well, then," Oñate said with a graceful wave of his hand. "If you force my master to kill you, he must do so. But he will not take you tonight. He does not wish to have you at an advantage. He wishes to meet you when you are not tired from a long journey, but when you are rested and steady of nerves. Then he will gladly meet you."

"You brown-faced rat!" called Berners. "All I'm gonna do is to find him and make him. . . ."

"Furthermore," Pedrillo stated, "my master prefers to meet you in the morning, when there is daylight. Lamplight or moonshine or sun, are all the same to him, but he does not wish to take any advantage of you."

"I've come here a-bustin' and a-ragin'," said the warrior, "and I've had short sleeps and I've rode long hours, and now I find that the sneak is gonna stay in a hole until tomorrow morning."

"But," Pedrillo continued, his imagination coming strongly to his rescue, "my master wants to make this as close to a fair fight as he can. Therefore he offers you any advantage that you may wish. He will let you have your gun in your hand, while his remains in the holster until the signal for the shooting. . . ."

"Advantage?" shouted Laurence Berners. "Have you gents all gone crazy? D'you let a greaser talk about anybody givin' me a handicap in a fight?"

"Laurence," Chick Murphy said solemnly, "the greaser ain't four-flushin' or bluffin'. We've seen this guy, Fernald. We've seen him work. You better take what you can get. You may be sorry, if you don't."

"I'll be dead first," said Berners. "But what's this stuff about shootin' at a signal? I dunno nothin' about signals, but I'll hunt for your boss in the morning, Mexican, and, when I find him, I'll send him to another world. You go tell him that."

Pedrillo was very glad to leave the saloon. He wanted to get to his master before Robert heard the report that his enemy had reached the town and started to meet him.

In fact, he got to Fernald's room at the very moment that Robert was clapping on a hat, preparatory to leaving the hotel.

Pedrillo told him everything, making the most of what he had seen and what he had heard and said.

"You do not wish to kill Berners by night," Pedrillo said with a grin. "You wish to give him the advantage of daylight. . . ."

"Advantage!" Robert gasped. "But he sees as well as I do, I suppose."

"You sent me to tell him that candlelight or starlight were all the same to you . . . but you would let him have the sunshine to die by."

"Pedrillo!"

"*¿Señor?*"

"You have been boasting to him in my name."

"No, *señor!*"

"If you have, I'll make you. . . ."

"No, no, *señor,* but I knew that you would not want to fight a nervous, tired man. . . ."

"Ah, that is true, of course," said Robert. "Poor Pedrillo, I have been suspecting you, and, all the time, you have been thinking only of my honor."

This made the Mexican easy.

"And your life," said Pedrillo, but he said it softly to himself, for he knew that, if Robert suspected that trickery had been used on his behalf, he would be in despair. "At ten o'clock in the morning," added Pedrillo, "you are to kill *Señor* Berners."

XIV

The dread of Pedrillo had been lest his master should balk at these arrangements that he had made with such care. But once he was sure that Robert would be docile, his pleasure and his confidence knew no end. He went from the room of Robert Fernald and called at the saloon where Berners was now drinking whiskey in wholesale quantities and vowing terrible vengeance upon Fernald for the latter's insolence in daring to come to Berners's own city.

To him, Pedrillo said calmly: "*Señor*, my master bids me tell you that at ten o'clock in the morning he will wait for you on the verandah of the hotel. He begs you to have your gun in your hand at that time. He himself will step through the door onto the verandah at ten o'clock with his gun in its holster. Or, if you wish a greater advantage than this, *Señor* Fernald is willing to listen to any reasonable request."

"You fat-faced Mexican fool!" shouted the irate Berners. "Go back and tell him that I'll take a fair start with him and that I don't want a handicap from any man in the world . . . or any two!"

So said Berners, and glared around him expecting to meet with applause, but he saw that all eyes were looking steadily at the floor, as if they feared that their looks might be held against them on another day, and that they might be quoted as having given comfort to the conquered. So Berners interpreted their silence. For his own part, he wanted to slaughter them all, but slaughter them all he could not. So he stamped out of the saloon, thinking that the entire world had gone mad. He took himself to the house of his mother, that cruel woman of iron, and there he fell into a bed and tried to sleep.

In the meantime, strange scenes went on in the saloon of Chick Murphy which was doing all the business this evening for the good reason that Pedrillo Oñate saw fit to give the place his patronage. And there Pedrillo heard the odds offered and taken on the probable outcome of the fight the next morning.

Last Buffalo had great faith in Laurence Berners. There was hardly a man in that saloon who had not with his own eyes had a chance to see the exploits of the gunman, or at least their effects. But on the other hand, Robert Fernald was a mystery—a mystery that carried with it a sort of advance agent in the form of Pedrillo Oñate. Therefore the townsmen were loath to bet their money upon their own hero. Two to one was freely offered upon Fernald. Three to one was asked and given. Four and five to one were finally the closing bets, and at this figure Pedrillo Oñate did not scruple to put down his money, which consisted of a scanty $15.

The night wore away. The townsmen began to drift toward their beds. Pedrillo, finding himself without an audience, went back to the hotel and to his own cot. There he lay down, but with the first gray of the dawn he was up, for he wished to enjoy this mischief from the first taste to the last, missing nothing.

All the city was stirring by sunup. Breakfasts were hastily eaten. And while the smoke still curled out above the tops of the houses, the people began to gather.

10:00 was far away, but there were choice places to be gained, and the townsmen wished to have them. So a murmuring, whispering, eager throng gathered and filled the verandah, crowded the doors and the windows of the houses just across the street, and packed the windows of the hotel that opened upon the porch.

9:00 rang clear and loud by the big clock within the hotel hall. Shortly afterward, there was a ripple of interest up and down the town.

Berners had left his house and was seen sauntering slowly down the exact center of the street. He carried a rifle in his hands, at the ready, and two heavy revolvers were in his belt. In this fashion he advanced to the steps of the hotel. There Berners took stock of the people who were crowded in waiting— and made a single gesture with the gun.

"Get out of this!" he commanded.

At once the verandah was vacated. Berners sat with his rifle across his knees in a chair that faced the door of the hotel. Presently he seemed to feel that a rifle was not just the weapon for work at this range. He discarded it, picked out the two revolvers, and sat on guard with a weapon in either hand.

Then he heard the voice of rumor, like a snake hissing in the crowd: "Look! Berners is going to take his handicap. He's going to have his guns out."

"You lie!" Berners shouted to that sinister and sneering comment, and forthwith jammed both guns back into their holsters. He began to grow nervous. It was only 9:30, and thirty mortal minutes lay between him and the appointed moment. He made a cigarette, but, halfway through the making, a spasm of terror seized him, for he thought he saw a movement among the shadows inside the door of the hotel. Instantly the cigarette dropped from his hand, and he snatched out both his guns.

"His nerve's gone," said a whisper in the crowd, like the voice of a snake.

Berners heard that whisper, also. He half believed it. This was far different from galloping into a town with a gun smoking from either hand. This was different from rushing into a room to do a deed. This was different, far different, from the rage and sudden challenge such as comes before a barroom brawl. In short, quivers of cold began to pass up and down his back. And still nearly half an hour to wait. Before the time elapsed, he was holding himself with a mighty force. All whispers had ceased now.

Then, within the hall of the hotel, the loud-voiced clock began chiming the hour of 10:00.

Berners leaned forward in his chair, tense, sick, white about the lips, and at the same time he heard a deep voice saying: "Here comes the finish of Berners." He wanted to turn—he was fiendishly tempted to whirl about and drive a bullet through the heart of that prophet. It would have done him good to ease himself in that way. It would have prepared him for the fight to come.

XV

In the meanwhile, in the hall of the hotel, young Robert Fernald waited in a corner, his hands folded in his lap, his eyes half closed. People peered earnestly at him, but the shadows obscured his face and its pallor. And the watchers were overcome with awe at the thought of these two—one waiting silently within—one waiting silently outside.

At the first chime of the clock, Robert rose, fumbled inside his coat to make sure that his automatic was held easily, and then started slowly toward the door of the building. Outside, where the sun glared like the blast of a furnace, death lay for him, perhaps. And yet he suddenly knew that he would not have wished himself in any other place. Cavaselle had been right. Danger was what he loved.

It made him tremble, but it made him coldly, terribly ecstatic. He shuddered with a fierce joy. He tried to make his face grave and thought that he had succeeded, but in spite of himself a faint smile was showing at the corners of his mouth. When he walked out of the shadowy corner, twenty people were watching, and they gasped when they saw that smile.

"He's happy. He likes it. He ain't hardly human."

He heard them keenly, and understood. Perhaps they were right. He heard everything. Every breath in the crowd, so it seemed—even the rustling of the clothes of the people who waited, crowded around the verandah.

Then, lightly as the clock struck its last chime, he stepped through the doorway onto the verandah. Not straight out, but with a cat-like stride to the side that brought him around the corner of the door and into the open.

As he stepped, he saw that Berners had changed his mind once more. With the first chime of the clock, he had jerked out both his guns again, and at the first glimpse of Robert, he tipped up the muzzles and sent a pair of balls *humming* through the doorway that Robert had stepped into and out of. One of those balls literally fanned his face.

So swiftly and completely was Robert seeing all things now, that he noticed the twitching of the gunman's body, and the manner in which he had half risen from his chair, like a jockey in his stirrups, riding a terrible finish. Death was the penalty for not winning this race of theirs.

To those who watched, it seemed that Robert moved like lightning. That one short step into the doorway, that swift glide to the side, and then a gun glinted in his hand and a spurt of fire came from its muzzle.

Berners lurched backward, floundered over the chair in which he had been sitting and waiting, and with a loud cry toppled upon the floor of the verandah. As he sprawled there, Robert leaned above him and laid the mouth of his pistol in the hollow of Berners's throat.

It was not a very severe wound. The bullet had driven through

Berners's shoulder, and the weight of the blow had staggered him.

However, he soon lay in bed, staring at Robert Fernald who sat beside him, while Pedrillo Oñate was in the saloon of Chick Murphy explaining: "He didn't want to kill Berners. He wanted to keep him alive to talk at the trial. Of course, that was what he wanted."

No one in the saloon doubted it. No one dared to doubt. Robert Fernald had earned the right to be considered invincible.

Now, in the room beside the bed of the wounded man, Fernald was saying: "You ride south with me to Catalina as soon as this wound is well, Berners."

"And what'll I do when I get south?"

"Tell the court what you have done."

"And you'll take me?"

"Yes."

"Ride right along with me?"

"I'd never trust you to the hands of any other man to guard or bring you there."

Berners closed his eyes. He was seeing in a vivid flash of imagination the picture of himself, the once terrible and feared Berners, riding tamely into Catalina at the side of his captor, the girl-faced, pink-cheeked Robert Fernald. And it was worse than the bitterest death to the gunman.

"Suppose that I got nothing to tell the court?"

"Let the court do the judging, Berners."

"Fernald, suppose that I was to *confess*. Would, you take that confession along . . . and leave me here to take my own chances of escaping?"

"And why not?" said Robert.

It was a neat and brief confession:

I went to see Lovat at his own invite. He wanted me to take a hand in a crooked deal, to take the job on that Tom Gill had

*had before me, of running cattle out of Larkin Valley. Because
Lovat wanted a chance to buy that valley cheap and he wanted
to make it too hot to hold the girl that runs it now. He wrangled
about terms. Finally we got hot. He cursed me. He even went
for a gun. Then I killed him.*

(Signed)
Laurence Berners

Robert Fernald took the precious document and rode south,
with Pedrillo grunting on muleback behind him.

Two days later a double item of news appeared in the papers.
The silversmith, Bede, had been freed from prison, and the
confessed murderer, Berners, most daringly had escaped from
his guards in Last Buffalo in spite of his wound. Now he was at
large and thought to be drifting north toward Canada.

"All is well, and the honest man is saved." Robert sighed.

But that same night, Fernald sat with Tim Cavaselle and
Chollie and Austin Bede in the house of the latter—in the
kitchen, for only the kitchen fire could keep them warm, the
mountain night had turned out so cold. And he said: "I have to
ride on a long journey to Larkin Valley. I only wish to ask one
question. Why were you cleaning a gun in the kitchen, Miss
Bede, the night that Mister Lovat was killed?"

Miss Bede turned white. "Are you the devil?" she cried.

"Young man, I'll tell you what she was doing," said Austin
Bede.

"No, no, Dad!" cried the girl.

"I'll tell him," persisted the silversmith. "She was cleaning
the gun with which I had just shot Lovat. And I would shoot
him again if I had the chance given me again. The fight between
us was an old one, Mister Fernald. It was for my wife first of
all, and I won. He came back. It was for Chollie, then, and I
thought his money was going to win. I went to his room. We
fought it out . . . man to man. But my stiff old arm was faster

than his. I killed him."

Robert choked, gasped, stared. "And the jewels?" he murmured.

"I don't know what became of them," Bede said, "unless it was that Berners may have got into the room and stolen them immediately after the shot was fired."

"But the money you had?" asked Robert.

"Honest money," Bede explained. "I'd saved it to let my girl afford to marry an honest man. But she made me spend it on my creditors. So there's the story, Fernald. Now you can call for the sheriff if you wish."

But Robert had no such wish.

He stumbled out into the night. He felt very hot in the face. But, after all, he was not sure that he had been a fool. Only, he knew that human nature was far too bewildering for him ever to understand it in the slightest. Now Larkin Valley lay ahead of him. What would he find there that was not a human mask, hiding the reality of the soul?

★ ★ ★ ★ ★

THE TIGER

★ ★ ★ ★ ★

I

If you have seen Pedrillo Oñate in the days of his poverty, when he was kicked from pillar to post in the town of San Joaquin, it may be interesting to observe him once his fortunes had changed. He stood in Pat McGuire's saloon, the leading drinking parlor in the town of Crawfordville, and held the place of honor—that is to say, he kept his post at the farther end of the bar, where he could turn his shoulder to the side wall and watch all who entered—and be watched from behind by no man. There were other men crowded before that bar and the bartenders were exceedingly busy. Teamsters and cowpunchers were there, enjoying the damp coolness of the place, for the floor is sprinkled every two hours with wet sawdust that is then swept out. The pungent odor of beer and the sour fragrance of rye whiskey lingered in the air, and every time the swinging doors were opened, they cast a cloud of smoke before them, rolling it far into the saloon and sending it bulging out of the farther windows. For, of course, everyone was smoking. Some smoked to give relish to the drinks. Some smoked to kill the taste of the cheap, poisonous liquor. There were ranchers, miners, lumbermen, tramps, fugitive yeggs and other criminals, officers of the law, outlaws of no vocation except battle, beggars, thieves, and confidence men. All these were crowded together in the saloon, and the deep sound of the voices of strong men rose and fell like the noise of waves along a beach.

There was another sound, steady as the dropping of water on

the floor of a cave—the chime of silver and gold dropping into the three tills ever yawning to receive more coin. This musical chatter, small but clear, kept steady pace with the music of the voices; when there was much talk, much confusion, much bustling and heaving and pushing in the crowd, then the *clinking* of money grew louder and steadier. What a steady tide of money was flowing into the pockets of Pat McGuire. In a month of such a trade as this, he must have become a rich man, one would say. But as a matter of fact, there was a flaw, a leak in the pocket of Pat. Across the street in Sweeney's place was a game of faro that never ceased, day or night, and once a week into Sweeney's place went Pat McGuire, his pockets bulging with money. Once a week Pat was a rich man; once a week he came back, humbled, weakened in spirit, poor in cash. Once a week he swore that never again would he attempt to beat the cursed game of faro, and once a week, certain as fate, he would wander back to the faro game across the street, scowl at it, curse it, snarl like a wounded wolf. But, before long, he would be playing; before long he would be losing.

Pat McGuire was the greatest man in Crawfordville, the boldest, most famous spirit, and in his saloon all the celebrated people of the period and the range appeared, but no one in that saloon caught the eye so clearly and quickly as did Pedrillo Oñate.

Standing there at the far end of the bar, he glowed like a beautifully feathered tropical bird. And, indeed, he was a mass of color and of metal. His lofty sombrero was banded around with heavy golden ornaments. It made one's forehead burn even to think of enduring such a weight in such weather. He wore a jacket of yellow deerskin, threaded and chased with golden thread and embossed with masses of silver. It was a short jacket—for, otherwise, one might have missed the miracle of crimson sash that engirdled his waist. Men said that the sacrilegious dog was wearing an altar cloth woven by the patient hands of Indians, a miracle of labor and of beauty. But to Pedrillo it was no more than a sash—a little ornament. His shirt was bluest of blue silk, buttoned down the front with golden buttons. It was open at the throat, and, lest the flaps of the shirt should fall apart too far, they were held loosely together with a delicate golden chain that supported in the center a great ruby. The boots of Pedrillo shone a dull, mahogany-red glow, his trousers were ornamented with solid silver conchos, and the holsters that supported his two guns—what use had a one-armed man for two guns?—were of the purest white leather worked and chased with gold.

Oh, Pedrillo Oñate, what woman of your people could behold your magnificence, your shining, glorious presence, without completely opening her heart?

"Women are flowers," said the refulgent Pedrillo, "but, alas, they wither in a day."

His fat cheeks were still fatter now, and glistened as though they had been coated with polish and rubbed hard. His black eyes seemed blacker and brighter. And he smiled continually, out of the greatness of his sense of well-being.

There were other Mexicans in that crowd in Pat McGuire's saloon, and they were distinctly of the upper class. They were gentlemen. Yet they were little regarded. They were served last. They were slighted by their companions in the place, and most of all by the bartenders. They were shouldered and crowded to the wall.

How different it was with Pedrillo, although he had only one arm, although certainly he could not pretend to gentle birth. Around him there was preserved a little space into which no man intruded. All the rest of the bar was packed. But this portion was clear, open, free. And that was a little miracle.

Pedrillo pretended not to notice. But this little attention, this little tribute of fear and awe from the crowd was to his soul as the music of the spheres. He drank tequila slowly, sipping the white fire drop by drop, spending half an hour over a single glass. Others swallowed whiskey with a gulp before they were crowded from their places by thirstier drinkers. But Pedrillo took his time, leaning his one elbow on the bar, at ease, cool, smiling, content. Of how many hundreds of dollars did he deprive Pat McGuire by taking so much time and so much space at that favored end of the bar?

Pedrillo liked to compute that loss. It amused him.

Presently he said: "I'm taking up a good deal of room here. Shall I move along?"

The nearest bartender shook his head violently. "Stay where you are, Pedrillo," he said. "Anything wrong?"

"Oh, no, not at all," Pedrillo said, and returned to his glass of tequila. Meantime, his ears were busy listening to a hundred broken conversations, piecing them together, making of them the groundwork upon which he will rear a fabric of inventions later on. For of all the careless speakers in a country of careless speech, of all the gossips, the inventors, Pedrillo Oñate was the very greatest liar. His magnificent combinations, his glorious flights of fancy, his soul-stirring fabrications were unmatched in a country where even the children can tell such tales as make the listening angels shudder.

Yet the attitude of Pedrillo was not entirely that of a man who listened idly, gathering gossip as a hummingbird gathers the honey of a blossom. In it there was something more narrowly attentive. There was an air of eagerness and an air of patient expectation combined. Study the face of a fisherman, and you will see the same expression. For what did he wait there? For what was he fishing, this transfigured and radiant Oñate?

Presently out of the crowd came a fellow dressed like any

cowpuncher, a man of middle age with fat jowls, a hawk nose, and eyes glittering with a wonderful brightness. Even a dog could have guessed that this was a man of evil. But Oñate did not seem to care. He noted the approach of the other from the corner of his eye, and pretended to heed the newcomer not at all. But that was not the truth. His expectant attitude had ceased. His expression had changed. Oñate now had a fierce glitter in his eye, a fierce but contented glitter, so that he looked no longer like the merely idle fisher. Now he had something on the hook.

Once, twice, and again the man of the hook nose and the bright eyes looked earnestly at Oñate. Then he came closer. He stepped into the little enchanted clearing that surrounded the Mexican. He waited, almost reverently, quietly, his eyes attentive. Still Pedrillo paid no heed.

All the time, like a hawk watching a sparrow, Pedrillo was watching this newcomer, judging him, regarding especially the size of a diamond ring upon his finger.

At length, the stranger stepped briskly up to the bar and looked Pedrillo in the eye. "You're Pedrillo Oñate, I guess," he said.

"I am," Pedrillo replied.

"Well, then," the stranger said, "I think we can do business together. And back yonder is a little empty room where we can talk. Come along."

When he had said this, he turned on his heel and walked straight toward the little back room that he had designated. Pedrillo stared. He wanted to follow, because he felt that this interview might be much to his advantage. But on the other hand, he did not like the assured manner in which this white man led the way, confident that Pedrillo would follow. It angered Oñate. It made him frown. But curiosity was stronger than resentment, and presently he walked, scowling, on the heels of the stranger and into the little back room.

II

How strange it was to see the completeness with which all diffidence vanished from the manner of the unknown. He sat at his ease among the shadows of the farthest corner, and rolled a cigarette. This he lighted, and, through the dimness and the smoke which he puffed forth, he examined Pedrillo closely—without malice but without friendship.

"Oñate," he said suddenly to the frowning Mexican, "do you know me?"

"No."

"I'm Sim Burgess of the Big Bend. Does that help you?"

"No," said Pedrillo, growing more and more haughty.

"Very well," Sim Burgess said, "I'll tell you a little bit about myself. You'll find it pretty interesting. I've got a big piece of land staked out down in that part of the world. Me and a partner staked it out, stocked it with cattle, and worked it into a going ranch. We worked like brothers. He's my heir, and I'm his heir. We wrote out that one will and we filed it away in a bank. Neither of us could change it. Neither of us could take that will out of the bank vault without the permission of the other man. You understand? Now, Pedrillo, we had a little falling out. No matter about what. Each of us thought that the other fellow was wrong. And so we had that falling out. He got more of the boys behind him. I was run off the place. You understand? Well, he gives me a pension, but he won't let me come back. You understand? I have to stay away and live like a dog on the two or three thousand a year that he sends to me. Now, Pedrillo, you can see where you come in. You get him shot for me, and I hand you a big wad of dough. Is that clear? Is that simple? You get him shot for me, and I get the ranch, because the double will hands it to me. You get a big chunk of handy coin. Now, how does that sound to you?"

Pedrillo rolled a cigarette—it was a miracle to see how he manipulated the paper, the sack of tobacco and all, with one hand, rolling the cornucopia-shaped smoke with a single twist—and thrust it into his mouth. He lighted it. Through the smoke that he presently sent upwards in great exhalations, he studied the idea that had been presented to him.

"Your partner is Pete McCoy," said Pedrillo.

Sim Burgess nodded.

"McCoy is a grand fighting man."

"Yes."

"That makes the price high, *señor.*"

"Of course. I understand that."

"And then, it is a big ranch, I think. I have heard about it."

"It's not so big as you've heard, maybe."

"You make fifteen thousand dollars a year on that place, *señor.*"

"It's a lie," said the other, "we've never cleared more than twelve." Then he bit his lip, because, by the smile of the Mexican, he saw that he had been tricked into giving important statistics. "And that was our banner year . . . we've never had another like it," he added.

The smile of Oñate was as radiant as before. He ordered drinks and tasted his before he would speak more about business.

"I think that we shall agree, *señor,*" he said. "I never believe in a hard bargain. I know that people must live. They cannot be taxed too heavily. But still, this is a great affair. Twelve thousand dollars a year income . . . many hundreds of good cows on the ranch . . . to say nothing of the fine land that may be developed . . . and I suppose that the whole property might come to a value of about a hundred and fifty thousand dollars. And you are shut away from that ranch. You only get a part of the income.

And the pity of it is that you cannot even leave the property to a son, because you have no children."

"Now how do you know that if you don't know me?" asked the rancher sharply.

Pedrillo smiled again. There was a good deal of devilishness in that smile of his, and some share of humor.

"Marriage writes its own story in the face," said Pedrillo. "However, *señor,* you want that ranch in your hands. Before you have had it a year, there will not be much left for the heirs of *Señor* McCoy. And then you can retire. Am I not right?"

Sim Burgess threw away his cigarette and folded his hands across his chest, saying: "You go on talking. Keep it up till you're tired. You're sort of funny to listen to."

"Ah, very well," said Pedrillo, waving his fat hand airily. "We become good friends. I can understand you. You can understand me. There is nothing to be wished for. All that I have to do is to strike a price with you. Suppose that we say twenty thousand dollars for this job, *señor?*"

Sim Burgess rose slowly from his chair, as one partly startled and partly dismayed. It seemed as though he were being dragged upward by the hair. Standing above the Mexican, he stabbed a finger vaguely toward him a few times as one not yet able to speak. "Twenty thousand," he said at last. "Are you nutty?"

"Or fifteen thousand," Pedrillo suggested gently, seeing that he had overstepped himself a little.

"Oñate," Mr. Burgess said hotly, "I'll pay fifteen hundred for this job. Does it sound good to you?"

Pedrillo waved the unhappy idea away. "Let us finish our drinks," said Pedrillo. "Let us have another round at my expense, if you will. But let us talk business no longer."

Mr. Burgess lost some of his fury and began to argue; first he tapped off his points, forefinger on palm, then he smashed them off with a clenched fist. "What's hard about it? A little trip. Just a fine little jog. Then you meet up with McCoy. He's got a temper strung on a hair-trigger. You touch him and he explodes. But of course he wouldn't have a chance against your man. And, well, Oñate, ain't it perfect for you? I know your Fernald. He's a sort of half-wit. Hunting for action and trying to do good, like something out of a kid's book. Well, he runs into this perfect set-up for him. Ain't it easy? Here's me that has been kicked out of a partnership by a big brute of a gunfighter like McCoy. Why, what more could Fernald want if his tongue is hangin' out to do a good deed? You tell me, kid. You tell me, will you? I'll listen. You've got your spiel made up for you. Why, I could've gone straight to him and told him the sad story. I wouldn't've had to pay a cent."

"The way is open, *señor*," Pedrillo said with a wave of his fat brown hand. "You have still a good chance to speak to him."

Mr. Burgess hurled himself into his chair and scowled. He made another cigarette, and then rubbed it to pieces between his fingers. He sat up, and then he slid down. Twice he began to speak, and finally he said: "*Aw*, I understand. You queer any deal except the ones that you promote. Look here, Oñate, I'll stand for five thousand, but that's the upper limit."

"Fifteen thousand, I said," replied Oñate. "I take my life in my hands. I go to *Señor* Fernald and tell him a sad story about you. I tell him that you are wronged, that you are. . . . Well, my dear friend, after he has killed McCoy, what if he learns the truth?"

"What truth?" asked Burgess, growing uglier than before.

"That you are . . . why, *señor*, let us remain polite."

Sim Burgess grew crimson with passion, but, after all, he was a businessman. He put his pride in his pocket, saying: "You talk free and loud, Oñate. I'll tell you . . . I'll raise the ante a little. I'll make it ten thousand flat."

"I split the difference with you," the Mexican said graciously.

"I am not a robber. But one must live, *señor*. I split the difference and call the price twelve thousand five hundred dollars."

Mr. Burgess drummed his fingers against his chin, but at length he nodded. "All right." He sighed. "But you've got a nerve with you. Twelve grand for . . . well, I'm the sucker. When do you start?"

"Before tomorrow morning. And now to bind the agreement, *señor*?"

"To bind the agreement? Here's five hundred, Oñate."

"Thank you," Oñate said, and deliberately he spread out the bills and counted them. "Correct," he said. "Five hundred and that diamond ring, *señor*?"

"This?" cried Burgess. "Oñate, I'd hate to tell you what kind of a shark you are. By heaven, I would. But the fact is. . . ."

"Yes, *señor*?"

"Well, take it and be hanged."

He tossed the ring on the table, and Oñate picked it up between fat thumb and fat forefinger. It was a deep little well of light, and it threw a radiance even to the inmost heart of the Mexican. It would not fit except on the little finger, and there he placed it, then turning his hand gently back and forth, admiring, it seemed, the deep wrinkles at the wrist.

"This will do very well," said the Mexican.

"Will it?" Burgess snarled. "Now you tell me, will you, what sort of surety I get that the job will be done?"

Oñate raised his eyes reluctantly from the brilliance of the jewel. "Ah, *señor*," he murmured at length, "as for that, you have the word of a gentleman."

So he said, and returned his attention to the ring, while Burgess rose and went slowly out into the broad, bright flare of the sun. Not until he had reached the outdoors did the full sting of the Mexican's last sentence enter his mind. He turned as if to go back, but again he altered his purpose and merely shrugged his shoulders, like a good gambler who has risked his last stake upon a long shot.

III

Something has been said about the gifts of Oñate as a natural liar. Now there is a chance to see him in practice. Observe him, therefore, at work in the presence of his master. He sat with his head in his hand, sighing profoundly. And here was Robert Fernald, who the years cannot change, the sun cannot tan, and the deeds of his life cannot make older. Grave, simple, earnest, looking on wide-eyed at life, he had evidently been cast in a mold that cannot be altered without breaking.

"What is wrong, Pedrillo?"

"It is for the evil that I find in the world that I sigh, *señor*," said Pedrillo.

"That is true," replied Robert Fernald mournfully.

"But what would the *señor* say of a man . . . good, sincere, brave, and honest . . . who becomes the partner of a villain, builds up a great ranch, loves his partner like a brother, so that he agrees to a mutual will in which each leaves all his property to the other, and then . . . alas, little father, I cannot tell you."

"That is the picture of a good man, full of trust," Robert said, much moved. "Tell me more, Pedrillo."

"Will you believe that there can be such a villain? Yet I tell you, on my honor, the scoundrelly partner gathers the men of the ranch together, bribes them, and fills their minds with poison, and then drives away the honest man. Think of this, *señor!* With bribery and treachery he corrupts the men of the ranch . . . they drive out the good man whose brains and whose money have made the ranch rich. . . ."

Robert rose from his chair. He was stiff with indignation. His chin was high in the air. "What is the name of this devil of a man, Pedrillo?"

"*Señor Don* Peter McCoy."

"I shall remember. Where can he be found?"

"In the Big Bend, *señor.*"

"Would it not be a good work, Pedrillo, to find this cur and rid the world of him?"

"Ah, little father, think what you say. To risk your life . . . because he is a terrible fighter. . . ."

"Is he?" Robert Fernald asked softly, gripping his slender hands into fists. "Is he such a terrible man?"

"Ah, *señor,* the list of those he has slain. . . ."

"He is a great man with guns, Pedrillo?"

"Ah, yes. If you were to stand against him, it would simply be death to you, *señor!*"

"A man may die only once," Robert Fernald said gravely, "and why not in a good cause?"

"What have I done?" cried Pedrillo, the cunning one. "No, little father, I never shall cease. . . ."

"I have decided," declared Robert Fernald firmly. "Learn where the ranch is to be found in the Big Bend. Then bring me word of it at once."

"No, no! We now are on the way to Larkin Valley, where you long ago had promised to be. . . ."

"I have made up my mind, Pedrillo. Nothing can change me. Who is the poor man who was driven away from his rights?"

"*Señor* Burgess. The world knows that he is an honorable man."

"Your word is enough for me. Hurry, Pedrillo. Find out everything. Let me know at once."

"Ah, little father, I beg you to think. I shall be an unhappy man forever. What will poor Pedrillo do when . . . ?"

"Go, go."

So, with seeming reluctance, Pedrillo was driven from the room. Once outside the door, he shrugged his shoulders, took on a different appearance, and went smilingly down to the street where, at the first corner, he encountered Burgess.

"Greaser," said Sim Burgess, "what's been arranged?"

Pedrillo overlooked the insulting nickname. "It is finished," he said, "except that the coffin for *Señor* McCoy has not been ordered. But you will attend to the burial, my friend?"

"You've got Fernald on the job?" Burgess asked, his eyes glittering with pleasure and excitement.

"He is eager to go. He is filled with a terrible compassion for the wrongs that you have suffered, *señor*. He burns when he thinks of the scoundrel McCoy."

Burgess grinned slowly and wickedly. "Now, keep the kid under cover all the way to the Big Bend," he said. "Don't let him have too much air, for, if you do, he'll hear something that'll poison his mind. He'll hear folks talking about McCoy, and damn me if ever you hear anything against him. He's got people hypnotized."

"I shall take him," said Pedrillo, "by such ways that even the eagle hardly knows them. We shall not meet others by the trail I travel."

Burgess grinned again. "I dunno," he said, "but somehow I feel as if the ranch was in my pocket already. Tell me, Pedrillo, how it comes that your boss never sees the inside of a jail, the number of fights that he's been in?"

"There is a simple reason. He does not fire until the other man draws a gun. And he rarely kills. A shoulder or a hip is his target."

"Is it?" Burgess murmured. "But this is different. A wounded McCoy ain't a thing to me. It's a dead man that I want."

"He is dead already," said Pedrillo. "And before we come to the ranch, *Señor* Fernald will wish for nothing in life except to kill this scoundrel." And he looked down to the glittering diamond upon his finger.

"If you was to double-cross me," Burgess warned, filled with a new emotion, "there wouldn't be nothin' in the world that would keep me from you, old-timer. I'd just nacherally have to hunt you down, even if you was to lay a trail clean around the world. You understand?"

"Nothing could be clearer. But you forget . . . my master never fails."

"If he should slip. . . ."

"I return you the money and the ring. That is settled."

"Pedrillo," said Mr. Burgess, "of all the low-down crooks in the world, you take the prime prize. But suppose, Oñate, only suppose, that your boss was to get half an idea of the sort of a gent that you really are?"

Pedrillo glanced over his shoulder, as though in dread lest this speech might have been heard. Moisture broke out on his forehead. However, he regained his confidence at once. "*Señor*," he said, "he would kill me over a slow fire. But that time never shall come. I can lead him with a silk thread . . . with a spider's thread."

"Tell me one thing, Oñate. What's in the head of Fernald?"

"Books, *señor*. He does not think. He simply remembers printed words that he has read."

Here they parted, and Burgess wandered slowly down the street, hurrying a little through the patches of burning sun, and loitering through shadow. His mind was far in the future. Already he had the sense of great property. It was placed literally within the grip of his hands and he had only to close his fingers over it. He saw himself established as the ruler of a domain like the domain of a prince. And he flattered himself that, even if he were not a miracle of industry like McCoy, at least he would be able to hire the proper people to run the place for him.

In the midst of these thoughts a voice hailed him, a voice

straight out of the heart of his dream, and Burgess, with a start and a groan, whirled and blinked up at a tall, lean, brown-faced man who had reined a mustang to that side of the street.

"McCoy," murmured Burgess. "Good Lord, what are you doing down here?"

"Why shouldn't I be here?" McCoy asked, stern and cold. "Now that I've seen you, I want to talk business with you."

"Come over here to the saloon," said Burgess.

"I don't want to talk to you over liquor," McCoy answered with a certain amount of disdain. "I want to talk business, not old times."

"Then fire away."

"I want the ranch."

"That's a funny thing. So do I."

"There's a difference, though."

"I don't see it."

"I'll pay for what I want . . . and you'll only steal what you want."

Burgess scowled, shifted in his place, and then changed his mind. He said sullenly: "Look here, are you gonna stop here only to insult me, McCoy?"

"I don't want to insult you. I was simply showing you a difference. Now, Burgess, I want you to listen to some hard facts."

"Go ahead, then. I'll listen."

"I'll pay you fifty thousand for your share in the ranch."

"You will! And you makin' between twelve and fifty thousand a year . . . and every year more. You'll pay me fifty thousand?"

"Don't be a fool, Sim. I make that money by hard work."

"So could I. But you run me off of the ranch. What chance have I got to show you what I could do with the place?"

"You showed it long ago. The year that you worked it with me, we had a deficit. You know that. You threw away money right and left . . . you fired the best hands or made them so sore that they quit. You spoiled everything that you tried."

"That's what you think. Simply because my way ain't yours."

"The proof of the pudding is the eating. After you quit, I made the ranch pay . . . when you were there, everything went to ruin. Now, Sim, I'm offering you a nice fat sum. Fifty thousand can bring you in three thousand a year . . . dead easy. Do you want it, or don't you?"

"Is three thousand half of twelve? No! You want to rob me, McCoy."

McCoy started to speak and again changed his mind. He reined back his horse into the street. "I've made you a proposition," he said, "and you can think it over for a while. I'm gonna be in town for a few days. You can find me and tell me what you want to do." So saying, he turned his horse and rode it up the street, a stiff, erect figure in the saddle, looking neither to the right nor to the left.

Burgess looked after him with disgust and with awe commingled, for he never had been able to understand the power that was in the honesty of his partner. There was no subtlety in McCoy. There was no cleverness. He simply did what every other rancher tried to do. Except that McCoy worked longer hours, took fewer chances, and lived, dreamed, hoped, prayed, labored only for the success of his ranch.

Yet the awe remained in Burgess, although he despised the starved existence of his partner. He sneered, but he envied at the same moment. And although he would not have changed lives with McCoy, how gladly would he have exchanged accomplishments.

There was a solution to all his difficulties, however. And he tapped the butt of his Colt. Not that he would use a gun. But by a gun should this dispute be put to an end.

IV

There was great haste in Sim Burgess now. He wanted to get to the Mexican at once, so he hurried back to the hotel. There he was informed that Pedrillo had left the hotel, and that his master, Robert Fernald, was now in his room, having given orders to have his bill prepared, for he was leaving at once.

All this was very well, but Sim Burgess wanted nothing less than the departure of these two for the Big Bend, now that their quarry was in the town. He went to the stables. Oñate was not there. He returned in a froth of impatience to the verandah of the hotel and sat down there to wait.

While he waited, he saw McCoy come out on the verandah and stand, tall and silent, by the pillars near the steps. He looked up and down the verandah, impassive, unhurried, always intent on some purpose. And no one on the verandah spoke to him. He was not a person to be lightly addressed.

Without moving, without rolling a cigarette, without stirring from his place even to lean against one of the wooden pillars, that statue of a man remained on watch. And now he had the reward of his patience, for a little cavalcade came riding down the street: three men and two women—three hardy cowpunchers with all the signs of their calling about them, and two women of whom the one rode like a true daughter of the West, with a fine, free, careless swing, and the other was elderly, and mounted on a side-saddle on a long-limbed thoroughbred. Such a cavalcade would have drawn more than a passing glance in any city; in this little town it became the cynosure of all eyes, and Sim Burgess, forgetting the hopes and plans that were revolving in his mind, came to the edge of the verandah and watched the newcomers.

They halted at the hotel; two of the men took the horses, and the third, with the two women, entered the hostelry. Sim Burgess, and all the idlers nearby, strolled casually in to hear what they could hear and see what they could see—particularly the face of the girl, for she was a black-eyed beauty with such a store of good spirits that she smiled continually. No shrinking, timid, bashful girl of the range was she, abashed by the stares of so many men; with a keen glance she gave back their regards, and looked them over from head to foot, after the fashion of one who knows men and how to judge them.

The idlers and Sim Burgess heard her ask the proprietor if there were a guest in his hotel under the name of Robert Fernald.

"Robert Fernald is here, ma'am," said the proprietor. "I suppose you've heard a good deal about him?"

"I'll tell a man I've heard a good deal about him," said the girl. "And I've ridden all the way from the mountains to see him."

All the way from the mountains—those enchanting, cool, blue heaps against the far-off sky. All that distance to see young Robert Fernald. The air suddenly tingled with the spice of romance and excitement. What could have brought her?

"Dan," she said to the big fellow who had been signing the register, "will you try to find Robert and bring him to our room? Come along, Aunt Harriet, will you?"

She and Aunt Harriet went up the stairs, and Dan followed them, guided by the fat proprietor who had huddled himself into a coat in order to do honor to these new guests. The room of Sim Burgess, by chance, stood next to that of Robert Fernald, who spent most of his time in his chamber—busy, rumor had it, with a book, or spending hours and hours in studious practice with his guns, drawing and pointing at a crack in the door, or at a nail head, or at a rift in the ceiling, and going through his maneuvers seated or standing, or walking to and fro and whirling to aim again.

It would have been folly in another person. It was not folly in

Robert Fernald, but a necessary protection, for did he not have deadly enemies here and there through the entire course of the mountain desert? How many had he struck down with bullets, how many had he turned into mortal foes—brothers or fathers or cousins or friends of his fallen men? Therefore he must spend these hours at practice with his weapons, and if he dared to relax or give over the work, then he would fall. Fall he must, sooner or later. So declared rumor, so announced tradition. For those who live by the gun must die by the gun. That is the law of the West.

Mr. Sim Burgess hurried up to his room, therefore, keen with curiosity to learn what was about to happen behind the paper-thin partition that separated his chamber from that of the gunfighter. He paused only to glance at the hotel register, and there he found inscribed the names of Harriet Atkinson, Daniel Parker, and Beatrice Larkin.

Beatrice Larkin! That linked up suddenly with the tradition that had to do with Robert Fernald. It rather took the breath of Burgess. So many tales had been breathed across the desert of the wild exploits of this mild-faced youth that one grew to thinking of them rather as fancies than as facts. And here was a legend that seemed to have a body—that legend that told how Robert Fernald had gone to Larkin Valley and there had captured Tom Gill, whose cattle rustling promised to break the girl who had inherited Larkin Valley from her famous father.

With this idea tucked away in his mind, Burgess reached his chamber. He did not enter it in a rush, for all his haste, but with a soft-footed ease, such that any casual passer-by would have shrewdly suspected him of being a thief. Like a thief, then, he entered his own room, making not a sound. There he took a chair and sat still as a mouse. That done, it was easy enough for him to hear everything that passed in the adjoining room.

The occupants barely had exchanged their first greetings, and

Robert Fernald was saying that he was glad to see Dan Parker, and saying it in such a voice that it seemed as though he meant it.

"Now look here, old-timer," Parker said, "it's a queer fact that Larkin Valley can't get along without you. I've come down here to take you back."

"I'd like to go," said Robert Fernald. "And as a matter of fact, there's no other place in the world where I'd be half so glad to go. I want to go there, and to the grave of my father, Dan. But just now I can't."

"You're tied down?"

"Yes."

"Got some big job on hand?"

"Yes," said Robert earnestly.

"Life and death matter?"

"Yes, it is."

"You couldn't tell me about it?" Dan Parker asked at last in an oddly dry voice.

"I can't, Dan. It's not a thing that I can talk about very well. I'm not held back by any promise. But the fact is . . . it's a very private affair."

Sim Burgess, listening, quaked in his boots. For if this mission to which he had inspired Robert Fernald should be known, his own life would probably be ended by the hands of a lynching party.

"This private affair . . . it means that you're going off on a death trail, Fernald."

Robert was silent.

"Of course it means that. But look here, old fellow. Miss Beatrice has come down here a long ways. . . ."

What a ring came into the voice of Robert Fernald. "She has come. Come here?"

"She has."

"For me, Dan?"

"Yes, for you."

"Is it possible?" cried Robert Fernald.

But before he could say more, there came a light tap at his door.

"Come in!" called Robert.

Then the door creaked, and a breath of silence followed, after which the eavesdropper heard Fernald say in a husky voice: "Miss Larkin, I'm so happy . . . I mean surprised . . . I mean . . . how do you do . . . and won't . . . won't you sit down . . . and . . . ?"

"Bobbie," said the voice of a girl, laughing, "you are the silliest child in the world. Sit down yourself. You look much more in need of support."

V

Sim Burgess, listening, forgot his recent terrors and was convulsed with silent laughter, still more when he heard this most simple and most terrible of gunfighters stammering: "But I mustn't sit down, you know. It isn't polite . . . I mean, when there is a lady. . . ."

"Bobbie," said the girl, "you're coming to Larkin Valley with me."

"I, Miss Lar . . . I mean, Beatrice . . . I . . . of course it's a thousand times kind of you to ask me . . . but the fact is . . . I have to do a little work. . . ."

"For whom?"

"For a good and just man who has been deprived of. . . ."

"Something by a villain?"

This crisp voice of the girl seemed to scatter the dreamy thoughts of Robert Fernald.

"The fact is, Beatrice," he added suddenly, "this is a terrible case of cruelty and ingratitude. . . ."

"And you have to kill somebody, accordingly?" she asked.

"I don't know . . . ," said Robert, "as a matter of fact. . . ."

"Tell me yes or no. Are you going out to commit murder?"

"Murder? Good heavens!" cried Robert.

"But tell me . . . isn't that what you intend to do?"

"Ah, Beatrice, how can you ask me such a thing?"

"Because I've heard enough about the things that you've been doing. Knocking off ninety percent of the stuff for gossip and lies, that leaves ten percent. Strike out half of that as exaggeration, and subtract another twenty-five percent of the cases because they've been good ones . . . but there still remains a considerable list of murders at your door, Robert Fernald."

"I've never heard of such a thing," breathed Robert.

"Of course you haven't," said the girl, "because everybody in the world is afraid of you and afraid to tell you the truth about yourself."

"Beatrice, will you try to believe me when I say that . . . ?"

"That you never shot a man through the back? Of course I'll believe that. That doesn't make your killings anything but murder nevertheless."

"I don't understand," said Robert. "You accuse me of murdering . . . but that is a terrible word, Beatrice."

"Robert Fernald, how many men have you fought?"

"Not very many, really, only. . . ."

"Well, I'll leave out the men you have wounded or shot down with your devilish skill. I'll count only the deaths. How many dead men lie at your door?"

"I . . . I don't know, Beatrice," Robert said faintly. "Very, very few, I hope and trust."

"You hope and trust," the girl said scornfully. "Well, I can tell you of a few. There was that poor fellow in El Paso, young Gregory, who you shot down in the street. And there were the Tucker boys in Idaho, and Charlie and Brent Hotchkiss in Butte City, and Lambert and King and the old. . . ."

"Don't," said Robert. A little silence followed this. And then Robert Fernald added: "They were wicked men, Beatrice. And every one of them had more than a fair chance."

"What do you call a chance?" asked the girl. "You give them a chance to make the first move to their guns. But they are people who haven't nerves as keenly strung as yours. Their hands can't move as fast. And perhaps they have something to do other than practice with weapons all day long. You say that you give them a chance . . . but I'll tell you, Bobbie, that to pit yourself against most men is like pitting a wolf against an ordinary dog. The dog may be bigger than the wolf, but he can't live ten seconds against the biting of a lobo. Bobbie, you've killed eleven men . . . and I make no count of the rumors that give you a lot more. I make no count, either, of the Indians and the Mexicans. But you've killed eleven white men."

"Eleven villains!" cried Robert. "Really, you must grant that!"

"Who judged them villains?" Beatrice asked angrily.

"Why, everyone knew. . . ."

"Are you twelve men and a judge, all by yourself?" asked Beatrice Larkin. "What right have you to judge men?"

Another silence, terribly heavy, followed.

"Beatrice," Fernald said at last, "you are very hard on me. I've always wanted to do only what's right."

She said ironically: "I suppose that's all you've been wanting to do . . . just help the weak and the defenseless . . . like a knight out of a book?"

"I . . . really . . . I wanted to help those that couldn't help themselves."

"We have a law in this land to help such people."

"Yes," said Robert, "but in this district . . . isn't it rather weak?"

"Perhaps it is, but does that give any one man the right to

take the law into his own hands? It does not. You ought to know it. You're a college graduate."

"I do know it," Robert said more faintly than ever. "But. . . ."

"What do people say about you now?"

"I don't know," asked Robert. "Will you tell me?"

"You bet I'll tell you. They say you're a professional gun-man."

"No, no!"

"They say you make your living with your guns."

"It isn't. . . ."

"Then how do you make a living?"

"Beatrice, I've never taken any sum of money for a killing. . . ."

"But when you've downed a man, you let his enemies make you a present . . . of a fine saddle . . . a bridle all covered with gold . . . a magnificent Mexican sombrero . . . a glorious diamond. You take those presents, and then you say, like a hypocrite, these things are much too fine and gay for me. I'm only a simple, quiet fellow. You sell those gifts as a matter of course . . . and you use the money for living. Tell me, Bobbie, if that isn't a fact?"

He looked vaguely, almost helplessly at her.

"And that's blood money," the girl said fiercely.

"I never thought of it like that," he responded.

"Of course you didn't. But isn't it the truth?"

"I want to think it over," said poor Robert Fernald.

"Ask other people," said the girl. "Ask Dan, won't you? Is Dan Parker an honest man?"

"I don't want to be in on this," protested Dan Parker.

"Don't back down, Dan," urged the girl. "Tell him straight from the shoulder."

"Why, then," said Parker, "I suppose there's a good deal in what you've been telling Fernald."

"They think that I'm just . . . a murderer?" cried Robert.

There was no direct answer to this, and it seemed that silence was a sufficient speech.

Finally the girl said: "I've come for you, and I'm going to have you, Bobbie. I'm going to start back for the ranch tomorrow morning, and I'm going to take you with me."

"I want to think a little . . . ," Robert began.

"Go out and walk around the block. We'll wait for you right here," she replied.

Presently Sim Burgess heard Robert leave the adjoining room. His first impulse was to hurry after his man of the guns and hurry him out of town on the blood trail. But he was greatly tempted to remain where he was and hear whatever might be said between the girl and Parker. He could remember, now, that Parker was the foreman in Larkin Valley, and a man held in the highest trust by the girl who employed him.

"You bore down on him pretty hard," Parker said after Fernald was gone.

All her surety seemed to have left her. She said in a trembling voice: "Do you think that we'll be able to get him, Dan? What do you think?"

"I dunno," replied Parker. "He's got something on his mind."

"It's the Mexican who leads him around by the nose from one deviltry into another . . . and sooner or later Pedrillo will get him killed. I know it. I've been dreaming it all this time. We've got to take him with us, Dan," said Beatrice.

"It's a pretty important job to you?" Parker asked.

"Well," said the girl, "you think it out for yourself. Of course it's important to me."

"But there's Larkin Valley as quiet as can be," said Dan Parker. "There ain't even so much as a mouse stirring up there without permission. I dunno that you got any great need for a gunman like Fernald, Miss Beatrice."

"You silly man," she said, and laughed a little—a very uneven, uncertain laugh.

"Is that the way of it?" murmured Parker's gruff voice.

"Of course it is," she said.

"*Humph!*" said Parker. "But I'll tell you this. You'd no sooner get married to him, than one of his old enemies would turn up ready to fight. You'd be a widow almost before you was a wife."

"I'll guard him like a handful of diamonds," replied Beatrice Larkin. "Hush. Here he comes."

Robert came hastily back to the room. He spoke in a sharp, broken voice: "Beatrice, I want to go back with you. But I've given my word of honor to another man. I have to try to help him. And then. . . ."

VI

The instant that Sim Burgess made sure his gunfighter *par excellence* was so devoted to his word of honor, he determined that he must prepare to have the blow struck before the iron was a single degree cooler. No matter what the pull of duty and honor might be to this deluded Fernald, Burgess had a great deal of trust in the power of a girl as beautiful as Beatrice Larkin to do as she pleased with almost any man. For his own part, it seemed to Burgess the height of insanity for a grown man to dare to cross a single wish of such a beauty. She held in her hand a fortune great enough to enrich a dozen. And upon this fortune, Fernald was at present turning his back.

Well, whatever madness induced Fernald to act in this fashion, Burgess was certain that he must make the most of his ally's assistance during the next few hours, for, otherwise, the golden opportunity might well be lost. The girl had browbeaten and scoffed at Fernald up to this point. If she once descended to appeal there would be an end of Burgess's fine scheme, and Robert Fernald would be whirled away to Larkin Valley, to peace and happiness for the rest of his life.

That was the reason for the haste of Burgess. When he got into the lobby of the hotel, however, he had to pause, for there was news sufficient to make any Westerner open his ears.

A most notorious character had arrived in town—Tiger Brennan, famous for a thousand wild and brutal acts, Tiger Brennan and his coterie of trained assistants. Trained, in fact, by the hand of the master, so that they would be useful in the performance of any act of crime that might prove profitable. There had been a time when Brennan roamed the range alone, doing whatever his patron, the devil, put into his mind, but that old and careless period had ended, and Brennan had learned how to make crime earn something more than various terms in jail.

He stood there in the corner of the lobby, surrounded as always by a crowd. The majority was more interested, idle spectators, but, with a single glance, Burgess could pick out the cohorts of Brennan from the rest. Three tall, straight, lean-faced, young men with restless eyes and sternly set mouths, they showed that their master had selected them with care and trained them with patience. They were the remainder of a larger company. How many crimes were committed by these same youngsters, men only could guess. They were not constantly busy. It was said that Brennan planned every job with the utmost care, and that he struck but once.

Nothing was too big for him to undertake. Nothing was too small, if his pride were enlisted in a difficult undertaking. It was said that he had robbed trains, banks, messengers, stages. But nothing could be proved. Hardly a year went by that did not find him on trial for some spectacular breaking of the law. But he always escaped. In one way or another he could build up an alibi. He had friends scattered throughout the length and the breadth of the mountains, all more than willing to swear to whatever Brennan wished. He had skillful lawyers who knew how to frame his cases for him. And so he went scot-free.

He looked his full age now. An iron-gray man was he, close to fifty, without surplus flesh, active, wiry, and a little straighter and faster with a gun than ever before, men said.

Mr. Burgess paused and regarded the great man with a measure of awe and a measure of envy. There was hardly an achievement of Brennan's that Burgess would not gladly have made his own. He looked. He admired the trained, keen-eyed, quiet legionaries who watched the crowd, searched every face, and made sure that no danger approached their well-guarded master. What a glorious life, then, to keep such fellows as these consistently at one's beck and call.

Burgess, shaking his head, and with a sigh of envy, went out from the hotel to the open street. He found Pedrillo where he expected to find him—in the saloon, at the farther end of the bar, where there was a space cleared for him, as usual, and where his narratives could be heard by the discerning.

Burgess went straight up to him. "Oñate," he said, "there's complete hell to pay."

"Alas, *señor,* do not say so," said the fat Mexican, his good-natured self-satisfaction entirely unruffled. "What can be wrong where there is so much good liquor?"

"Do you remember Miss Beatrice Larkin?"

"The *señorita?*" Oñate said, shrugging his thick shoulders with such violence that his entire body shook. "Ah, yes. And what of her? She had a cruel, bright eye. It went through one like the blade of a knife, grazing the heart. What of her, *señor?*"

"She's come here for your master."

The Mexican gaped. "Holy Virgin!" he breathed, and hastily swallowed a glass of tequila.

"It's the truth," said Burgess. "And you know that McCoy is here in town? But I tell you that, unless you work very fast, the girl will get Fernald away before he's had a chance to fight with McCoy. Now, greaser, if you love the money that I've promised you, start to work, and start *pronto!*"

Oñate clutched the edge of the bar. So doing, his eyes caught the large diamond of his new ring. It fascinated him, not like a jewel, but like a great watching eye. To Oñate it had become more than human, and he would have done almost anything in this world rather than lose possession of it. "Stay for me here," he said at last. "I shall go get my little father and bring him here to talk with you. He must know you, *señor,* before he will do such a thing."

So Burgess, with a rising hope in his heart, waited for the coming of the young killer, and, when Fernald arrived, all three walked in the yard behind the saloon, a big stretch of ground, dotted with poplars.

There Burgess told his story of lies with all the conviction that he could summon. And young Fernald listened with a grave air, shaking his head from time to time as he considered the villainy of which the persecuted Burgess spoke.

"It is all as Pedrillo has told me," Robert said at last. "A good man fallen into the hands of a villain. Mister Burgess, if there is anything I can do that will help you, count on me. Let me know where to find this scoundrel, and I'll go to him at once."

Burgess gripped Robert's hand and wrung it with a mighty pressure. "He's in this town . . . in this hotel," said Sim Burgess. "The devil that has brought him luck all his life has deserted him now. He's left the Big Bend and come up here. God bless you, Mister Fernald, if you can help me."

"Here?" asked Robert, his eyes gleaming with a light that robbed his face of its fresh boyishness. "Here at this hotel?" And without another word, he turned on his heel and strode from the yard and into the building.

Burgess exchanged glances with Pedrillo, mopping his brow the while.

"It's done, *señor*," said Pedrillo, "and McCoy is a dead man this minute." So saying, he looked up at the hotel, and there he saw, staring down at him through a closed window, a face that made him gasp and turn gray-green.

"*Señor!* Look!" Pedrillo gasped.

"What is it?" asked Burgess, starting violently.

"It is *Señor* McCoy . . . at that window . . . no, he is gone from it now."

Burgess stared up, fascinated. "Why did you jump and carry on like that when you saw him?" Burgess snarled. "Will you tell me that? Now, if there's a suspicion in him, you've sure brought it to the top of the pool."

"He couldn't hear what I said," Pedrillo said, still uneasy. "But I said that he must be dead now . . . and then looking up and seeing him . . . it was like seeing the evil eye . . . the face of a ghost . . . and I think that there's an end to my good luck." He stood still, staring blankly at the ground. "There's an end to it," repeated Pedrillo. "And I shall be back in rags, in the very dirt and dust of the street."

Burgess recovered his good spirits at once, as though the depression of his companion stimulated him to better thoughts. "McCoy has an eye like the eye of a ferret," he said. "But he can't have heard a thing . . . and he can't have guessed what I'm up to. . . ."

"Why not?" exclaimed the Mexican. "He knows that you want him dead. And he's sure to guess at something, seeing you here with me and with the little father. God forgive all my sins. God forgive them! I am going to offer at the shrine of. . . ."

He found himself talking to the air, for Mr. Sim Burgess was walking off toward the rear entrance of the hotel with a carelessly confident swing to his gait, whistling as he went, for he had noted that evil gleam in the eyes of Fernald, and it promised to him the realization of all of his hopes, and at once.

Pedrillo got no comfort from this. He looked up again at the window where he had seen McCoy, and, although that window still was blank, it seemed to him that the grim eye of the rancher was fixed upon him from empty space. So, bowing his head, he skulked into the hotel in his turn.

VII

What did Robert Fernald do when he reached the hotel? He went as straight as a hound on the trail to the room of his quarry. He tapped on the door. There was no answer, except the muffled echo of the noise that he himself had made. There he paused a moment.

He was on fire with a double reason. On the one hand, he felt that he had committed himself to a good cause. On the other hand, he felt that he had to do it with a practiced warrior of the range. For both reasons, he would not have had to do with a better affair. It was suited to his hand in every respect.

He wandered down into the lobby to make inquiries, but he did not have to search far.

"Where's Mister McCoy?" he asked.

"Sittin' right out on the verandah now, sir," said the proprietor, and he rubbed his fat hands together and smiled upon Robert.

There was such a rush of important guests on this present day that the hotelkeeper would have been affable even to a Mexican. How much more so, then, to as distinguished a character as Robert Fernald, battler extraordinary?

Out through the doorway stepped Robert.

Let us accompany him not only with an observing eye, but entering into his flesh and spirit. There had been a time, when he first issued from his college doors and came West to seek adventure, when he feared only lest he should reveal himself to himself as a natural coward. That time had ended. Even Robert himself knew that there was only one thing that gave spice to life, and that was danger. He still was blind to the moral danger of such an attitude, even though Beatrice Larkin had not so long ago pointed out the hard facts to him in harder words. However, here he was like a drunkard in the immediate presence of an ocean of liquor.

Yonder on the verandah sat a possible opponent, a dangerous fighter, a mature and crafty brain. Yonder was an evil man—he had the word of Pedrillo for it. And through the doorway, Robert stepped with a heart as light as the heart of a hawk when it sees game rising from the covert far beneath.

It was not that he was certain of victory. What he loved was the thrill of the encounter, the facing of death, and, above all, the dreadful moment of pause that generally preceded the actual battle. Other men were unnerved by that instant. To Robert it was like wine, a thing to be tasted, and prolonged in the tasting.

Such was his spirit, then, as he stepped onto the verandah, and, as he came out, he saw his quarry at once, seated in a chair at the farther end of the porch, tilted back against the wall of the building, with a few idlers on either side of him.

McCoy was in the very act of counting out a thick little sheaf of bills into the hands of a gray-headed fellow beside him. And the latter, as he stuffed the money into his wallet, looked up to Robert, who was approaching with a step as light and gay as the beating of his own heart.

"Here we are," said the gray-headed man. "You've just made your dicker in time."

Robert stood before the chair of McCoy. "You're Mister McCoy, I believe?" he said in his gentle voice, but with his eyes as cold and bright as the eyes of a hunting bird.

"I'm McCoy," said the lean man.

"My name is Robert Fernald. May I have a few words apart with you, sir?"

"Words?" McCoy asked dryly. "D'you mean words, or bullets?"

Robert started, and flushed. He could hardly believe his ears.

"Is that what you mean?" McCoy said. "Well, lad, this ain't my day to be murdered."

Robert gave back a little. It was a stunning surprise to him. For he had figured to himself a little stroll with McCoy down the street, and during that stroll he would suddenly confront the evil rancher and tell him in plain words his judgment of his companion. That done, of course guns would flash at once. There would be scores of witnesses to see that it was a fair fight—and then. . . .

It was a simple plan. It should have worked. But here was an odd matter. It was as though McCoy had listened to the interview that had just taken place in the back yard of the hotel. But no matter what McCoy thought, he had been written down for Robert as a bold and courageous scoundrel, and pride should have made him rise to accept any challenge from a single opponent.

Instead, he leaned back in his chair and regarded Robert with perfect calm, and all the time his eyes were as the eyes of one who reads in a book. One who sits securely by the fire and reads.

"Mister McCoy," Robert said, "I think that you've said something that requires a little explaining."

"Have I?" replied the rancher indifferently. "Well, you tell him, partner. You got the right to tell him, I guess." He gestured to the gray-headed man beside him.

"All right. I'll talk," said the latter, regarding Robert with a curious interest, not entirely hostile. "Kid, you don't know me?"

"I don't," Robert said, more and more bewildered, and his

face growing hotter and hotter as his wits failed to keep pace with this odd situation.

"I'm Brennan."

"You're Brennan!" cried Robert, turning very pale.

"You know me, eh?"

"You're Tiger Brennan," repeated Robert, whiter than before.

"That's me, kid."

"I'm glad to know you," Robert said, standing stiff and straight as a soldier. He was beginning to tremble a little, too. "And you have something to say to me . . . for Mister McCoy?" he added.

"I have, youngster," said Brennan, who was beginning to smile. For he felt that he recognized these symptoms of fear. He had seen them many a time before like this. And the same smile appeared on the faces of the lean, grim young men who were seated upon either side of the criminal.

"I'm waiting, sir," Robert Fernald said, and suddenly he smiled in turn, a mere flash of expression rather than an actual smile, a glance of light, as it were, but it had a great effect upon Mr. Brennan, for suddenly he could see that what he had taken for fear was not fear at all, but really a tense, overmastering, soul-absorbing joy in danger. It altered his own attitude at once.

"My lad," said Brennan, "you're here lookin' for trouble and wanting it real bad. But you ain't going to get the kind that you want. You want to make a show out of this here, and what would please you would be to have a stand-off fight with guns. But you ain't going to get the gunfight, kid. Not that way. There was a time," he added, "when I would've taken you on quick and finished you off, too. But my time is too dog-gone' valuable and I got too many important things on my hands to waste myself scrapping now with every young fool that wants to get famous. Matter of fact, youngster, all that you'll get out of us is a killing. Here's me . . . and McCoy . . . and here's my three partners, all ready to turn loose at you. And if you so much as raise a finger, kid, we'll surely blow you to bits."

He leaned forward a little as he said this, and Robert looked him fully in the eye—then flashed a glance on either side.

McCoy remained at ease in his chair, smiling faintly with satisfaction. The three young men were leaning forward a little, tense and quivering like eager hounds straining at the leash. There was not the slightest doubt that they would be at him the instant he made a dangerous move. Then a terrible temptation took Robert by the throat. There were five of them, to be sure, and they were all fighting men celebrated for their skill with weapons. McCoy and Brennan were known, and these three young disciples of the latter were doubtless chosen because they were experts with weapons of all kinds. Yet suppose that he should whip out two guns and plant two bullets—that would finish one pair out of the five. Then fall to the floor, shooting as he fell, and, with a little luck—because certainly these men would not be expecting such a frontal assault against such odds—why, if he were to do such a deed as this, he would be raised at once to that dizzy pinnacle where the one and only Wild Bill now stood above the rest of the world. He would become an historic figure. . . .

That wild temptation stung the heart of Robert, and who can tell what he would have done, had not the hard, cold voice of McCoy cut in on him.

"Don't do it, kid. You might get famous. But you'd get dead, too."

Robert straightened with a long, soft sigh. "Brennan . . . and the rest of you," he said, "I'd like to know what is the meaning of all this?"

"I can tell you, sonny," answered McCoy. "I've bought and paid for protection, and I've got it. You can go back to the dog that hired you and tell him that his medicine is no good. He's out of this here. He's tried to double-cross me in every other possible way, and he's failed. Now he'll fail again. And he'll always fail. Because I've got his number, Fernald. He came high when he got you. But I came higher when I got Brennan. That's all. Now run along . . . you're late for school." And he chuckled a little, with a deep inner content.

Robert, quite baffled, went slowly away, and twice he paused to look back at the group on the verandah.

Instantly one of those tall, athletic youths who were with Brennan stood up.

"Where you gonna go, Chuck?" asked Brennan.

"Gonna take a lil' stroll," said the other.

He was a mighty man, slender about the waist, Herculean around the shoulders and in the length and weight of his arms. And he stared earnestly in the direction of the hotel entrance through which Robert had just disappeared.

"Sit down, Dashwood," said the master.

Dashwood hesitated, frowned, and then obeyed. But he was very restless, shifting back and forth in his chair as though he were terribly ill at ease.

"You want to take him by the throat, Chuck, don't you?" Brennan asked with a grin.

"And why not? The little runt . . . ," muttered young Dashwood.

"It don't take a strong man to pull a gun," Brennan said wisely. "What good would all of your beef be against Fernald?"

"Have I got nothing but beef?" asked the youth quickly, and he turned his bold, bright eyes upon his master.

"You've got something else," Brennan admitted, "and you're gonna get still more in time. But you ain't up to Fernald just yet."

"The proof of the pudding is in the eating," observed this sullen youth.

"Exactly. And though you've done a good deal of eating, kid, don't you get away with the idea that you can't be et in your turn. And that pink-cheeked kid is just the baby to turn the trick."

"I don't see it," Dashwood muttered, growing a violent red.

"Look here, Chuck, you're a brave kid. But would you tackle five men like the bunch of us here?"

"Well, no," said Dashwood. "I ain't that much of a flathead, I hope."

"Of course you ain't. Well, lemme give you an idea about Fernald and the kind of a gent that he is. When he was standin' here, he wanted terrible bad to get at you and the rest of us. When I talked big over him, he came within an ace of letting drive at the bunch of us."

"Him?" grunted Dashwood. "He was scared white."

"He was white with wanting to tear us to pieces. That was all. Don't make no mistake, Chuck. You can't read men yet. You need more training. Ask McCoy if the kid wasn't on edge to jump the whole gang of us?"

"I was never closer to dying," McCoy said calmly and judicially. "I knew that he would get you, Brennan, and me, with his first pair of shots. Maybe your boys would shoot him to bits afterwards, but the pair of us would've gone down first. That was why I spoke. I wanted to break the spell. And when he paused a bit, walkin' away from us, why, he was sayin' to himself . . . 'Ain't there a chance? If I was to turn back, ain't there a chance that I could kill the whole bunch of them by fast shooting?' That was the way that he was working things out in his head. And maybe he could. Anyway, it threw a chill into me."

Chuck Dashwood lost all of his restlessness and settled back in his chair; he even shuddered a little, as a man will do when he has had a narrow escape.

Brennan said at last: "I've seen 'em big and I've seen 'em small. I've seen 'em that fought for money, and I've seen 'em that fought for fame . . . but I've never seen one before that loved guns for the sake of the death that was inside of them. McCoy, I took on this here job too cheap."

VIII

There was more than one reason why Robert should feel as though one half of the world had crashed about his ears. In the first place, he felt that he had been shamed, even though by numbers a little too great to be faced with good sense. But, in the second place, he was bewildered because he did not see how true Westerners could have acted as these fellows had done, for he had made a fair proffer of battle, and they had driven him away by the pressure of vastly superior numbers. It was quite beyond his understanding, for he could not help feeling that these were no cowards but truly brave men.

If Robert's vanity had been developed a little more, he might have hit upon the correct explanation, but, as it was, he missed it entirely, and went to find Mr. Sim Burgess. He found that worthy in close consultation with Pedrillo Oñate, and the pair of them raised brows furrowed with hope and trouble.

"Something's gone wrong," Robert heard Burgess say to the Mexican. "Something's gone wrong, and, if he's missed at the first try, he's missed altogether."

To them, Robert explained briefly what had happened; how he had confronted McCoy and found that that hero had bought the protection of no less a man than Brennan and all his coterie of promising young gunfighters. What, then, was to be done? Robert suggested that he leave town with Pedrillo, and then, when McCoy departed in turn, Mr. Burgess could announce the event with a smoke signal.

"Stay here in town with all of them devils?" gasped Burgess.

"I'd be dead in one hour after you left, of course."

That settled this suggestion. They talked a little longer, and then retired to Robert's room to carry on their consultation. Here, as they entered, Pedrillo adroitly scooped up a letter that had been passed under the door. And when he and Burgess left the room a few minutes later, the latter was quick to ask why the missive had been purloined.

"There was no stamp on that letter," Pedrillo said. "And who would be writing a letter to the little father in this town? It's the *señorita* . . . to get him back to Larkin Valley."

"I understand"—Burgess grinned—"and once you get back with him to Larkin Valley, you stop being a big gun. You're just an ordinary sort of piker. Ain't that it? You can't stand around in the saloons, then, and blow about the things that your boss has done and the things that he pretty near done. And, worst of all, you wouldn't be getting any little commissions, like this here one from me." And he cast a sour glance at the diamond that sparkled on the little finger of Oñate.

"Ah, *señor,*" said Pedrillo, "have no fear whatever. We have been checked, but we have not been beaten. It will not be as quick as I expected . . . but we'll manage to win. The little father never stops until he has reached his man, and, when he reaches his man, the man dies. It is always true."

So saying, he ripped the envelope open with his teeth and took out the enclosed letter. He read aloud:

My Dear Fernald: From what I've heard of you, you don't pick on honest men. And that is what I claim to be. What sort of lies have been told to you by Burgess I don't know, but I can imagine. I've even heard that money can't corrupt you, and, if that's the case, you've been hoodwinked by some clever, lying story.

Now, Fernald, I want to tell you the true story of what happened in my partnership with Burgess. As for the proofs, it's commonly known all through the Big Bend, where his credit isn't big enough to gain the attention of even the Mexicans.

These are the facts. I had an old mortgage on a stretch of land that had belonged to. . . .

Here Burgess snatched the letter away.

"¿*Señor?*" asked the startled Pedrillo.

"That's enough of that!" Burgess scowled. "Leave the letter be. It's all nothin' but lies."

"Lies that the whole of the Big Bend would swear to, *señor?*" asked the Mexican, and then he chuckled softly, a chuckle rich in understanding. "I ask no questions, *amigo*," he said. "What you say is enough for . . . a friend."

"Greaser," Burgess said sourly, "you talk too much. Leave off, will you?" He added: "Now, I'm gonna tell you something, Oñate. Unless McCoy is a dead man inside of two days, I get back everything that I've given to you. You understand?"

Oñate, turning a little green, moved the diamond ring so that the jewel was securely hidden inside the fat palm of his hand. "You are very hard, *amigo*," he said gently. "But I shall do what I can."

So they parted, and Mr. Burgess, going gloomily up the main street a little later, came squarely into McCoy as the latter rounded a corner. McCoy, but not alone. On either side of him marched as a guard of honor one of Brennan's chosen men of war.

They halted before Burgess, who shrank back into a doorway, clutching the jamb, ready to leap into the interior at the first sign of trouble.

McCoy, however, merely smiled. "You've missed again, Sim," he said, "and you'll always miss. The reason is, old-timer, that you don't think straight enough to be honest, and you don't think well enough to make a successful crook."

Chuck Dashwood was one of the guards, and now he said

thoughtfully: "It looks to me, McCoy, as if you had a pretty good case ag'in' this rat. Why don't you let me polish him off for you?"

Burgess shrank deeper into the doorway, his eyes glittering with terror, but tall McCoy merely answered: "I couldn't do it. The fact is, Chuck, that I don't go in even for the killing of vermin . . . and, besides, this here gent was a partner of mine, once, and I liked him well enough to trust him."

"It's your business, not mine," replied Dashwood. "Leave him be, then. And maybe he's got enough poison inside of him to finish him off one of these here days. Only, Burgess, keep clear of me. And keep clear of the rest of us. We don't like your looks, and they's a price on the scalps of coyotes down in my part of the country. I might make a little mistake."

He grinned at Burgess most evilly, and then the trio marched on down the street without so much as a single backward glance at Burgess. For his part, he had enough of a shock to send him skulking into a back room of the saloon, and there he sat down to whiskey—whiskey straight, red, and raw—and drank until the fear was burned out of his brain and a red-stained mist filled its place.

IX

Now when Robert Fernald got back to his room, he fell into a quandary that lasted him all the rest of that day and kept him awake most of the night. He had only one visitor during this time, and the visitor was Dan Parker, who strode into the room and sat down on the end of the table.

He found Robert pacing restlessly back and forth, an extremely nervous young man, sometimes fidgeting at the window that looked onto the street, and again hurrying up and down the room as though in search of something he had lost.

"Bob, old fellow," said the ranch foreman, "tell me the

straight of it. Are you coming back with us now?"

"Coming back?" Robert snapped, grown irritable.

"That's what I said."

"How can I come back, Dan? I've given my word to. . . ."

"To kill McCoy?"

Robert gaped.

"The whole town knows about it," explained Parker.

"How?"

"You can't walk up to five men and ask for trouble without having the news spread around, Bob. But what makes the rest of us wonder is this . . . how'd you ever get mixed up in any job on the side of a gent like Burgess?"

"And what's wrong with him?"

"Why, he's a bad egg, that's all."

"You're generally right," said Robert, "but the fact is that you're completely out in this case, Dan. McCoy is a villain. And Burgess is the man he's wronged."

"Who told you that?"

"I had it from Burgess himself."

Parker bit his lip. He wanted to scoff at this testimony, but he knew something about the child-like simplicity of Robert Fernald, and therefore he held his tongue.

"Had it from anybody else?" he asked.

"Yes, from Pedrillo."

"Oñate!" burst out Parker. "I knew he was at the bottom of the whole idiotic business."

"Ah?" Robert breathed, and raised his head, a cold light in his eyes.

Dan Parker scowled at him. "I know what you mean," he said. "You want to pick a fight even with me, Bob. But you can't. Because I'm not fighting you, you see. Suicide ain't my line. I get excitement other ways. But Oñate . . . the fat pig . . . the fat snake, I ought to call him. Why, Bob, you're letting him lead you around by the nose for his own profit."

"Profit, Dan? Pedrillo's profit?"

"Who else?"

"I don't understand."

"How did you find Oñate," Parker asked, beginning to tap out his points against the palm of his hand.

"In San Joaquin."

"Where?"

"In the street."

"Wearing silks and lots of gold lace?"

"No, he was a ragged beggar, of course."

"Is he a ragged beggar now?"

"Not at all. He has a good deal of luck at cards, you see, and he makes money in that way. He really looks quite splendid now, don't you think?"

"Why didn't he make money at cards before he hooked up with you?"

"How can I answer that? His luck was out, I suppose. That's all."

"Bob, lemme tell you something,"

"What?"

"You're his luck."

"I?"

"I mean you're his card game."

"I don't follow you, Dan."

"Well, make a hard try to, because I've got the straight of this."

"You have?"

"Pedrillo is simply making a gold mine out of you."

"Ah, there in the very beginning you're all wrong. As a matter of fact, it's a wonderful thing that, although Pedrillo has worked for me all this time, I simply can't make him take money."

"Bob, you make me want to curse. As a matter of fact, the brown-faced swine is simply taking a commission for every job that he gets you to do."

"Job?"

"Who worked you into this case of Burgess against McCoy? It was Oñate. And look back and you'll find that he's led you into the other fights that you've been having. Somebody profits out of those fights. Who? Why, Oñate, of course. His commission is what makes him a rich greaser right now."

Robert merely shook his head, and he smiled upon Parker with a calm superiority.

"You're like most people, Dan," he said. "You can't see that, as a matter of fact, there are some folks who do good for the sake of good, where there are others who have to be paid for it."

"And Oñate is one of the first kind, is he?" asked the foreman, his lips curling in angry disbelief.

"Let me tell you something about him. He and I have to take some hard trips. Well, Dan, on those trips through the mountains or across the desert, Oñate is like a personal servant to me. He does the cooking, and never complains, no matter how long the trail that we've ridden over since dawn. He keeps up a cheerful front in all weathers. He'll even groom my horse for me, if I'll let him. In every respect he looks after me."

"Go on," Parker said, more gloomy than ever. "I see what you're driving at, though."

"And in reward for these services, I've tried to make him take something in the way of regular wages from me. But he won't do it. I've even slipped money into his pocket. But the next morning I'm sure to find that he's slipped it back in mine." Tears came into the eyes of Robert. He fairly trembled as he contemplated the goodness of the Mexican.

"And between us, Dan," he said, "there's a real attachment. I assure you that it's real on my side, and I know that it is on the side of Pedrillo."

"Bob," snapped the foreman, "gimme a chance, and I'll knock that idea of yours into a cocked hat. I'll show you as a fact that Pedrillo is only a hound and a loafer, playing you for an easy mark who. . . ."

Robert shook his head with finality. "I don't want to have my faith in him broken," he declared. "In the first place, I know that it can't be. In the second place, I don't like to have you try. Pedrillo is all right. You can't fool me about him, Dan, no matter what wrong impression you may have on the subject."

Fernald said this with such emotion that Parker pursued the subject no further but left the room and went to a certain earnest and resolute young lady who was waiting to get a report.

Seeds of suspicion had been planted in the mind of Robert Fernald, however. He might deny that they had touched fertile soil. And, if they sprouted, he might hoe them up resolutely. Yet, nevertheless, the mind is in its own place—as more than one profound observer has noted—and our control over it can never be more than a mild tyranny. It is apt to rise and assert itself with rebellious strength at any moment.

So the sway of Pedrillo Oñate was seriously threatened, although the danger might not come to a head for a long time. And Robert was left alone with increasingly serious thoughts, pacing back and forth in his room, and finally throwing himself face downward on his bed. He had reached such a state of utter depression that he began to be acutely aware of all the small things in life around him. The sounds in the street—the smell of cookery from some nearby kitchen that blew faintly through his window—and then the pattern of the bedspread. Mixed with all these sense impressions was an overwhelming gloom that invaded his mind with an irresistible force, for he could see more and more clearly that what he had wanted to be, he had failed in attaining. He had wished to go through the world like a perfect knight errant, redressing wrongs. He had failed. For now men were beginning to look upon him as a hired bully. It was very unjust, but it was true. He could not avoid the realization that this judgment was so very widespread that now he was looked upon askance, and he sank under the burden of that thought. He suddenly fell into a troubled sleep.

When he wakened, the room was dim with shadows. He found that a blanket had been laid over him carefully, and the unmistakable fragrance of a Mexican cigarette filled the air. He raised his head. Pedrillo sat in the corner near the window. The cigarette was marked by a tiny glowing spot of red, and the face of Oñate was lost in shadow.

Emotion rushed through the heart of Robert. "Pedrillo!" he cried.

"*¿Señor?*" Pedrillo came swiftly to him, the room shaking a little with his heavy step.

"Pedrillo, a thought occurs to me."

"Yes, little father."

"Now and again, I'm short-tempered, peevish, and use bad words to you. Promise me to understand that my heart never changes. My trust in you is absolute, Pedrillo."

"*Señor,* how could I doubt it? We have traveled too many trails together."

"Give me your hand, Pedrillo."

They shook hands, and Robert sighed. Sleep had smoothed much of the pain and the trouble from his mind, and now he felt that all was well. Let the rest of the world misunderstand as much as it pleased, but between him and Pedrillo there was a perfect harmony. And what could a man expect more than one understanding spirit?

X

The sun was not up when trouble returned to Robert Fernald; the gray light filled his room when he was wakened next morning, and again it was by the entrance of big Dan Parker who was in a fury, cursing at every step he took.

"What's wrong?" asked Robert.

"Wrong? Everything's wrong! Miss Beatrice and her aunt are gone . . . spirited away . . . flown . . . and no trace of them left behind."

Robert sat up in bed and stared. "It doesn't seem possible," he said.

"Don't tell me what seems possible or don't . . . I tell you what's happened. They told me to wake them just before daylight so's they could get a flying start this morning on the trail back to the ranch. I went and rapped at their door. No answer. I banged loud . . . no answer. I pushed the door open. By heaven, the lock of it was broken . . . it had been forced. There I found everything in disorder. And no sign of the pair of them. I ran downstairs to the stable, and there I found that their horses were gone. The stable boy was drunk, didn't know a thing. And, Fernald, your man Pedrillo probably has had a hand in some dirty plot . . . and maybe you have, too."

He raged out these words in a shapeless jumble, so that Robert barely could make out his meaning. But when he did understand, he swung to the floor and stood up. He began to dress with frantic haste.

"Dan, they've simply started on ahead of you for the ranch trail. . . ."

"Started on alone? Without me? Without even a word to me? No, I tell you, there's been crooked work."

"How could it have happened?" Robert asked, fighting to disbelieve the worst possibilities. "Something would have been heard."

"In the middle of that windstorm last night?"

Robert had slept through the storm. Now he merely blinked.

"Besides," said Parker, "a touch of chloroform would have made the women quiet enough."

"Chloroform?" Robert cried. "Man, man, what is it that you think has happened?"

"Is it the first time that women have been kidnapped in this country?" asked Parker, raging more than ever. "Put your wits together and make it all out for yourself."

Robert could make out nothing. His mind had been reduced to a blank even by the terrible possibility. Now he was finishing his dressing.

Pedrillo, who slept on a cot at the other side of the room, was likewise dressed, accomplishing his work with wonderful agility, considering his single hand.

Parker turned savagely upon the Mexican. "He's behind it, Bob!" he shouted. "You'll find out that the greaser had his hand in the thing."

"You talk like a madman, Dan!" exclaimed Robert.

"*Señor* Parker," Pedrillo pleaded, writhing with emotion, "I swear . . . I vow . . . I give my honor!"

"Your honor!" The big foreman sneered "You ain't got none!"

"There's nothing gained by abusing Pedrillo," broke in Robert. "But what under heaven can we do? Have you raised the town? Have you sent for the sheriff . . . ?"

"What good will that do? We need to start and ride," Dan Parker stated. "Will you come with me, Fernald?"

"Alas, *señor*," Pedrillo said in haste, "you have given your word to. . . ."

"To what?" broke in Dan Parker. "To kill McCoy? Is that what you mean, Oñate? Bob, that is proof of what I told you. The scoundrel is urging you on into an. . . ."

"I've given my word," Robert said earnestly, "but I'll redeem it later without fail. What's the life of McCoy compared to the happiness of Beatrice Larkin? God forgive me if I hesitate. Dan, let's get to our horses . . . Pedrillo, raise the town . . . call out everyone."

Pedrillo, with a deep groan and rolling his eyes like a man turned suddenly faint, went from the room, while Parker said: "We'll take a last look in their room . . . there may be some sort of clue. . . ."

Into the deserted room of the two women they stormed, and almost at once Robert saw the thing that, in their hearts, they half expected. It was pinned against the rough wall with a splinter, a piece of paper that fluttered in the wind of their coming. Robert caught it from its place and found that it was covered with a roughly made writing consisting of separate, straight strokes of a pencil, so that it looked at first rather like a series of meaningless scratches than a legible message. However, as soon as one's eyes grew accustomed to the system of the markings, it was possible to make out the words:

Bring $10,000 to the foot of Crystal Mountain a week from today. They won't be harmed.

"A kidnapping," Robert breathed, growing very sick.

He even had to steady himself by resting a hand against the broad shoulder of Dan Parker, who had snatched the paper from the limp fingers of Robert and was busy reading it in turn.

"I knew it," Parker groaned. "I guessed it with the first look. Lord, what'll we do?"

"Start now for our horses . . . and then ride with the devil behind us," said Robert through his teeth, resuming his energy with a sudden start. "Are you ready, Dan?"

"Ready, lad. Yes, yes!"

Shoulder to shoulder they rushed down the stairs.

"Who could have done it, Dan?"

"Brennan."

"Brennan?"

"Why not Brennan? Isn't he the man for such a job as this? No one else would have dared." Then Parker shouted: "Here's Brennan's room! Try him here. . . ."

They beat at the door. It was locked, and silence answered them. Parker did not hesitate. One thrust of his powerful shoulder cast the door wide, and he lurched into the chamber. A glance was all they needed. The room was quite empty of any man or even blanket roll, and the bed had not been slept in.

"God help us! God help us!" Robert gasped. "Hurry, Dan!"

The house was rising now. Men were stumbling out of their rooms, most of them with guns in their hands, for in the distance there was the dreadful voice of Oñate, howling like a wolf. The proprietor, half mad with dismay, met them at the stables. They told him the story in half a dozen words. Then they flung the saddles on their horses. Others had heard the tale by this time, from the throat of Pedrillo Oñate, and swarms of men rose up around them, saddling horses and making ready with much noise to take up the trail.

What trail? And where could it lead? Toward Crystal Mountain?

In five minutes groups of restless riders were sweeping this way and that around the village, cutting for sign in frantic haste, and finding nothing except several minor clues of their own leaving.

But this much was known. With the two women, Brennan and his three companions had disappeared, and it did not need much forethought to connect the disappearance of the one with the disappearance of the other.

Robert and Parker, riding together, kept away from the other searchers until the snorting mule of Pedrillo brought that matchless trailer up with them. He had saddled as fast as he could to follow them, not because he wanted to be in on the work, but, no doubt, because he dreaded to be left behind in the village where McCoy could get at him—to say nothing of Sim Burgess, who would be wanting certain sums in cash and a jewel of value refunded.

So Oñate joined them, and, being with them, he could hardly help but use his rare talents. Put pencil and paper before an artist and a drawing must result. So it was with Pedrillo on the trail. He could not help but hunt, and it seemed that he could hardly help but find.

The wind of the night apparently had wiped out all traces, but, on a stretch of firm ground beyond a draw, Pedrillo found what he wanted—the prints of the hoofs of six horses.

"We have a long hunt before us," said Pedrillo. "They left when it was still quite dark, and they were riding hard."

"How do you tell that, Pedrillo?"

"You see the distance that the horses were striding? That shows the speed of their gallop. And notice how close two of them came to that tree. They must have had to duck the branches. If it had been daylight, they would have swung wide. I'll call in a dozen of the best men," Pedrillo went on. "We'll need all their help if. . . ."

"Wait for nothing," Dan Parker urged with much resolution. "Twelve men can't keep pace with six. And I saw Brennan's horses. He's mounted for a race."

"You two against four?" cried Pedrillo, gaping.

"Are you willing?" Parker turned to Robert.

"Ready and willing," said Fernald. "Go on, Pedrillo. Hunt down this trail as you never hunted before!"

And he spoke to his pinto, and that hardy and beautiful little horse swung into a reaching gallop that consumed the ground as easily as the canter of a greyhound. They headed straight across the desert. The town dropped out of sight behind them.

In silence they rode. The heat began to drop heavily from the heavens and wash back to them from the glowing surface of the sands. The surface grew yielding. They had to slow to a walk, and there is nothing so disheartening as a chase continued at a walk. The sand slushed softly around the hoofs of the horses; the stirrup leathers *creaked;* the horses puffed and snorted the blow-sand from their nostrils; they were proceeding rather like a plow team than a fleet-footed posse.

Then the Mexican said: "Listen to me, *señores.* You say that *Señor* Brennan has done this thing for ten thousand dollars. It is not possible."

"Tell us why, Pedrillo."

"*Señor* Brennan has many men working for him. He cannot afford to waste his time on small game. And ten thousand is not much to him. Besides, this is not the sort of thing that he does. Here he has shown his hand openly. Everyone in the world would know that he has done this thing. It is not possible. He is as secret as a fox."

"The whole world knows that he has done this thing," Dan Parker said scoffingly, "and yet you say that he has not done it?"

"I talk against myself. That is because I am trying to think honestly," said Pedrillo. "But does such a man as *Señor* Brennan take a chance at prison for two or three thousand dollars? No, little father, that cannot be."

"A lion will eat a mouse, Pedrillo," said Robert Fernald.

"You have the facts in front of you, Pedrillo," commented Dan Parker. "How will you dodge them?"

"He seems to have stolen the two ladies," said Pedrillo, "and yet he cannot have done it. He has stolen them and yet he has not stolen them. And if this seems like madness, wait a little while, and you will see."

XI

A day passed, and another. They were days of scorching heat, endless labor. Again and again the trail was blotted out before their eyes. Nothing but the incredible skill of the Mexican was able to recover it, so it seemed.

Dan Parker was both cheerful and resolute. Robert Fernald was as a man devoured by a terrible fear. His face grew drawn. He stared constantly at the wavering heat lines along the horizon. But both Parker and Fernald were comparatively silent, whereas the tongue of Pedrillo Oñate rarely ceased wagging.

"I am the eyes," Pedrillo said, "and I see the way into danger, and yet I cannot help going into the cave. There we shall be torn to pieces. What are two men against four? Four such men! I saw them. Like four mountain lions. You are no more than mountain sheep. You will be cut to pieces. Afterward, they will strip me and turn me out to starve or let the desert sun burn me to a cinder."

"You never could starve," big Parker said. "You've got enough fat between your skin and your bones to keep you going like a camel for a month. Besides, Pedrillo, your skin is so wonderfully thick that the sun never could burn through it. So have no fear."

"Ah, fear eats me," Pedrillo said, smiting his hand against his stomach with force. "Fear eats me like a wolf. I lie in the shadow of this danger."

"Listen," said Parker. "He's dealing in proverbs now, but I know a few to match them. Pedrillo, all the weapons of war cannot arm fear."

"I do not wish to be armed. I wish to go home," said Oñate. "Fear has big eyes and sees the truth."

"On the contrary, fear has no understanding."

"Fear is one part of prudence, *señor*. Fear guards the vine-yard."

227

"He that fears not the future may enjoy the present," said Parker.

"Ah, *señor,*" replied the Mexican, rallying himself to this duel of memory, "he that fears danger in time seldom feels it."

"I have lived too long near a wood to be frightened by owls," said the foreman.

"Wise fear beats care," answered the Mexican. "Fear makes lions tame, says the proverb. And who, *señor,* would not prefer a tame lion to a wild one?"

"Listen to him." Parker laughed. "He has made out a case to prove that a coward is wiser and better than a brave man. But I'll try him on another subject. You are always talking, Pedrillo, and yet silence is golden."

"The silent dog is the first to bite," answered Pedrillo.

"Silence brings friendship," said Parker, "it is a fine jewel though it is seldom worn . . . it is more eloquent than words . . . it is the answer to anger . . . it is wisdom . . . it never betrays you . . . and it reaps what speech sows."

"To all of this," Pedrillo replied, grinning, "I will make only one reply . . . *silence is the virtue of a fool!*"

This stinging proverb, so aptly applied, brought an oath from Parker, but Pedrillo was greatly contented, and rolled from side to side in his saddle, chuckling and nodding.

"You will never beat him at that game," Robert advised, smiling at the red face of Parker.

"He is fuller of proverbs than a porcupine is of quills," admitted the foreman. "But I think that all proverbs were invented by lawyers . . . they talk on both sides of the case. Let's stop here a minute in the shade of this rock. My horse is fagged. Have you a proverb on stopping, Pedrillo?"

"The best time to stop is the beginning," Pedrillo declared.

"Confound him, he has always something to say. What's your meaning this time, greaser?"

"That we never should have begun this trail!"

"Now, Pedrillo," Robert said, "tell me honestly that you have missed the trail and that for the last three hours you have been riding blindly. Certainly I haven't seen a sign or a ghost of a sign. Have you, Dan?"

"Not a trace. Confess, Pedrillo."

"I am aiming," Pedrillo explained, "at those two gullies that open in the hills, yonder."

"Aiming at both of them?"

"Yes, because in one of them we'll pick up the trail again."

"Are you sure?"

"Alas, *señor*, I am more than sure. For I know that the men we are following do not want us to miss the trail."

"What the devil are you talking about?" Parker exclaimed. "This is rank nonsense, Pedrillo."

"*Señor*, it is true nevertheless."

"Tell us what makes you think so."

"Because these people we are following know how to make a trail problem, but the ones that they have left for us are so simple that a child could solve them."

"Are we children, Fernald and I?" asked the big foreman, frowning again.

"No, no, *señor*. Not in all things." Pedrillo grinned again. He was as fond as a woman of making his point.

"One can never corner the scoundrel," admitted the big man. "But go on, Pedrillo. You haven't explained enough."

"It is this way, *señor*. They do just enough to make most people think that they are trying to cover their trail. But I know that they could be cleverer if they wished."

"Well, Pedrillo, for three hours, as you admit, we've had not a ghost of a trail to follow. Explain that."

"Easily. Their trail this morning pointed for those same valleys in the foothills. They knew that, if we lost the sign, we would cast ahead toward the hills."

"We'll see," murmured Parker. "I think this is nonsense."

"Nonsense, perhaps," Fernald agreed, as they resumed their journey, "but I'll tell you, Dan, that the Mexican is seldom wrong when he makes up his mind in earnest."

"Do you think so?"

"I've seen him at work too many times."

"Perhaps so. Well, I still have the privilege of doubting. We'll get a better idea when we come into those gullies."

They came into the first of the passes between the hills in the late afternoon. There was no trace of the six horses, but the Mexican did not delay for a long search. It would be the other valley up which the six had gone. "And depend upon it, my friends, that we shall find the sign immediately we enter."

As he suggested, so it happened. They found the complete trail written at large in the crossing of a claybank. Parker and Fernald stared at one another.

"But," Parker said, "of course they had to get up this gulch and they couldn't avoid this bank."

"Yes." The Mexican nodded. "There is that loose sand on the other side that would hold a trail no better than water."

"Their horses were too tired to ride them through loose sand."

"*Señor,* a frightened man is never too tired to make himself safe."

"Tell me, Pedrillo," Robert said in some heat, "what makes you think this? And what could be in the head of *Señor* Brennan?"

"It is very simple. A child could understand," said the Mexican. "He is drawing us after him into the heart of the mountains, and there he will suddenly draw us into a trap. Look up yonder. Somewhere behind the cactus, one of his men is lying now with a glass trained on us, studying everything that we do."

Fernald and Parker looked up instinctively.

"That is an old trail," Parker said with decision. "They're still a great distance ahead of us."

"That trail, *señor*, was made no longer ago than noon."

"What is your reason for that?"

"This is a moist claybank . . . the hoof prints are dry in the center, but still moist in the hollows on each side. If the horses had passed this way yesterday, the whole print would be dry now . . . if they had passed only within an hour, the whole print would be dark and moist."

Parker looked at Robert and nodded. He was much impressed.

"I've wondered how you could follow such long trails in the past," he said, "but now it's explained. You carry a hunting hound with you. I think that he's right, and Brennan may be holding a trap for us. We'll have to watch every wrinkle on the face of the hills as we go . . . we'll have to ride rifle in hand, old fellow."

Robert shook his head. "We have Oñate still with us," he said. "And one can trust to him. He can scent danger as far as a wild horse. And if there's the least danger ahead of us, you can depend on him to smell it out."

"Very well," said Parker. "But now comes the crux. I think we'll be dead men . . . or famous . . . inside of the next twenty-four hours, Bob. What do you say?"

Fernald said nothing. He had grown pale, his lips were a trifle compressed, and he looked forward up the valley with a peculiar eagerness. Dan Parker studied him with interest that was seasoned by a peculiar fear. For what would have been panic in another man, in Robert Fernald was the sudden and fierce working of the desire to kill. Parker watched, therefore, with a species of awe and wonder. But they did not speak to one another for some time. Although the day was wearing late

231

and the sun was low in the west, it shone down the length of that shallow valley and turned it into a meager trough of fire that turned the sweat on the horses to white salt, and seared the very eyelids of the riders.

The Mexican, in the meantime, rode his horse nervously in an irregular line that waved back and forth from side to side of the ravine as he went from one vantage point to another.

"Look," Parker said, "the impertinent scoundrels have brought their captives almost straight back to Larkin Valley."

He had hardly finished speaking when Oñate came flying back to them, bowed over his saddle horn to make the better speed.

"Turn back, friends!" he gasped at them as he went flying past with gray, pulpy face. "They are all there on the farther side of the hill!"

XII

"Come back!" Fernald called harshly. The Mexican spurred his weary horse only the more vigorously. "Come back, Oñate, or I'll shoot you out of the saddle!" And Robert actually whipped his long rifle out of the scabbard that ran down the side of his saddle beneath his right knee.

"Good heavens, man, will you kill even Pedrillo?" exclaimed Dan Parker.

But Pedrillo was taking no chances with death. He glanced over his shoulder at the danger from the rear and instantly reined up and came back to them slowly, shaking his head in violent protest.

"They are all there on the farther side of the hill. They are all there, *señor*! Four devils, at least, and maybe more."

"The ladies, Pedrillo. Did you see the two ladies, also?"

"I saw the bait they are using for their trap," said Pedrillo. "But they are not women. They are not women, I swear to you!"

"He's gone out of his head," Parker said sternly. "Bob, let's you and I press ahead and pay no more attention to this gibbering idiot."

"Ah, ah, ah!" Pedrillo gasped. "Then you are in the plot, also, *Señor* Parker! You are working for Brennan! You are in the plot, also!"

"You yellow-faced devil!" snarled big Parker, and reached for the fat throat of Oñate, and found it, sinking the fingers deep in the rolling fat, until Oñate's tongue thrust out and his eyes rolled up toward heaven.

"Don't hurt him," Fernald said without heat, but in the manner of one who must be obeyed instantly.

Parker obediently released the Mexican. "He needs to be flayed alive, Bob," he commented. "Did you hear? He said that I was . . . by heaven, I shall beat him to a pulp."

He made another pass, but Pedrillo sought refuge behind his master. All the while his tongue was busy.

"Beware, *señor.* Beware, dear little father!"

"Be still, Pedrillo," Robert Fernald snapped impatiently. "Parker is one of my oldest and best friends."

"Better an open enemy than a false friend," said Oñate. "And avoid a friend who covers you with his wings and destroys you with his beak."

"By heaven, I'll kill the dirty dog," Parker hissed, reaching for a gun, his face very black.

"Hold on, Dan, old fellow. Just let him talk it out. He can't do you any harm with me, of course. Go on, Pedrillo, and get this nonsense out of your system."

"Look! Look!" Pedrillo cried, still keeping his sheltered place behind Robert, and pointing his fat, quivering arm at Parker from the barricade. "Look at him! He's changing his color. There is treachery in his heart."

In fact, Parker was a little pale, although he had been terribly red before.

Fernald merely laughed. "Pedrillo, you are worse than an old woman," he said. "You try to make every speck in the sky into an eagle."

"Look, *señor*, he is shaken. I only guessed before, but now I know. He is working in some manner with that murderer, that cut-throat, that devil of a man-eater, Brennan, El Tigre."

Robert laughed, and waited for more, nodding and smiling at Parker, who seemed to take these remarks from the Mexican with a singular bad grace.

"First," the Mexican said, "Parker rushes away with you on this terrible trail. He never argued when you wanted to get more men to take the trail. But he was eager to ride on it . . . just the two of you . . . he and you."

"Because he is a brave man," Robert said, smiling again at the tall foreman.

Pedrillo was becoming immensely disturbed. "Think only a little moment," he warned. "Is *Señor* Parker a fool?"

"Of course not. Does it follow that he's a villain, Pedrillo?"

"He is not a fool, you admit. Then he knows that he is not a great fighting man. Does he not? He is no Robert Fernald . . . he is no Brennan . . . and he is not even so good a fighter as any of those wild young men who live with Brennan. Is not that true?"

"Are you going to listen to any more of this sort of stuff?" Parker asked, raging with impatient anger.

"Let him talk himself out," replied Fernald. "I've learned before that words won't stay bottled up in him, and the easiest way is to let him turn the bottle upside down at once, even if it takes quite a time, for sooner or later I'll have to listen to every one of these words."

"Not if he was gagged with a rope," said Parker savagely.

"Listen. He is afraid. He would like to kill me," said the Mexican. "He would like to hang me up. He would like to drive bullets through my heart. Because he fears lest I should make you believe in the truth. That is the way with him." So said Pedrillo, bellowing with surety. He was hot with conviction. "Consider, *señor*," he went on, "that this same man, who is not a fool, was willing to ride off with you and a one-armed Mexican who cannot use weapons on the trail of the terrible Brennan. He did not ask any questions. He did not wonder what would happen when he met Brennan. He only said that he wanted to rush ahead to the fight. Tell me, then, if he is not a fool, why does he wish to throw his life away so soon?"

"Ah, Pedrillo," Robert said sadly, "you never could understand such a man as my friend Dan Parker. You cannot understand how a man could lay down his life for a friend. You cannot understand, therefore, why Dan Parker would risk his life on this trail to catch Brennan and his gang of devils."

"I? I understand everything!" shouted Pedrillo, infuriated at this aspersion upon his faith and his stoutness of heart. "I'll die ten times a day for my little father. But he . . . he's a paid man. He's a hired hand on a ranch. And you tell me that he is going to commit suicide for the sake of the *señorita* who employs him? *Bah*, he is only a. . . ."

The hard fist of Dan Parker shot straight for the chin of the Mexican, who dodged behind Robert Fernald, and the driving arm of Parker staggered the smaller man.

Fernald frowned a little, but then shrugged his shoulders. "Let Pedrillo alone," he said. "And you, Oñate, don't be such a madman. You say that you have just seen the whole party of Brennan, and the two ladies among them . . . and yet they are not women after all. Is that sense, my friend?"

"I saw them ride. I saw the way that they sat the saddle. I know that they are men, *señor!*"

Fernald considered Pedrillo more seriously. "He actually has seen something," reflected Fernald. "He has some sort of reason working in him, Dan."

"The scoundrel is frightened to death," Dan Parker said. "But I don't care what he's thinking, because my job is to close in on Brennan and his crew the minute we can come up with them. I'm going to ride over the brow of that hill . . . and, if Brennan and his gang are below, I'm going to shoot as I ride. Fernald, come with me or else stay here. I have my work cut out for me." With that he swung the head of his horse away and jogged briskly up the valley toward the rise of land beyond which, according to the Mexican, were Brennan's men and the women, or what seemed women, that he escorted.

Robert would have followed at once had it not been that the Mexican suddenly grasped his bridle reins and fell on his knees under the nose of Pinto.

"If you go, you are a dead man . . . beyond that ridge lies death or a terrible betrayal!" cried Oñate.

Robert looked down into a face that was convulsed with emotion, a fat, broad face that quivered and shook and turned pale with the greatness of his feelings.

"Pedrillo," Robert said kindly, "I believe that you have my interests at heart. I know that you wish what is best for me. . . ."

"Alas, *señor*," said Pedrillo, beginning to weep, "I love you like a father, and like a son. I have been an evil man. I have done much wickedness. I have lied to you terribly. But now believe me. Do not ride over that ridge."

"Take your hand from my reins," Robert Fernald stated a little sternly. "I believe that you love me, Pedrillo. But I tell you, if there were ten thousand fighting men on the other side of that rise, I would have to go with Parker against them."

Pedrillo released the reins. He fell face down in the sand, sobbing heavily, so that his whole great body shook and trembled like marsh land underfoot.

Robert gave him a final glance, shook his head as though banishing from his mind any last indecision, and galloped Pinto swiftly after Parker, who was now riding up the slope beyond.

After him came the voice of Pedrillo, thick, choked with sobs: "*Señor* Parker is a traitor! A traitor! Name of heaven and the Virgin, do not go with him!"

But Robert closed his ears to the warning voice. He called loudly to Parker, and the latter turned in the saddle and waved, as though to call him on.

It was plain that the big foreman did not intend to turn back, but to keep on and cross the ridge alone, to begin the battle. It filled the heart of Robert with a great burst of faith in humanity. Never before had he seen such heroism as this of Dan's. And he leaned forward in his saddle and jockeyed Pinto into a racing stride. Even so, he could not quite come up with the other.

He saw Parker, a few lengths before him, drive over the crest; he heard the shout of the foreman, and then the rapid explosions from the rifle of the big fellow as he charged down the other slope. Then Pinto flicked over the summit, and in the hollow Robert saw a band of four men and two figures of women, one sitting in a side-saddle.

The next instant, guns spoke from the hollow, and big Dan Parker reeled heavily in the saddle, and fell forward, clutching blindly at the pommel of his saddle.

XIII

When Robert Fernald saw this happen, he knew that Parker was gone so far as that fight was concerned, and Parker being gone, Robert gave himself up for dead. Had there been two or three men in that hollow—even such great fighters as Brennan and his gang—he would have felt that there was a ghost of a chance, but, when he looked down, he saw the four ready, alert, guns in hand, and he knew that he could not crush them all.

He did not turn back, or waver for an instant. But suddenly he saw the sublime logic in this event. For the whole last part of his life, he had been pointing straight toward this instant. For had he not been roving here and there, searching out the great adventure, matching himself with impossible deeds? Now had come the deed that truly was impossible. He must fail, but he would fail gloriously, with a smoking gun in either hand. He offered up only one prayer from his strange, half-childish, unworldly heart, and this was that heaven would deliver at least two of these men into his hand before the remaining pair shot him to bits.

He was about to straighten Pinto at the enemy when he heard a wild wailing cry behind him, and, looking over his shoulder for an instant, he had sight of the strangest picture, perhaps, that ever dawned upon human sight, and that was of the Mexican charging over the brow of the hill to do battle with his master, and yelling as he came: "Halt, *señor!* In the name of heaven, let me die beside you!"

What madness, then, had made Pedrillo spring from the ground, fling himself upon his mule, and come flying to the rescue? Was it the working of a painful conscience? Was it a vast devotion to his master, a devotion unsuspected by Pedrillo himself until the great moment came? Who could tell? Perhaps it was a blending of all of these things that animated Pedrillo.

But Fernald, amazed and staggered, merely shouted back to Pedrillo to save himself, and then turned Pinto toward the men in the hollow.

Three of them waited for him there, and now he saw that the seeming ladies had sprung down from their horses and thrown off their trailing mantles. They *were* men. A sort of masked battery, now ready to be turned upon Fernald in case of need.

Six to one! The thing became almost ridiculous. But Robert did not hesitate. How should he? How could he, being what he was, when he saw one figure detach itself from the rest and come straight out to meet him?

Yes, there was the magnificent form of big Brennan riding toward him. A gust of wind, or perhaps a desire to have his head free, had made the gunfighter cast his hat aside, and his long gray hair blew back from his face as he came forward at a gentle canter. Brennan! What a vast lifting of the soul there was in Robert at that moment. Now, at least, he would be sure of destroying one of the band, and the most important of all. Brennan must go down before him.

Yes, in either hand Robert felt an utter surety, such as comes to a self-devoted man. He felt that neither of the revolvers that he poised could possibly miss. And he laughed with a fierce joy, and Brennan, riding forth to meet this enemy, saw the laughter of grim ecstasy.

Yet Brennan did not turn back, and he did not swerve. Instead, he brought his pony to a halt and jerked the rifle to his shoulder.

"High and to the right," Robert said, looking at the level of the weapon. As though his words had directed the bullet, it flew above his head and to the side. The rifle spoke again—and the bullet *hummed* closer to the head of Fernald.

Then he fired in turn. He was at rather long range, but he had no thought of missing. Carelessly, half blindly, as a good pistol shot will do, he snapped his gun into place and fired. And then he opened his eyes with amazement.

Brennan had not fallen. No, there he sat in his saddle, the wind ruffling his long hair into waves of silver, his rifle poised for the third shot. Yes, and he was smiling.

The very bottom of the world fell out for Robert. He had missed. Missed utterly—and the target was a man and a horse.

As fast as he could pull trigger, he showered five bullets from alternate guns.

Behold, there sat Brennan upon his horse, his rifle still poised for the finishing shot—and every one of Robert's bullets had failed of its mark. A sort of hysterical cold came upon Robert Fernald then. He was closing upon the outlaw with the last fury of Pinto's rush.

He cast aside the guns that had failed him. He drew the long hunting knife from his belt, and he waved it above his head with a shout.

A change came in the face of Brennan; the smile went out; the gun spoke loudly. And poor Pinto pitched down head foremost in death. Over his head he flung his rider.

Robert saw a blue flash of heaven lit blindingly by the westering sun, and then all light went out. As the darkness rushed across his senses, he heard the scream of the Mexican far behind him as the other guns spoke.

Had Pedrillo gone down, too?

Yes, and in exactly the same fashion. The rifle of Brennan had spoken at the proper moment as he saw Oñate plunging down the slope at him. A wild picture, for Oñate had seized the reins in his teeth, and so left his arm free to grasp his revolver. He came on, shooting blindly, foolishly. The steady rifle of Brennan was tipped up; it spoke, and the mule rolled in death, casting Pedrillo far ahead, and laid him senseless.

So here were two of the three assailants helpless upon the ground.

Brennan's men rushed eagerly around them. Oñate had a leg twisted under him, unquestionably broken and broken badly. But Robert Fernald lay face up, with a bloody gash upon his brow. No, he was merely stunned, unless there were internal injuries.

What of Dan Parker? It was a most amazing thing to see him

ride straight in on the Brennan band and, when he was among them, stop his horse and drop to his feet, and then sink upon a rock.

"In the name of heaven, are they both dead?" Parker cried, white of face.

Brennan himself came back to Parker. "They're not dead," he declared. "They'll come around in time, but they're out for a few minutes. Old boy, you played a good part there. But even at that, I thought I was going to be a gone goose at the last minute. Look here." He pointed to the hunting knife of Fernald, sticking deep in his saddle. "He threw it as his horse fell," said Brennan. "And bless my heart if I didn't think I was gone when I seen that streak of silver. And every shot that he fired was a bull's-eye, Dan. He sprinkled me with lead dust every time. Look here." He pointed to his shirt; it was flecked with dots of black.

"What did you put in those slugs, Dan?" he asked.

"It was a hunch that I got a long time ago." Parker grinned. "It's lead, you see. Real lead. But it's only crystals that are packed in under an outer film. It looks smooth and hard, and it weighs like lead. But when you fire, it scatters like dust in the air. Now, dammit, get his fallen guns and his cartridge belt and load them with real bullets, will you? Since I put in the phony ones at our camp last night, I've been in a stew."

"Afraid that he'd take a crack at something along the way?" Brennan nodded understandingly.

"Yes, and find out that there was something wrong with the ammunition, you understand?"

"Chuck," Brennan said, "get the belt off Fernald and line it with new bullets. Same number that there are in it. Shake the cartridges out of his guns, too, and put in real ones. We'd have nothing but wasted work if he was ever to find out. And here, Sam, help to get a bandage around Parker's head, will you?

Prick your finger and get some blood on it. It's got to look as though you were grazed by a bullet and knocked silly that way, Dan."

Four of the men were working over the fallen warriors, and now they could hear the loud groaning of the Mexican up the slope, although still he was unconscious.

In the meantime, the bandage was wrapped around the head of Parker. His gun belt was taken away, and his hands were tied before him.

"Will it do any good, though?" said Parker. "Ain't he going to find out?"

"If he finds out," Brennan said with a shudder, "God help us. I was a dead man six times, Dan. I never seen such shooting from the back of a running horse. Six times he dusted me. And when I seen him coming like a madman . . . the first two bullets I fired to kill . . . and missed. Then I seen that you'd done your work right, when he opened fire. So I waited, and let the poor horse have it at the last jump. If it's possible to break the nerve of any man, Dan, this ought to keep Fernald from wearing guns again. But . . . I have my doubts. He's a wildcat. He ain't human!"

"And if he should ever guess," Parker said with a groan. "If he ever should guess that this was a put-up job. Why, the greaser had a hunch at the last minute, and I thought that I was a gone goose. Would have been . . . except that Fernald never suspects anyone who he calls a friend."

"A hard job." Brennan sighed. "I wish that I'd never started it. But who could resist, with a girl like her cryin' and beggin' for my help. She loves him, Dan, the way that few men ever have been loved."

"Aye," Parker said, "and, besides, she's paying big. What did you do with the pair of them?"

"Just as we planned. They shifted from their horses at the

point where Chuck and Sam met us. Took their horses and headed for Larkin Valley. And they're waiting there for news. I'll send in a boy with the good word . . . if you can call it good."

XIV

No hint of these happenings came to Robert, of course, as he lay senseless. And when he recovered and opened his eyes, he saw nothing to betray the plot that had revolved so cunningly around him. What he observed was Dan Parker, his hands bound together before him, his head encircled by a blood-stained bandage, and then, as he sat up, Robert heard the terrible groaning of Pedrillo Oñate, who, in turn, had recovered his senses, urged on by an incessant spur of sharp pain.

Brennan in person was at work over the Mexican. Men said that in early days the lone rider had been a doctor. At least it was certain that he knew much of the ways of a healer. And now he was putting his art to a practical use as he encased the broken leg of the Mexican in rudely improvised splints. A great dram of brandy gave Pedrillo force to endure his present pain. His groans diminished.

Robert, his own hands tied in front of him, was permitted to go to poor Oñate and sit beside him.

A flash of joy struck across the face of the Mexican. His eyes glittered with happiness. "They told me that you were alive, *señor*," he said. "But I thought that the devils were lying. Glorious Virgin of Guadalupe! It is because I vowed six tall candlesticks of pure beeswax. She saved you. She turned the bullets from you and made them strike Pinto. *Señor*, little father, let me have your hand and feel that it is yourself and not a ghost that is here and. . . . *Hai!* Hellfire take them! They are killing me! Stop them, little father!"

He clung to the hand of Robert, and remained clinging to it until the operation was finished. Then another dram of brandy, combined with the exhaustion of great pain and the aftereffects of a shock of nervous excitement, washed Pedrillo deep into a gulf of sleep.

Brennan, stiff-lipped and stern from the surgical work that he had been doing, stood back from the Mexican and looked to Robert Fernald with a faint smile.

"How did you manage it, Fernald?" he asked. "What medicine did you use to turn this great hulk of a coward into a hero today?"

Fernald made no reply, but he looked steadfastly into the face of the older man. It seemed to him that infinite wisdom was gathered in the calm, courageous eyes of the famous criminal. It seemed to him that he felt the power of soul that had beaten him from his horse and brought about his fall. And, falling, he had not been able to bring down a single one of his enemies. He could not understand. Striving to understand, he struck upon one possible solution: it was the force of a superior warrior that had beaten him. It was the overplus of a conqueror that had deprived him of his ability. Something in the dauntless bearing of Brennan, riding out to the encounter, single-handed, had served to unman Robert. For that matter, he could recall other instances when nerves had worked on his own behalf and had made famous gunfighters almost as helpless as children before him. He thought of some of those other occasions now, and he felt the full irony of his fate. And then a fiery pang struck through his head from the wound on his forehead.

Presently they prepared to march. A litter was made for Pedrillo and slung between two horses, then the party journeyed on up the valley, turned sharply into a little twisting ravine, and, where the stream spread in a small pool, they made their camp.

Robert was with Pedrillo, who was coming back to his senses again with deep groans and occasional loud yells of pain.

"Patience, *señor*," said the Mexican. "We shall have them yet.

If they cannot be trailed to this place, all the men in the desert are blind as bats. Patience, *señor*. A moment's patience is ten years' comfort, and he that can be patient finds his foe at his feet. They will trail us here and bag all the villains, *señor*."

Robert could not reply except to say: "Be quiet, Pedrillo. Keep your strength. You have been through a great deal. Now save yourself. God knows how long it will be before you can be moved from this place to the care of a good doctor."

"*Señor*," the Mexican said, "you give me foolish advice and worse comfort. God defend me from all doctors, I say first of all. When the doctor comes in at one door, death comes in by another. Death is the shadow of the doctor, *señor*. And it is by death that the doctor lives. No, God defend me from doctors, I say. Above all, do not tell me to be silent. If it is not for the music of my own tongue, I shall go mad thinking of the pain in which I lie here. Let me talk and talk, *señor*, for talking stops thinking, as drinking stops thirst. Let my tongue be busy with words, or my throat will be busy with screams. And stay close to me, little father, for no one will listen to me with half your patience."

In this manner Pedrillo talked, twisting himself to and fro, and never resting until Robert had propped up his head a little. He rolled a cigarette for Oñate, and the latter smoked it with great sighs of relief. But still he talked, making the smoke bubble and break at his lips. He talked, indeed, until he seemed quite to forget his pain from the broken leg.

"He doesn't need an opiate," Brennan said, pausing to listen. "Not so long as he can keep hinges on his tongue."

When Pedrillo at last fell asleep again, Robert had a chance to talk with Parker. The two were left quite alone, and allowed to talk freely and secretly with one another. Their hands were bound, and they were not spied upon unnecessarily, but there were two of Brennan's young men constantly on guard, their rifles across their knees when they were seated, or tucked under one arm as the guards walked up and down. And there was something in the carelessness with which they handled those weapons that augured ill for the man who attempted to bolt to the shrubbery at the side of the ravine. There was something, too, in the keenness of their eyes that discouraged any attempt at trickery.

But Robert had no trick or shift in his mind. With his bound hands, he took the imprisoned ones of Parker and pressed them hard.

"Old fellow," Fernald began, "I've seen a good many brave things done. But I've never seen anything finer than the way you drove over the top of that hill. Only, tell me this, why did you do it? Why didn't you wait for me? Then we could have made the charge together and perhaps . . . God knows . . . we might have done something, working together."

Parker frowned at the ground, and then peered at the dusky sky, for it was long after the sunset.

"It was Pedrillo," he said, speaking rapidly and in a mumbling voice. "It was Pedrillo. He'd tormented me with his infernal tongue. I had to do something to show you. . . ." Here he stuck, and frowned again at the ground.

"*Tush,*" Robert said. "As though I could have doubted you. As though I could have doubted you for a second. But . . . what do you think Brennan will do with us?"

"God knows," said Parker. "It seems that his main idea, after the ladies gave him the slip in the middle of the desert and after he found that we were following, was to trap you and fight with you hand to hand." Here Dan managed to raise his head and look Robert in the eye. But Robert was staring gloomily into the distance. "He wanted to beat you," went on Parker, "and. . . ."

"And he did it," Robert said sadly. "But now what?"

"I think he's holding you in the hope that, if he could not keep Miss Larkin for ransom, at least he may be able to make her ransom you."

Robert shook his head.

"Why not?" asked Parker. "We've both done something for her. And she has money enough to help us."

"It would do me no good," Robert said. "I've been thinking the thing out, you see."

"Thinking to what end?" Parker asked, his voice turning very sharp.

"For you, yes. The ransom would be all very well for you, Dan. Of course you should get your freedom. But it's a different matter with me."

"I don't see that."

"It's this way. I never could live happily, remembering how I stood up to one man, and was beaten like that."

"Do you mean it?"

"Yes. I mean that I have to have another chance at Brennan. Now . . . or later."

"Another chance?" cried Parker. "But, old fellow, don't you see how it is? He met you fairly and squarely. He beat you certainly. You can't expect to be the best man in the world, you know."

"I understand that he's the better man," Robert said, falling back into his gloomy thought. "And I'd rather be a dead man than a living man with that thought. He beat me fairly and squarely, as you say. And I wish that the bullet had killed me instead of dropping poor Pinto. That was a brave little cayuse, Dan." He sighed.

"You mean," interpreted Parker "that, if you're ransomed here, you'll keep on the trail of Brennan until you have a chance to fight the thing out with him again?"

"Of course," answered Robert. "There's nothing else for me

to do, really."

Parker said no more. He fell into a brown study, and his reflections did not seem to be very pleasant ones. In the meantime, a campfire had been lighted. Brennan and another came back from a brief hunting tour of the ravine loaded with rabbits for the evening meal. And in a few short moments the odor of roasting meat was drifting across the air.

The stars came out, the dim and distant desert stars. The hungry men were so silent that, now and again, one could hear the horses grinding their forage in the darkness. The fire *crackled* merrily. Never had there been a scene of greater peace. But for two there was no beauty in the scene—to Robert, seated on a fallen log and staring at the stars with sightless eyes of thought, and to Parker, who hunted out Brennan for a private conference.

XV

Brennan, for his part, seemed in the best of spirits. After all, he had undertaken a most delicate and ticklish business and had brought it through to an apparently triumphant issue with the secret help of Dan Parker. Therefore, he was whistling softly as he took his share of roasted rabbit to one side and sat down to eat. There Parker joined him. He sat in silence, regardless of the share of food that had been given to him.

"Hello," said Brennan, "is there sand in that meat, Dan?"

"Damn the meat!" said Parker.

"You didn't get your slug of coffee, then?"

"Damn the coffee," Parker said.

"Then, what's wrong?"

"It's as wrong as any man could wish," Parker declared sourly.

"What's wrong?"

"Guess, then."

"You mean the kid? Why he seems to be pretty well in hand.

He ain't said a word, hardly."

"He never was a talking kind," Parker mused. "When he first come up to Larkin Valley, I used to bully-rag him a little. I thought he was a cross between a fool and a coward. And he didn't say nothing. All that he did was to go out one day, and come back with Tom Gill in tow. No, the kid never was great on talking."

"What are you aiming at with that?" demanded Brennan briskly, but lowering his voice. "What's your drift, Dan?"

"Why," Parker explained, "what's the main job here?"

"To bust the spirit of the kid and show him that he ain't almighty with a gun. What else?"

"Nothin' else," said Parker. "That's exactly the main job. To sort of gentle him down, so's he'll be willing to retire to Larkin Ranch and marry the finest girl in the world and settle down with her. That's the main job."

"It's done," Brennan said with decision. "He's had his lesson."

"Old son," Parker informed him, "he's just after telling me that he'll never live happy until he's had a chance to fight the thing out with you again."

"Fury and fire," breathed out Brennan. "Do you mean that?"

"I mean that. Now, how will it be for you, Tiger, to stand up to that kid again?"

"I'll see him hanged first," said Brennan without the slightest hesitation. "He dusted me with six bullets running. I was a dead man six times over before I managed to bring down his horse. No, no, Dan. I take my chance with any man, even old as I am, but I don't take any chances with a shooting machine like that same kid. Missing a shot just ain't in his makeup."

"Suppose he's ransomed? Then he immediately starts on your trail and sticks to it until he gets a chance to. . . ."

"I'd simply have the boys lay for him and massacre him, Parker. Suicide ain't in my line."

Parker lighted a cigarette, and he sighed deeply. "He's over there admiring you," Parker explained. "He's been telling me how much better a man you are than him. And at the same time, he couldn't live, y'understand, knowing that he's been beat, even when he was beat fair and square. But suppose, Tiger, just supposin', he should ever get wind of what really happened . . . or even should he find out that I really wasn't knocked silly by a bullet, but that I was in the game on your side from the start . . . ?"

Tiger Brennan whistled. Then he added: "We'll wait till we get word from Miss Larkin. Then we'll see. We'll see what's to happen."

So they waited. And the messenger sent to the Larkin Ranch returned the next morning before noon with a letter for Brennan. The letter was brief and amazingly to the point:

You've done wonderfully well. I hardly see how you managed it. I'm enclosing another check for $5,000—just to show you how I appreciate the skill you've used. Get Fernald to the ranch as fast as you can. And, for heaven's sake, never let him guess how this has happened.

Then Brennan called Parker and young Robert Fernald before him.

"Boys," he said, "I'm mighty glad to say that Miss Larkin didn't waste no time. She's sent down the coin that I needed. And so the pair of you can go free. But you don't go free until you make a bargain with me. I've used you a bit rough, and no doubt you have a hankering to get even with me. Now, lads, I want your promise to me that you'll never take my trail and never pull a gun against me. I'll take your word for that, because you're a pair of honorable gents."

"Certainly," said Parker. "I'm not fool enough to want any

more of your game, Tiger. Here's my hand on it."

"Thanks, Parker. Then you're free. Wait till I cut this rope. There you are."

The rope fell instantly from the hands of Parker, and Brennan directed one of his men to restore the guns and belt to the liberated prisoner. Then he turned to young Fernald.

"The same deal goes with you, Fernald," he said kindly. "Just shake on this deal and. . . ."

"I think you mean very well in this," said Fernald. "But the trouble is, Brennan, that I can't do it."

"And why not, then?"

"Because, sooner or later, I've got to get at you, Brennan. We've had one fight, and all the winning has gone to you. Perhaps you're a better man. But I want to stand up to you once more and finish the deal. Living is no good to me with a better man just around the corner."

Brennan strode close and towered above Robert, five feet and eight inches. "Kid," he cried, "are you plain batty? Are you askin' me to blow you to hell? Because once there, I can't blow you back again."

Fernald merely smiled. It seemed that this blustering only served to give him more strength of purpose. "The sun is right over our heads," he said, "and so it can't shine in the eyes of either of us. Why not take this time, Brennan? Why not take this time and have it out? I'd as soon be buried here as anywhere."

Brennan turned on his heel and strode away.

"You've made a fool of yourself," Parker said anxiously to Robert. "You've really made quite a rare fool of yourself. Let me call him back."

"Why did he quit me?" Robert asked, bewildered.

"Because he's not an idiot," Parker said with a ready wit. "He's beaten you once, and let you live. Why should he risk himself against you a second time . . . even if the risk isn't

251

much? He's a gold digger, not a gambler, Bob."

Brennan, sitting apart, turned the matter back and forth in his mind. He sat in the deep shadow of a projecting rock. All was deadly still in the shallow ravine. It seemed as though the fire of the sun had burned all life out of everything. Even the air was still, and not a breath stirred through the dry leaves of the shrubbery. The horses shrank the skin on their backs, time and again, as though to escape from the unceasing fall of fire that burned them, and the men mopped their foreheads incessantly.

For a half hour or more Brennan remained lost in his brooding. Then he rose with a grim face. He looked up and pointed to two or three small black spots in the sky.

"Let the buzzards finish this argument," he said. Watching, waiting eyes were fixed upon him. "Let the buzzards have the last word," he said. "I've offered this fellow his life . . . he won't have it on decent terms. Well, that's the end of him. Fernald, you're going to die here like a dog."

Fernald stiffened a little. "If you do it, Brennan," he said, "you'll be more detested than a mad dog through the range."

"I'll take my chance on that. Boys, stand him against that wall, will you? And give me that new Colt. . . ."

"Wait a minute, chief," big Chuck Dashwood said, gray with disgust and fear. "D'you mean that you're going to butcher him like . . . like a pig?"

"And what have you to say to that?" Brennan roared, but, as he whirled on Dashwood, he winked a broad and solemn wink, seen not only by Chuck but by the rest of the band.

"All right," said Dashwood, frowning to keep from smiling. "I'll stand him up for you. Bandage his eyes?"

"No, no!" Robert shouted. "You needn't fear that I'll dodge. And . . . I want to see it coming." He stepped back against the appointed wall.

Brennan cursed softly. And then: "Hold on!" he cried. "It

ain't right that the master should go before the man. Bring out the greaser and prop him up against the wall."

It was done. But when poor Oñate saw what was contemplated, he screamed like a woman. "*Señor* Brennan, noble and kind *señor*, I'll be your slave. I never will betray you. I'll be truer to you than to *Señor* Fernald. *Bah!* What is he to me? What is he compared with a great man like you, *señor*. But do not kill me. Oh, my God! I have a mother . . . and an old father . . . I have seven children to starve without me . . . I am. . . ."

"A pair of you hold him up by each shoulder," said the cruel Brennan.

"*Señor* Brennan, I swear that I shall give you my solemn honor!"

"Bah!" said Brennan. "You have no honor, you yellow swine. Hold him up, boys, and I'll soon have this over. . . ." He balanced the revolver in his hand.

Oñate was supported on either side, so that his breast was open to the bullet.

"One moment," Oñate said with a changed voice. "I defy you and spit in your face, dog of a pirate and cut-throat. *Señor* Fernald, little father, pity me and forgive me. I denied you because I loved life. But if God gave me the right to die for you and so set you free, I should go to my death smiling. Tell me that you believe me, little father."

"Ready?" said Brennan. "Say your last prayer, greaser, if you've got one to say."

"*Señor*," Pedrillo said to Fernald, overlooking the threat of the ready gun, "we meet in heaven. It is only one moment of pain. *¡Adiós, amigo!*"

"Brennan!" shouted Fernald.

Brennan stepped back a little, and scowled at his prisoner.

"Don't fire on him," Robert Fernald gasped. "I'll give you my word . . . I'll do whatever you want."

XVI

So by the wit and cruel imagination of Tiger Brennan, Fernald
was tamed and his career as a slayer of men was brought to an
end. An untimely end, in some respects, one might call it. For if
he had gone on with his red-handed work, there is no telling to
what strange heights of adventure he might have scaled.

For these were the terms imposed on him by Brennan: never
to seek the society of a dangerous man; never to respond to a
challenge to fight; never to draw a weapon, except in the actual
defense of his life.

And this, of course, was to condemn him never to fight at all,
for with the reputation that had been built up by Robert, there
was not one chance in ten thousand that he would ever
encounter a man rash enough to rush into war with him. Ten
men could be controlled by one fearless hero whose skill with a
gun had been proved. And so it would be with Robert Fernald.
If he were forced to give up the making of trouble, then trouble
most assuredly would not dare to seek out Fernald.

It was in this manner that the terms were concluded. Fernald
groaned and buried his face in his hands as he saw himself shut
off from all chance of vengeance upon Brennan, shut off, too,
from his avowed duty of executing the wrath of Sim Burgess
upon McCoy—the villain. But, as an alternative, he was told by
Brennan that he could have the pleasure of seeing his faithful
Pedrillo placed against a wall and shot through the heart.

So Robert submitted. An odd document was drawn up by
the hand of Brennan, stating in exact terms what was to be
done. "Because," Brennan said, "your memory might fail you
one of these days, but I'll keep a copy, and you'll keep the
other. And there you are."

How did it happen that Brennan was willing to trust merely
to the pledged word of this man who was a stranger to him?
Well, Robert was not really a stranger to anyone in the West. All

men had heard about his exploits, and all men knew a good deal about his work with guns and men; above all, he was famous for an unstained honor that never yet had broken faith upon great matters or upon small. So Brennan was willing to trust.

Half an hour later, Tiger Brennan was gone with his men, disappearing in a whirlwind of dust up the ravine, and leaving Robert, the stricken Pedrillo, and Dan Parker without horses, without food, without so much as a hunting knife as means of helping themselves.

However, they did not have long in which to wonder what would come of them. Over the edge of the western hill they heard the *rattling* of hoofs, and there came down into the ravine half a dozen stanch riders, who were recognized afar by Parker as members of his own crew, workers on the Larkin Ranch. They greeted Parker with much noisy enthusiasm. They greeted Robert Fernald with an awed respect, such as he received from most men from that time until the day of his death. And even to Pedrillo they showed a singular amount of attention.

They made a litter for him, the softest that could be fashioned, and started the trek across the hills, climbing up and up to the beautiful, cool meadow lands of the Larkin Valley and the Larkin Ranch.

Robert and Dan Parker walked together behind the procession for a time, but Robert was terribly in the dumps, and he could not raise his head to talk. So Parker hurried on to the others. They left Robert trailing behind, breathing their dust, the most bedraggled and woebegone figure that one could imagine. Certainly no one could have selected him now in this sad, dejected mood as one who would make a possible hero.

In the meantime, the party in the lead made merry, badgering Pedrillo.

"You greaser scoundrel," a grinning cowpuncher would say,

"tell me how come that you offered to let Brennan shoot you? D'you think that his bullets was made of paper, maybe?"

Pedrillo lay back in his bed of pine branches and puffed cigarettes and smiled upon them, for he was content with the world.

"Great things cannot be understood by little men," Pedrillo would say. "Pardon, *señor*, but you throw your shadow upon me."

So they laughed and tormented one another. But Pedrillo knew that he had left the ranks of the rogues and, against his own fondest expectations, established himself among the ranks of honest men. It made him feel very dizzy, but it made him feel that God was very great, being able to accomplish even such a miracle as this.

So the caravan wound on toward the upper plateau, reached it, and came in sight of the house, where a solitary rider swept toward them—beautiful Beatrice Larkin, her face drawn and her eyes brilliant.

"But where's the man you went to get?" she asked, cruelly overlooking Parker and poor Pedrillo. "Where's Bobbie Fernald? Where's he?"

He had disappeared.

"I'll get him in five minutes," Parker said, turning pale. "He was with us, I'd swear, not long ago . . . he must be back beyond that stretch of hummocks."

She cast one terrible and blasting glance upon him, and then her horse darted away, and the others rushed off, also, scattering here and there in a wild search.

But it was Beatrice who found him—far back—five miles back—in the center of a little circle of poplars that stood around a spring. There he was, sitting beside the pool, his face in his hands.

And when she rushed her horse through the trees and cried

out at the sight of him, he did not raise his head.

She flung herself out of the saddle and ran to him.

"Bobbie, Bobbie! I thought you were lost!"

"I am," he said, and stood before her. "I'm lost, Beatrice . . . shamed, disgraced, and done for. No man will ever want me for a friend again."

"And the women, Bobbie?" she asked.

"No proud woman ever would want me in her house as a friend," he said.

"Perhaps not . . . but as a husband, Bobbie . . . that would be a rather different thing."

"You're making a joke of me, Beatrice," Robert said with a sad dignity.

"Only half, Bobbie," she said.

Certainly she never stopped laughing at him, even when he was the father of her children, and certainly even the cowpunchers on the place used to smile as he went by, for to the end he remained rather a shrinking figure. And one hardly could have said whether or not he was a happy man. At least in many a way he was never truly content. There were only two people in the world who could make him laugh.

One was his wife.

The other was Pedrillo, who never left that valley so long as he lived. There is another matter that must be mentioned. Burgess failed to harm McCoy, and Burgess himself was killed by the kick of a powerful little mule.

As for the enormous hoax of the pretended kidnapping of Beatrice Larkin and her aunt, rumors about it flew everywhere; certainly big Brennan never was accused of it as of a crime, but as of a joke—but no convincing tale of the truth ever came to the ears of Robert Fernald. He had passed into a mildly happy dream. But still his eyes were fixed on the wild heights of life, and he despised the quiet ways in which he found himself.

ACKNOWLEDGMENTS

"The Terrible Tenderfoot" by George Owen Baxter first appeared in Street & Smith's *Western Story Magazine* (7/2/27). Copyright © 1927 by Street & Smith Publications, Inc. Copyright © renewed 1955 by Dorothy Faust. Copyright © 2008 by Golden West Literary Agency for restored material. Acknowledgment is made to Condé Nast Publications, Inc., for their co-operation.

"The Gentle Desperado" by George Owen Baxter first appeared in Street & Smith's *Western Story Magazine* (7/16/27). Copyright © 1927 by Street & Smith Publications, Inc. Copyright © renewed 1955 by Dorothy Faust. Copyright © 2008 by Golden West Literary Agency for restored material. Acknowledgment is made to Condé Nast Publications, Inc., for their co-operation.

"The Tiger" by George Owen Baxter first appeared as "Tiger, Tiger!" in Street & Smith's *Western Story Magazine* (7/30/27). Copyright © 1927 by Street & Smith Publications, Inc. Copyright © renewed 1955 by Dorothy Faust. Copyright © 2008 by Golden West Literary Agency for restored material. Acknowledgment is made to Condé Nast Publications, Inc., for their co-operation.

ABOUT THE AUTHOR

Max Brand is the best-known pen name of Frederick Faust, creator of Dr. Kildare, Destry, and many other fictional characters popular with readers and viewers worldwide. Faust wrote for a variety of audiences in many genres. His enormous output, totaling approximately 30,000,000 words or the equivalent of 530 ordinary books, covered nearly every field: crime, fantasy, historical romance, espionage, Westerns, science fiction, adventure, animal stories, love, war, and fashionable society, big business and big medicine. Eighty motion pictures have been based on his work along with many radio and television programs. For good measure he also published four volumes of poetry. Perhaps no other author has reached more people in more different ways. Born in Seattle in 1892, orphaned early, Faust grew up in the rural San Joaquin Valley of California. At Berkeley he became a student rebel and one-man literary movement, contributing prodigiously to all campus publications. Denied a degree because of unconventional conduct, he embarked on a series of adventures culminating in New York City where, after a period of near starvation, he received simultaneous recognition as a serious poet and successful author of fiction. Later, he traveled widely, making his home in New York, then in Florence, and finally in Los Angeles. Once the United States entered the Second World War, Faust abandoned his lucrative writing career and his work as a screenwriter to serve as a war correspondent with the infantry in Italy, despite his fifty-one years and a bad heart. He was killed during a night attack on a hilltop village held by the German army. New books based on magazine serials or unpublished manuscripts or restored versions continue to appear so that, alive or dead, he has averaged a new book every four months for seventy-five years. Beyond this, some work by him is newly reprinted every week of every year in one or another format somewhere in the world. A great deal more about this author and his work can be found in *The Max Brand Companion* (Greenwood Press, 1997) edited by Jon Tuska and Vicki Piekarski. His next Five Star Western will be *Nine Lives: A Western Trio.*